Praise for the Greenhouse Mystery Series

A MUDDIED MURDER (#1)

"Tyson gives us an evocative sense of place, a bit of romance, and dimensional characters with interesting backstories. Readers are left looking forward to the next book in the series and hankering for organic mushroom tartlets."

– *Publishers Weekly*

"A warmhearted mystery with an irresistible cast of characters, two- and four-legged alike. Tyson's small town setting is a lush bounty for the senses, and the well-structured plot will keep you guessing right up until the satisfying conclusion."

– Sophie Littlefield,
Edgar-Nominated Author of *The Guilty One*

"Tyson grows a delicious debut mystery as smart farmer-sleuth Megan Sawyer tills the dirt on local secrets after a body turns up in her barn. You won't want to put down this tasty harvest of a story."

– Edith Maxwell,
Agatha-Nominated Author of *Murder Most Fowl*

"Hungry for a great mystery? *A Muddied Murder* is a delight and Wendy Tyson is a natural. She delivers a perfectly plotted mystery with well-planted clues and a healthy dose of secrets. This first Greenhouse Mystery will only whet your appetite for more."

– Sparkle Abbey,
Author of *Raiders of the Lost Bark*

"An irresistible story with delicious food, scheming villagers, and a secret worth killing for. Her heroine, prodigal daughter of Winsome, PA Megan Sawyer, may not carry a gun, but she's packing brains, courage, and loads of integrity. Megan is a star."

– James W. Ziskin,
Anthony Award-Nominated Author of the Ellie Stone Mysteries

The Greenhouse Mystery Series
by Wendy Tyson

A MUDDIED MURDER (#1)
BITTER HARVEST (#2)
(Spring 2017)

A Muddied Murder

GREENHOUSE mysteries

WENDY TYSON

HENERY PRESS

Mys
tys

A MUDDIED MURDER
A Greenhouse Mystery
Part of the Henery Press Mystery Collection

First Edition
Hardcover edition | March 2016

Henery Press, LLC
www.henerypress.com

ISBN-13: 978-1-63511-008-1

Printed in the United States of America

*In memory of Mary, Rose, Jennie and Sophie,
in whose kitchens I realized the importance of slow food,
fresh ingredients and warm conversation.*

ACKNOWLEDGMENTS

First and foremost, I'd like to thank my husband, Ben Pickarski. He has the true green thumb in the family, and I've learned so much from him. What started as an economical past time (a way to eat organic foods in a cost effective manner) blossomed into a passion for both of us. He was my number one consultant for all things farming while writing A Muddied Murder. Thankfully, I have him on retainer for the next book.

I'd also like to thank my agent, Frances Black of Literary Counsel. The idea for the Greenhouse Mystery Series developed while I was at a book signing in a small town in North Carolina, and I called her that weekend to pitch the concept. She immediately understood my vision, and her encouragement, insights and passion helped bring the town of Winsome and all its quirky inhabitants to life.

Many thanks also to my Henery Press family. Kendel Lynn and Art Molinares believed in the project from the beginning, and the wonderful editors and staff at Henery Press—Kendel, Art, Anna Davis, Erin George, Rachel Jackson, and Stephanie Chontos—supported the book throughout the process. Their sharp ideas and intelligent editing made it a better novel.

Thanks to Rowe Copeland at The Book Concierge. Cheerleader, business manager, organizer, friend, first beta reader...Rowe does it all. And she does it all well.

I am grateful for the smart feedback and ready wit of my beta readers and line editors, Adrienne Robertson, Sue Norbury, Laura Coffey, and Carol Lizell. Thank you!

A big shout-out to my family. Ian Pickarski, Mandy Gohn, Angela Tyson, Greg Marincola and Ann Marie Pickarski—as always, they provided much-needed emotional and marketing support. And my twins, Matthew and Jonathan, may just be the best plot brainstormers and Revolutionary War researchers ever.

To all of the people who embrace an organic, more humane lifestyle and who are willing to question the status quo...you inspire me. Keep the faith.

One

Early mornings at Washington Acres were dead quiet. It was usually Megan Sawyer's favorite part of day, a time when the farm's inhabitants went about their daily routines silently, ghosts in a tranquil pre-dawn landscape. Today there was a disturbance in the air, an almost palpable sense of something amiss. Megan had felt it as soon as she climbed out of bed at four forty-five, and she felt it now as she was checking on the last set of tomato seedlings.

Standing in the old den that doubled as a nursery, Megan was thinking about the day ahead when something outside the window caught her attention. She paused, straining to see from her spot across the room. The sun had just risen, bathing the farm in a milky bluish glow muddied by a cold, steady rain, and all that was visible was the hazy outline of the trees on the horizon. You're imagining things, she thought. Still, a shudder ran the length of her spine. She blamed it on the chill of the morning.

Returning to her work, Megan ran a finger down the stem of a seedling, grateful for the full set of leaves on its thin stalk, and blew on it gently to strengthen the young plant. This set was strong enough to be transplanted outdoors. She adjusted the grow lights over the plants and sprinkled water on the seedling. She needed to get the tomatoes outdoors, alongside the broccoli, spinach, and other vegetables she planned to offer through the farm's store in town and at the local Saturday farmers market. Tomatoes would be a big seller. She hoped.

This task complete, Megan walked to the room's east-facing

window and gazed through the glass at the curtains of rain pummeling the ground. No, it wasn't looking good for planting. Ah, well...this new life was certainly teaching her patience. Mother Nature had her own opinions about timing, and she wasn't hearing appeals.

Megan stretched, yearning for release in her tired back and arm muscles. Less than two years ago she'd been tied to a desk, living in Chicago and defending big companies from environmental claims. She shook her head. Life can certainly take a turn.

Megan cracked open the window and took a deep breath, trying to wash away a building sense of unease. The earthy smells of rain and dirt mingled with the scent of her grandmother's baking bread wafting from the kitchen. Cinnamon-raisin swirl today. Her stomach rumbled. Despite everything, she loved this place. She loved the old shadowy stone farmhouse with its low ceilings, wide-planked pine floors, and deep window sills. She loved the massive stone barn, with its cool, packed earth and sense of history. She loved the shady spots under old-growth oaks that allowed for stolen moments of solitude with the latest mystery novel. She loved the feel of the earth in her fingers and the sound of her goats bleating in the distance.

Goats...bleating? Megan cocked her head, listening. Was that Bibi's voice coming from *outside*?

Megan slipped on her galoshes and grabbed a raincoat from a hook on the den wall. The Pygmy goats were adorable, but also a constant source of mischief. What had they done this time? She hustled through the hallway that led to the kitchen, certain that it was some minor mishap, and nearly tripped over the stray cat who was now a permanent resident of the farm. The cat, barely out of kitten-hood, was batting around what appeared to be a crumpled letter.

Megan reached for the paper. Spreading it flat, she quickly scanned the words on the page, color slowly rising to her cheeks. It was a failed inspection notice for the work that had been done on the barn and café. The inspections needed to be complete in order for Megan to start selling produce in a few weeks. And despite the work of competent contractors, the town's zoning commissioner, Simon Duvall, always seem to find something wrong.

Megan scanned the rest of the letter. At the bottom was a line with the next appointment date. Simon would be at the café. Today. At eight o'clock. Megan glanced at the kitchen clock, blood pressure rising. That didn't give her much time to get ready—or inspect the café before Simon arrived. *Damn.*

Bibi shouted again, this time louder. Megan glanced at the wrinkled paper before tossing it on the table next to the cat. She sprinted outside.

The rain had slowed, but the wind still whipped through the hilly courtyard between the old farmhouse and the barn. Megan pulled her raincoat tighter around her body and lowered her head against the drops. It was mid-May. Spring had been slow in coming to Winsome this year, and temperatures were well below normal. Megan followed the sound of her grandmother's voice through the courtyard and down toward the barn and the attached heated shed where the goats lived.

It didn't take long to discover the source of her grandmother's excitement. Heidi the goat was at the edge of the shed roof pawing at a gutter with one tiny hoof. A black leather glove dangled from her mouth. And Bibi, her petite body dwarfed by a man's raincoat, was dragging a ladder from the barn.

"Bibi!" Megan raced to her grandmother and took the wooden ladder gently from her grasp. Her grandmother had been "Bibi" since Megan was little, back when "Bonnie Birch" was too much of a mouthful. "Here, I'll get her down."

"That goat," Bibi paused to catch her breath, "is one stubborn animal."

Hmm, Megan thought to herself...who was calling whom stubborn? Megan knew better than to tell her grandmother the myriad of reasons she shouldn't be climbing up ladders or lifting ornery goats. Bibi wouldn't listen anyway, and, at some future point, she might do it simply to prove she could.

Megan shook her head, both admiring her grandmother's independence and cursing her stubbornness. The latter trait was a Birch family staple.

Megan was getting ready to put the ladder against the shed when she noticed the goat had opened the shed gate this time—a first for the industrious animal—and the gate was dangling from two hinges. Normally Heidi simply squeezed Houdini-like around or under the bars. Megan looked into the covered shed. Heidi's sister Dimples was nowhere to be found.

"Bibi, can you call Dimples while I get Heidi down?" Megan asked, worried. She climbed the ladder and, taking a deep breath, hauled a squirming Heidi off the roof. After doing another quick inspection of the inside of the shed, she put Heidi back inside and closed and locked the gate.

When a look around the perimeter of the large barn didn't turn up a goat, Megan sprinted down toward the greenhouses and rows of hoop houses. No goat.

Catching her breath, Megan paused to survey her surroundings, hoping to catch a glimpse of the animal. She needed to hurry. Her gaze shifted from the rain-soaked hoop houses to the stone outbuilding lined with stacks of firewood and bordered by chicken tractors, small enclosures on wheels that housed the chickens and could be moved around within the outdoor pastures. The tractors kept the chickens warm and safe at night, and by day the birds were free to roam. Heidi loved to chase the chickens; maybe her sister had picked up the habit too. But the tractors were closed up and quiet.

On the other side of the tractors, barely visible from this angle, was the neighboring property: the old Marshall house, a failed farm with an empty, dilapidated stone house. The Marshall house's fields, long overgrown with weeds and saplings, were empty except for a single crow, which perched atop a broken fence rail, its head cocked in Megan's direction. Megan pulled her gaze away from the crow, the bird's cold stare mirroring the sinking feeling in her gut.

Megan turned, looking up the hill from the chickens at a thick forested swath of land on the edge of the woods, which housed Barney Creek. Beyond the woods was the road. The thought of Dimples down near the street, maybe even hit by a car, twisted Megan's stomach into ropes.

"I see something!" Bibi shouted from the top of the small hill. She pointed toward the creek.

Megan joined her grandmother up by the house. If the goat was in the water, she'd drown. Though goats could swim, Pygmies were small—Dimples was barely eighteen inches high. With all the rain they'd had over the past weeks, the creek was a raging stream. The goat wouldn't have a chance.

Megan looked in the direction her grandmother was pointing. After a moment, she saw Dimples through the budding maple trees, her head barely visible on an elevated rock.

"Go inside, Bibi," Megan said. "I'll get her. You're soaking wet."

"I'm fine. Save the goat."

Megan ran alongside the house, away from the fields, and down the small embankment that led to Barney Creek, her feet slipping in the slurping mud. Dimples was near the brush that lined the creek bed, her head on the rock and her body partially submerged in the rising creek waters. She scooped the tiny goat into her arms. Dimples was alive, but barely. Her body was stiff and cold, her fur matted with what looked like mud and blood.

Back at the house, Bibi was already running a tepid bath. Megan lowered Dimples into the water. Blood-red circles fanned out in all directions from the goat's little body. "Call Dr. Finn," Megan said to her grandmother. She glanced at her watch and sighed. "Tell him it's an emergency."

"We need to stop meeting like this," Dr. Finn said in his Scottish brogue, an accent that became more pronounced when the vet was animated. The goat was on his lap, wrapped in a yellow blanket, and Megan's dog Sadie was under the table, her head on the veterinarian's foot. "Your animals seem to be going mad."

Megan smiled. She watched Dr. Daniel "Denver" Finn as he attended to her goat. Once the animal's body temperature was back to normal, he'd checked her from head to tiny tail and discovered only a few surface lacerations on her left rear leg and one gash across her side that required stitches. Now he was giving her a shot of antibiotics. The goat didn't flinch.

Nearly six foot four and somewhere in his mid-thirties, Dr. Finn had the musculature you'd expect from a large animal veterinarian used to handling horses and birthing cows. Megan, brought up on James Herriot novels, thought Dr. Finn possessed the characteristics she'd come to expect of a man in his position: patience, strength and a sense of humor born of acceptance of the cycles of life. His reddish-brown waves were always tousled, his smile was of the dimpled, crooked variety, and a pale jagged scar ran across the bridge of his nose. The result was a ruggedly handsome man with a wicked smile who seemed capable of handling any emergency. They'd been flirting—if you could call it that—for months, and friendly for longer than that, but Megan didn't have the nerve or time to make it more.

Dr. Finn patted the goat's head. "Your wee lassie will be perfectly fine." He smiled. "At least this time."

Megan leaned against the table, relieved. "Thank you."

"Happy to help."

Bibi was bustling around the big farm kitchen. She put a steaming cup of coffee in front of Dr. Finn and patted his shoulder. He threw her a grateful smile.

"Cinnamon bread?" she asked. "It's fresh."

"Oh, I wish, but I have appointments waiting." His warm response brought a smile to Bibi's face. To Megan, he said, "I'll come back tonight to check those stitches. In the meantime, the area will have to stay open to the air. Anything I put on there, the lassie will eat."

Megan nodded. This was the fifth time Dr. Finn had been called to the farm in the last two months alone. Usually his presence was required because one of the goats had eaten an inedible object—like shoestrings, electrical wire, or even a garden hose. Visits were so common, she had a line of credit with the clinic.

Dr. Finn ran a palm along the length of Dimples' body. Not for the first time, Megan noticed his big hands, surprisingly long, slender fingers bare of rings, and nails cut short, neatly squared-off.

"She must have slipped at the edge of the creek. Wedged herself down between the rocks. That's how she got cut." He stroked the goat's head again absentmindedly. "She's a lucky one to be alive." Dr. Finn looked up. "Do you know how she escaped her pen?"

Megan glanced at Bibi, who shrugged and said, "I looked outside while I was baking and happened to see Heidi up on that roof."

Megan frowned. "I wonder how she opened the gate."

"It should have been latched," Bibi said. "Maybe she kicked it in?"

"I don't think so. The gate looked fine." Megan glanced at Dr. Finn and said, "Heidi's clever, but she's not *that* clever. She's never been able to open the gate before."

"Maybe the other goat did it?"

Megan shook her head. "She's less likely to get out than Heidi."

Dr. Finn looked thoughtful. He took a sip of coffee, swallowed, and said, "I guess there's always a first time." He thanked Bibi again and stood, unfurling to his full height. "Goats are smart little buggers."

"But what about the cat?" Megan asked, remembering their newest family member and the balled-up letter. "Bibi, did you let the cat inside?"

"Not that I can recall."

Megan was still thinking about the cat when Dr. Finn looked at her and said, "Will you be okay for now, Megan?"

Megan nodded, still distracted.

The goat still nestled in the vet's arms, he said, "I'll get her settled back in her pen to make sure she's okay. Then I'll be back around six thirty tonight. Does that work?"

Megan agreed and thanked him. When the vet was gone, she grabbed her keys off the wall.

"I'll see you later."

Bibi looked startled. "Where are you going?"

"To the café." Megan grabbed the crumpled letter off the table and handed it to her grandmother. "Do you know when this letter arrived?"

"A few days ago." Her grandmother looked chagrined. "I forgot to give it to you. Those stupid letters. Permits, inspections, licenses...this farm has been standing since 1764 and now this arrogant man can tell us what we can or can't do."

"I know, it feels unfair," Megan said, keeping her tone steady to mask her own annoyance at the commissioner. "But we have to play by the rules. The fact that my father didn't is what got us in this predicament."

"Bah." Bibi waved her hand. "Simon never liked the Birch family. His mother doesn't like us either. Simon's only making trouble. It's what he does these days, make trouble for simple folk who want to be left well enough—"

Megan shook her head. "He's simply doing his job. And right now, I need to do mine by meeting him at the café." She looked down at her jeans and sweatshirt—now soiled by mud and pinprick spots of goat blood—and thought about changing. There was no time.

"Well, tell him we don't need his stupid inspection," Bibi said, but she looked worried. "We can get along perfectly fine without his blessing, right?"

Megan's lips twisted into the semblance of a smile. If only it were that simple. She kissed her grandmother on the forehead and thanked her for her help. "Don't worry, Bibi. I'll handle it. The farm will be up and running in no time, just as we planned."

Two

Megan drove through Winsome at a greyhound's pace, her truck striving to cradle the backcountry curves. Winsome was a quintessential rural Pennsylvania town, the kind of place where family trees were deeply rooted and neighborly alliances—and grudges—measured their ages in decades, not months. Only forty miles outside of Philadelphia, it felt like a different world. The landscape was notable for its old stone farmhouses, cobbled streets, and tiny, iron-fenced graveyards, a favorite with history buffs. Tourists loved Winsome in the fall, when the horizon was ablaze with the burnt orange, crimson red and molten yellow leaves of birch, mountain maples, ash, and oak trees, but they especially loved Winsome in the summer, when the Bucks County farms bloomed and the wildflowers lining Winsome's main streets painted the town in a kaleidoscope of vibrant colors.

Now, with spring slow to come and summer seemingly far off, Winsome's muddied landscape didn't seem all that endearing to Megan. She drove her pickup truck straight through what served as a downtown, navigating around pond-size puddles of standing water, and made a left onto Canal Street, Winsome's main thoroughfare. She pulled right in front of the sign for Washington Acres Farm Café & Larder.

Winsome's love affair with its Colonial roots had made naming her organic farm and café easy. Rumor had it George Washington had spent time in Winsome long before the town was a town, and that same rumor pegged the Birch homestead as the place he'd stayed. Truth? Megan wasn't sure, but truth didn't always matter much to people when it came to a good story. Or a good name.

She glanced at the sign and took a deep breath, saying a silent prayer for patience. Simon Duvall's brand new Chrysler Sebring convertible was parked two spots down, next to a bright green and white sign that read "Win Back Winsome!" Fitting, since the "Win Back Winsome" campaign had been his baby.

A few years back, Simon and a group of Winsome residents got together within the Winsome Historical Society and created a beautification board. The Board's mission: to refresh the town's tired main streets, especially Canal Street. Canal Street, creatively so-named because it ran parallel to the old canal, once transported goods between Pennsylvania and destinations north. It was the pride and joy of Winsome. The donkey tracks, still visible on either side of the canal, had been reinvented into walking paths.

Megan made her way along the spanking new pavement that lined Canal Street's businesses. She was late, but as she walked past the ornate benches, metal lamp posts, and small gardens—all new as well—that had been interspersed between the crumbling facades of centuries-old buildings, she wondered where the money was coming from. Every day, the Beautification Board seemed to add something. Winsome was not a wealthy place, and the cost for the changes caused by the "Win Back Winsome" campaign had to come from somewhere. Megan figured higher taxes made up a portion of the shortfall. And an impossible zoning process was making up the remainder.

Megan opened the café doors to find Clover Hand, her store manager, and Simon deep in conversation at the counter. At the back of the store, the Dorfman brothers, Megan's contractors, were putting the finishing touches on the new lunch counter.

"Simon," Megan said. "I'm sorry I'm late. We had a bit of an emergency up at the farm."

Simon turned to look at her, distaste evident on his face. "Yes, well," Simon said. "I have another appointment after this, so let's get on with it."

Megan nodded. She peeled off her dripping raincoat and placed it on a coat rack by the front door, taking her time. Out of the corner of her eye, she saw Neil Dorfman, a stocky redhead with a bushy mustache and a red-veined nose, watching her. Clover, too, seemed entranced. Her long, thin fingers covered the bottom half of her long, thin face. The room pulsed with tension.

Megan pulled the failed inspection letter out of her bag. "I received your notice, Simon. I hope we can clear up any misunderstandings today. You know as well as I do that in order to be up and running in time for the spring harvest, I need the town's approvals soon."

Simon took the paper from her, glanced at it, and handed it back. "Then I suggest you do as the inspector suggests."

"But Roger Becker did the last barn inspection, and he didn't *suggest* anything."

"I'm sure Roger gave you a list of things to fix."

"That's the only correspondence I have, and it's from you." Although, even as the words left her mouth, Megan wasn't so sure they were accurate. Bibi's reaction earlier told her that perhaps Roger Becker *had* sent her a list—a list that ended up in the garbage.

"That's not my problem, Ms. Sawyer. While you were busy being tardy, I took the opportunity to look around the café. I have my own list of things that need to be fixed or completed before you may open here as well."

Megan closed her eyes. "Simon, we're supposed to open Monday. I have orders to fill, shelves to stock. Perishables."

"By the grace of God, Ms. Sawyer, that is not my problem. We have rules here in Winsome. *Rules.* They may not have had many rules in Chicago, but in these parts, order matters. Safety matters." He narrowed his eyes. "Unless you don't care about order and safety."

"Oh, *please,*" Clover muttered.

Megan shot her a warning look. Simon was a pompous ass, but it wouldn't do to exacerbate things by baiting him.

"Look, Simon, let's be reasonable. You know that order and rules matter to me, but we've jumped through every hoop the town has set up to get the farm and café running. We've delayed the store's opening twice. I fixed absolutely everything you asked me to—"

Simon walked toward her, gut first, wearing a diamond-patterned knit vest over a ruby Polo shirt. Simon's appetite for power was only rivaled by his appetite for craft beer. Or so Megan had heard. Eyebrows raised, he thrust something at her, the skin under and above his salt and pepper beard a livid red.

"Everything, Ms. Sawyer?"

She snatched the paper and read through the handwritten list. "Fire extinguishers? We already purchased them."

"They're not stored properly."

"You never told us how you wanted them stored." Megan scanned the list further. "The numbers marking the street address are too small?" Megan eyed him, incredulous. "They're a hundred years old and carved into the brick fascia."

Simon shrugged. "Rules."

"And the café sign is six inches too large?" At this, Megan tossed the list on a workbench and spun around to face the zoning commissioner. "Six inches too large for what?"

"It creates an eyesore."

"That sign cost three thousand dollars!"

He shrugged again, looking smug. "Perhaps you're in over your head, Ms. Sawyer. An organic farm? A café? Your father tried this route before and found it led nowhere." He bent to pick his umbrella out of the stand by the door. He took the list off the bench. "I'll have our secretary type this up and send you a formal letter. Once you get that, you have thirty days to comply. Only then will you get the permit."

Megan flinched at the comment about her father—because it was true. She said, "And the farm?"

"Do what my inspector told you to do."

"But your inspector gave us no specifics." Megan looked at her contractors, who had also done the bulk of the work on the barn and produce prep areas. "Right, guys?"

Both Dorfmans stared at their shoes. Dave, who, unlike his brother, was tall and lanky and completely bald, mumbled something unintelligible. They were afraid of Simon, Megan knew. No one, especially those in the construction industry, wanted to be on Simon's bad side. Frustrated, Megan turned back toward the commissioner.

"I'm opening next week."

"Thirty days. Protocol." Simon waved his hand. "Good day, Ms. Sawyer."

"Oh, for goodness sake," Megan exclaimed, but Simon was already gone.

"Bastard," Clover said. "You're a lawyer. Can't you do something about this?"

Megan sat down on a milk crate, head in her hands. She'd come to Winsome in part to escape the practice of law. A legal battle with her hometown was the last thing she wanted. "I'm not going that route—not unless they give me no choice."

"Well, what he's doing—what *they're* doing—isn't fair. I told him that, but he wouldn't listen." Clover pouted. Clover had a face that, at twenty-three, still looked sixteen, and when she was upset, she had a tendency to pout. She also had a tendency to wear very little clothing, and today was no exception. A green canvas miniskirt ended right below her derriere, and a tight brown t-shirt ended a hair above her belly button. But that was Clover, and Megan had come to love her just as she was.

"You're right. It's not fair," Megan said, heart heavy. "Simon is a zealot. He believes he's doing something good, which can make him even more dangerous."

"But why stall on the farm?" Clover asked. "You're fixing up an eyesore—no offense to your family—and you're producing food for the community. What could be wrong with that?"

It was Megan's turn to shrug. "Simon wants things his way."

"That ain't it," Neil Dorfman finally spoke. Clover and Megan both looked at him, surprised. Neil rarely spoke, and when he did, it was usually in grunts and monosyllables.

"Then what is it?" Clover asked.

He looked at Megan. "I heard your property was supposed to be sold to the Winsome Historical Society."

Megan's eyes widened. She couldn't see Bibi selling that house to anyone, much less the Historical Society. Bibi despised local politics almost as much as she despised the permitting process. Her grandmother did not have much love for rules *or* the people who made them.

"Who told you that, Neil?"

"Your Aunt Sarah."

"Aunt Sarah?" The mythical Aunt Sarah? Megan's grandfather had been the middle child in a family of three kids. She vaguely remembered her father and Bibi speaking of an Aunt Sarah, her grandfather's younger sister, but only in those hushed tones used to discuss terminal illness and sexual predators. Indeed, any inquiries on Megan's part had been met with a rapid change in topic.

Neil repeated, "Sarah Birch."

When Megan still looked blankly at him, he sighed and said, "Oh, never mind. You must have known about the offer, right?" When she shook her head at that too, he stared, disbelieving, and said, "The point is, Simon was not happy when you came back to town."

"So he's taking it out on my businesses?"

The Dorfmans shrugged simultaneously.

"That's his way," Dave said. "It's why most everyone hates him."

Clover nodded. "He even has a rough relationship with his own mother."

"Ridiculous," Megan uttered. "Simon wanted Washington Acres for himself—or for the Historical Society—so now he's denying the permits?" She felt the walls of the café closing in on her, the creeping, crawling sense of unease now fully realized. She needed some air.

"What are you going to do?" Clover asked.

"Why not delay the opening?" Dave said. "Postpone it a month or two. That will give us time to get the work finished."

"All those vegetables will go to waste," Clover snapped. "Megan? What's our next move?"

"I'm not sure." Megan stood. She grabbed her raincoat off the rack. "But it will be something more drastic than letter-writing. It's about time someone challenged Simon Duvall."

Despite her brave words, Megan was feeling pretty heartsick. She'd left Chicago and a financially lucrative—if not emotionally satisfying—legal practice to come back to Pennsylvania. She hadn't lived in Winsome for the last fourteen years, since she went away to college, but the town never lost its call. It was where she met Mick, the love of her life, killed three years ago in Afghanistan. And now if Simon Duvall had his way, her vision of what the Birch properties could be, properties that had been in her family for over seventy-five years, would be dashed. She wished Mick was here. Together, they'd figure out what to do.

Megan sat in the truck for a few minutes, nursing her hurt. She plugged in her iPod, searched for Bruce Springsteen, and took off. Winsome was surrounded by back country roads, roads with a high speed limit and no one around to notice her blaring music or screeching transmission.

She drove north, past the town center, past Washington Acres, and headed toward the Episcopalian church that sat high on the hill. Windows down, face soaked with tears, she flew past the elementary school, the town mill yard, and the only synagogue for miles around and still kept going, Mick's death stinging like a million tiny knife wounds. But he'd loved Springsteen, and with "Thunder Road" on and the wind mussing her hair, she almost felt him beside her.

Almost.

At the next intersection, she made a right and then a quick left, still climbing toward the church. Once there, she made her way down the other side of the hill to the gravesites.

She parked the truck, scrambled out, and made her way to Mick's grave, hidden away under an oak tree on the edge of the graveyard. The American flag waving next to it made it easy to spot.

She sank down on the wet ground, fighting back tears. Answers would come.

It was well after five when she finally stood to leave. She remembered that Dr. Finn was coming to see Dimples. She needed to get going.

All that thinking time with Mick helped. She would fight the zoning board, if she had to. And she would win.

Three

When Megan arrived at the farm, Dr. Finn was already there. She found him sitting with Bibi at the kitchen table drinking tea. Bibi made her own tea from a variety of herbs she grew in a small garden out back, and Megan was convinced she added a touch of whiskey to "keep the bad away." Megan didn't have the heart to tell Dr. Finn. He and Bibi looked quite content. In cahoots, one might say—that one being Megan.

"You two up to no good?" Megan asked, smiling her first real smile of the day.

"Megan, where have you been? Dr. Finn's been waiting."

"I'm early," he said apologetically. He stood and grabbed his jacket. "Thanks for the tea, Mrs. Birch."

Dr. Finn followed Megan through the courtyard and down to the barn shed. The rain had given up its hold around noon, and the sun was finally peeking out between the clouds, just in time for sunset. The courtyard was muddy, and they negotiated their way around the puddles, Megan's dog Sadie trailing along behind. The chicken tractors, off to the side and near the other end of the barn, were full, the chickens inside for the evening, but the birds squawked loudly, their own private jeering section.

Sadie turned her head hopefully in the direction of the chickens. Although she'd never been around farm animals before moving to Winsome, the dog was gentle with the goats and barn cats. But sometimes she looked at the chickens with an expectant expression that made Megan uneasy. Megan was pretty sure Sadie thought the birds were moving squeaky toys.

"That dog's got some Newfoundland in her," Dr. Finn said.

Megan took another look at her canine companion. "Really? I don't see it." Sadie tipped the scales at eighty pounds despite a slender physique. She was a Mr. Potato Head of a dog, with a German shepherd face, a greyhound body, and a golden retriever tail. Her coloring was that of a shepherd. Megan didn't see Newfie any more than she saw Dachshund.

Doctor Finn grinned. "Aye, have a genetic test done. I'll bet you dinner."

"I may take that bet," Megan said, surprising herself.

"I hope you do."

Their eyes met. Megan looked away first. They'd reached the covered shed, and Megan unlatched the gate and went inside the goat enclosure.

Dr. Finn picked up Dimples. "Seems to be feeling better. Let's have a look at those stitches."

He handed the goat to Megan. She held her up to the light while he traced the spot he'd shaved earlier today. The skin that had been stitched was slightly red and puffy.

Dr. Finn pulled something from his pocket and sprayed it on the wound. "Just to be safe." He handed Megan the bottle. "Three times a day. If it starts to look worse, or if she's acting off, call me right away. I left some oral antibiotics with your grandmother. Give them—"

His words were cut off by Sadie's sudden barking. Sadie rarely barked—it was what made her a great city dog back in Chicago—so when she did, Megan took notice. The dog pawed the gate. She barked again, more insistently.

Megan looked at Dr. Finn, whose head was cocked to the side, listening. "Someone must be here."

She placed Dimples back in her straw bed and she and the vet left the goat enclosure. Sadie ran ahead, sniffing the ground as she went. She bolted around the corner toward the main barn entrance.

"Sadie!" Megan called. "Sadie, come back here."

Dr. Finn said, "I've never heard Sadie bark like that."

"Me neither."

They followed the dog into the pitch black barn. The massive structure was made up of three sections: a newer, cavernous space at the front, an empty older portion in the back, and an addition containing a wash room, an office, and horse stalls. The Dorfman brothers had gutted parts of the barn as part of the renovations. Now the newer section was mostly one giant, tool-strewn room. Megan fumbled against the wall from memory and grabbed a hoe. She handed it to the vet. Her toe kicked another tool lying on the floor, near the back wall, and she picked that up too. A shovel. It would have to do.

Sadie had stopped barking. Megan tip-toed to where the light switch was, a feeling of urgency washing over her. She flipped on the overheads, which brightened the center of the barn, bathing the corners in shadows. She grabbed a flashlight.

Megan and Dr. Finn stood stock-still, eyes searching for movement. "Sadie!" Megan called, hearing the panic in her own voice. "Sadie!"

Sadie barked. Relief flooded over Megan and she looked at Dr. Finn with a reassured smile. But he didn't look satisfied.

"Call her again."

Megan did, but Sadie didn't come. Raising her shovel, Megan said, "Sadie, now." Megan gripped the shovel harder, feeling the hairs on her arms and neck stand straight. Her stomach clenched and unclenched. "Sadie," she called again.

This time Sadie came running. She stopped in front of them, barked, and headed back toward the farthest stall, where the overhead lighting didn't reach.

Megan started to jog to cover the distance when her flashlight beam swept the floor. She stopped dead in her tracks. "Denver, look."

He looked down to where Megan was pointing, then back at Megan. Their eyes locked.

"Oh no," he said.

Oh no, she thought.

Sadie had left paw prints all along the floor—bloody paw prints.

They rushed quietly the rest of the way through the barn. In the stall, they found Sadie, barking madly again, standing over the body of a man. He was facedown on the floor, wedged between a hay bale and a row of rakes, shovels, and hoes that had been hung from the wall. His skull was bashed in. Blood splattered the floor and walls behind him.

Megan didn't need to roll the man over to know who he was— the diamond vest and rotund body told her that. Simon Duvall.

The murder weapon wasn't hard to identify either. There was one tool missing from the rack on the wall—a shovel. Her best shovel. With increasing horror, Megan shined the flashlight onto the shovel in her hand, the one she'd picked up at the entrance of the barn. Streaks of blood marked the metal. She hadn't even noticed in the dim light. The tool clattered to the ground when she let it go. Her stomach lurched. She swallowed a scream.

Denver knelt down, careful to avoid the pools of blood. He lifted one outstretched arm and felt for a pulse. "Dead." He stood, looking around. "Whoever did this must have run through the main portion and then out through the rear of the barn."

"Bibi. We need to make sure she's okay."

"I'll check on Bonnie," he said. "You call the police."

Bibi was fine. They found her in the living room watching television and eating potato chips and sour cream. Megan hugged her fiercely. She told her what they'd found while Dr. Finn checked the rest of the house.

"Well, that's a new one," was Bibi's response when Megan finished the story. "Your grandfather died of a heart attack in the bathroom, and old Mr. Newsome was shot by a hunter down by Barney Creek. Never had anyone murdered here before, though."

"One is more than enough." Megan pictured Simon's skull, the gray matter that had spilled onto the barn floor. She was no forensic expert, but she figured the murderer had been enraged enough to make the first blow count.

"Where's Sadie?" Bibi asked.

"On the porch. I have to wash her before she comes inside. She has blood on her paws. Dr. Finn is going to carry her to the bathroom tub for me."

Bibi looked at her sideways. "He's single, you know. Wife left him years ago. Wanted a man with regular hours, she said. And didn't like dogs, imagine that. Dr. Finn never remarried."

Megan shook her head. A man had been murdered on their property and Bibi was playing matchmaker.

At that moment, Denver walked in.

"House is clear."

"Thank you."

Sirens blared in the distance. Winsome had a police force of exactly five, and Megan knew who would be coming. A murder would mean the whole force. And the crime scene investigator. And the district attorney. There would be warrants and searches and police tape. She was still queasy from finding Simon's body, but years as a litigator had given her a good idea of the circus that was to come. The noise of the police cars got louder.

"Rescue is on the way," Bibi said.

"Bibi, it's no time to joke."

But Denver only smiled. "I'm sure whoever did this is long gone."

Megan nodded. Still, she suspected that sleep would elude her tonight. "I'll bring the cats in the house. I'd bring all the animals in, if I could."

"Maybe you and Bonnie should stay somewhere else tonight."

"We'll stay here," Megan said.

"We'll be fine," Bibi echoed.

Denver shook his head. "I guess." He walked to the window and looked outside. "I'll wait until the police take our statements, and then we'll get Sadie cleaned up. Okay?"

Megan nodded. The happenings of the last hour, of the whole

day, really, hit her and she sat down heavily on an armchair. Simon Duvall. Dead in *her* barn. The argument they'd had earlier. Her rash words, her fingerprints on the shovel. It didn't take a law degree to realize the police would look at her first.

She glanced at Denver. "Thank you. For everything."

"Do ye need me to stay? I can stay."

She glanced at Bibi, who had buried a husband. Megan had lost her husband and lived through it. We Birch women persevere, she thought.

"I'll be fine."

Denver grabbed her hand, gave a quick squeeze and let go. She found she wanted him to hold on.

Four

The next day brought cloudy skies and madness in the form of more police activity. The Winsome police force, all five officers, had cordoned off the barn and a portion of the grass behind it the night before in order to preserve evidence. The county coroner had arrived some time past eight and pronounced Simon officially dead before removing his body. Crime scene investigators took pictures and videos, dusted for fingerprints, used luminol to examine the rest of the barn, and searched outside for footprints—a mostly thankless task, given the recent rains. When Megan argued that she needed access to the barn in order to work, she was told firmly "no"—police business. She'd have to wait in case the police needed to regain entry to the crime scene.

And here they were to continue their investigation. They'd kept their promise.

"Megan, tell me again where you were between the hours of twelve noon and six in the evening on May fourteenth."

"She's already told you that five times," Clover said. Clover had arrived at the farm right after Police Chief Bob King pulled in, so soon after that Megan suspected she'd followed him.

"Well, Clover—" he glared at his girlfriend "—she can tell me again."

King looked at Megan for a response. Megan wiped her hands on her jeans and turned to look at Winsome's young police chief. "I've repeated the story *at least* five times over. This is not a television show. You're not going to get a different answer on try six."

But King remained stalwart. "Humor me."

And so she did, all the while continuing her task of collecting last night's eggs. She had to keep her wits about her, and murder or not, there was work to be done—hard as it was to concentrate. When she had finished, King jotted down a few more notes in his small spiral pad.

"What can you be writing in there, Bobby?" Clover asked. "She told you the same story every time."

King, a tall, broad man with a blonde crewcut and more determination than common sense, looked at his on-again, off-again girlfriend with annoyance. They were outside by the chicken tractors. He had been following Megan from task to task, ignoring Sadie's plaintive requests to play fetch. Because the store opening was delayed, Clover said she was here to help with the farm chores, although the term "helping" was only loosely applicable.

King ignored Clover. "So you go to the church cemetery often?" he asked. "To talk to your dead husband?"

Clover elbowed him in the stomach.

"Clover, that hurts. I am a sworn police officer and someone died here. Please let me do my job." He turned to Megan. "I'm sorry if that sounded insensitive. Maybe someone saw you? Someone who can vouch for your whereabouts."

Megan stood, the basket of eggs hanging from her elbow. "Bobby, are you trying to tell me I'm a suspect in Simon's death?"

King's face colored. Although he was a few years younger than Megan, his family went back at least as far as the Birch family—and he'd never left. "Now, you know I have to do my job. And Duvall *did* die on your property."

"And you think I would be stupid enough to kill him, leave him there so that I could discover him with Dr. Finn, and then call you?"

Clover placed a single watercolor green egg in the basket and nodded emphatically. "You have to admit—that would be pretty dumb."

King gave Clover a withering look. "And maybe that's what she wants us to think. She could have killed Simon in a fit of anger and then panicked. She's a lawyer, Clover. She would be banking on us thinking she's too smart to do something that dumb."

Clover arched thin eyebrows. "Listen to yourself."

Megan left them alone to argue. She walked away from the chicken tractors, making her way through the mixed flock of chickens—Chanteclers, Delawares, Orpingtons, and a few Plymouth Rocks—and opened the padlock on the walk-in refrigerator outside the barn. She placed the eggs inside. Behind her, Clover's angry monologue said the pair were following her.

"Megan, tell him you didn't kill Simon."

"Of course I didn't kill Simon."

King sighed. "It's not that simple, Clover."

Megan closed the refrigerator door—without the store and café, what was she going to do with all those eggs?—thought better of it, and reached back inside. She pulled the basket back out.

"Bobby, I need to get into the barn."

"I'm afraid that's out of the question."

"Then you go in for me."

He frowned. "What for?"

"There's a big box by the doors, under a tarp. It's marked 'cartons.' Bring that out here?"

"Seriously, Megan?"

Clover looked at him beseechingly. She ran a finger down the arm of his uniform in a playful gesture. He shrugged her hand away, but Megan could see him softening. Clover was hard to resist.

He shook his head. "Fine."

He was back a minute later with the box. Megan opened it, pulled out three egg cartons, and knelt down on the still-muddy ground. She filled the cartons with the morning's bounty, taking time to mix the browns, blues and greens so that each carton looked balanced in color and size. There were still more than two dozen eggs left over in the basket—enough to satisfy Bibi. She handed one carton to Clover and two to Bob.

"Thanks," Clover said.

King looked down at the eggs in his hand. "What are these for?"

"Eating," Megan said with a smile. "One for you and one for your mother."

"Aw, thank you. She'll like that." King's blue eyes narrowed. "Is this a bribe?"

Clover scowled. "Bobby!"

Megan stood. "You really have seen one too many episodes of CSI." She placed the basket back in the refrigerator and secured the padlock. "Now, if you'll excuse me, I'm going to help Clay transplant tomatoes." She looked up at the sky, wishing for the warmth of the sun on her face. It would be nice if the ground would finally dry out.

"I have more questions," King said.

"Then by all means, join me." Megan glanced at Clover. "Why don't you run the eggs up to the house and check on my grandmother? If she has any of her cherry Danish left, bring it down. I'm sure Bobby and the others are hungry."

King gave her another suspicious look, which she dismissed with a wave of one chapped hand. "I have absolutely nothing to hide. Ask me whatever you want, but let me get my work done. One way or another, I have a farmers market to attend next week, and I need to be able to sell something other than mud." She looked around the farm, her eyes settling on Clay's narrow figure in the distance. She knew her need to work had as much to do with escaping thoughts of Simon's murder—and the fact that a murderer was still at large in Winsome—but she had to *do* something. Something was better than worrying, after all. "And as of right now, mud is about all I have to offer."

Undeterred, King followed Megan to the fields and through the deer fencing, where she picked up a tray of tomato seedlings and a small shovel. Clay Hand, Megan's farm manager and Clover's older brother, had turned over the bed, and Megan selected a row far enough from Clay that she could talk to the police chief without being overheard. She began to dig a small hole at one end of the row and waited for King's follow-up questions. She'd sent Clover to the house in order to give him some time to ask hard questions without his girlfriend's interruptions. The way Megan saw it, King had real potential, but youth and a desire to please had him convinced he could handle Clover and the investigation. As much as Megan hated this process, she had enough respect for the law to want it done right. She also wanted to be crossed off the suspect list—as quickly as possible.

"Would you like me to get you a chair?" she asked.

"I'll be fine." He paused and, although Megan's gaze was on the task at hand, she heard him rifling through his notebook. "I understand you had an argument with Simon the day he was killed."

"As I told you last night, it wasn't an argument. It was a disagreement."

"Over the permits for the store and farm?"

"Correct."

A pregnant silence forced Megan to consider her options. She knew her disagreement with the zoning commissioner would be the subject of town gossip, but she also knew she wasn't the only person in Winsome who had a beef with Simon Duvall.

"Megan, you know how this looks. What can you tell me to help me shift my focus? Who else might have wanted Simon dead?"

Megan looked up, surprised. She rubbed her temple with the back of her hand, leaving a streak of mud across her forehead. "Seriously? He was the zoning commissioner and the head of the Historical Society. I bet if you dig, you'll find a hundred people with something against Simon."

"How much money do you have tied up in this—" Bob stopped to look around "—project?"

"Do you think that's relevant?"

Bob looked chagrined. "If Simon was threatening your businesses—and your bottom line—yes, I think it's relevant."

"I'm in the black. For now, at least." Megan shook her head. "You want more information than that, you'll have to get a warrant.

Our finances are our business." She pushed the tip of the shovel into the wet ground and dug a spot about six inches deep. "In the meantime, you're barking up the wrong tree. Winsome has a killer on the loose, and he or she doesn't reside at Washington Acres."

"What about the bid?"

"What bid?" But Megan felt her shoulders tensing. The bid Neil Dorfman had mentioned yesterday? Was it somehow related to Simon's murder?

"Bonnie was entertaining an offer from Duvall. To buy the place on behalf of the Historical Society."

Megan placed her shovel on the ground. She straightened, kneeling on one knee, and met King's gaze. "My grandmother never mentioned that to me." Which was the truth.

"That doesn't seem right. Clover says you two are real close."

Megan shrugged. "If you want to know about my grandmother's dealings with the Historical Society, I'm afraid you'll have to ask her."

"You're going play hard ball with me? Really?"

"I can't tell you anything because I don't know anything. Ask Bonnie."

King took an audible breath. "You seem awful calm for a lady with a dead body in her backyard. Doesn't it make you wonder who hates you enough to frame you for murder?"

Megan kept her voice metered to hide her rising frustration. "I am angry, scared, and very sad for the Duvall family. But I'm not sure you can jump to the conclusion that I'm being framed any more than you can conclude I did it."

"Simon was a resident of this town his whole life. I think his murder is as much about you and this farm as about him."

"Did you find anything at the crime scene yesterday to support that?"

"You know I can't divulge that."

"Look, I don't think Simon was a well-liked man. It's quite possible someone simply followed him here. The fact that his murder took place on our property was happenstance." But even as

Megan uttered the words, she wondered whether they were true.

"Had you arranged to meet him here last night?"

"No. I don't know why he was here." Which, Megan realized, did call into question whether someone simply followed Simon. Why had he come in the first place? "Ask around, Bobby. Simon wasn't easy to deal with. I'm sure I wasn't the only person who had issues with him."

"Simon was a pillar of Winsome."

"Then Winsome is standing on some mighty unsteady ground."

King sucked on the end of his pen, contemplating Megan's words. "You're not planning any trips in the near future, are you, Megan?"

Megan twisted pale lips into a smile. She waved her hand in the direction of the fields, sodden and dotted with fledgling plants. "I'll be right here, where I belong."

He nodded, but his eyes said maybe Winsome wasn't quite the right place for Megan and her projects after all.

Clay had another opinion on the matter. He and Megan were turning over a small bed along the western wall of the house that would soon be home to wildflowers. In addition to brightening up the yard and attracting pollinators, the wildflowers would make great bouquets that Megan planned to sell at the café and farmers markets. Clay had started on one end of the fifty-foot bed and Megan on the other, but after a few hours of intensive labor—work that made Megan's muscles ache and reigned in her wandering, worried mind—they'd met in the middle.

"He was a bastard," Clay said. "I don't care what King says. No one liked Duvall, not even his mother."

Clay spoke between huffed breaths. He wore low-slung jeans and a thick plaid flannel shirt. As always, his beard was neatly trimmed and his longish brown hair was held back in a ponytail. One thick strand had come loose and flopped across his face as he worked. He wiped the hair back with impatient swipes of long, strong fingers.

A stunningly handsome man, Clay had Pierce Brosnan's eyes and Jake Gyllenhaal's smile, but without a hint of narcissism. He and his sister had grown up in a commune. Like Clover, there was something almost naïve about his honest approach to the world, and Megan was afraid that eventually the world in all its cruelty would rob him of that innocent outlook.

Megan raked a section of soil and sprinkled seeds in the shallow furrows. "King called Simon a pillar."

"There's the public face and the private face. If you ask around, people will say good things about Duvall, even now. Simon had power and no one wanted to cross him." Clay stopped, resting his arm across the top of his new shovel, a shovel he'd had to buy from Merry Chance's nursery because the rest of the shovels were tied up behind police tape. "But behind closed doors...well, that's when you'll learn how people really felt about the man."

"Like what?"

"Like he was a pompous, controlling ass who used his power to get others to do his bidding."

"And what bidding would that be?"

Clay shrugged. "Depended on the day. Voting for him to be commissioner, getting someone he didn't like off the zoning board, driving customers to or away from a given business, enforcing the Beautification Board's directives." He smiled. "Like I said, he wasn't well liked."

This wasn't news to Megan, but Clay's knowledge of the townsfolks' sentiments was a surprise. "How do you know that much about the zoning commissioner?"

Clay smiled. "Shocking?"

"You've never struck me as a gossip."

Clay shrugged, but some of the humor had left his eyes. "When you grow up the way I did, you learn to pay attention to people. Besides, the few times I've run into his mother, Lenora, I didn't much care for our interactions. She's...self-righteous."

Megan considered the little she knew of the Duvall family. She'd seen Lenora here and there but had never spoken with her. An iron-haired, tight-lipped woman with impeccable posture, she certainly hadn't struck Megan as warm and fuzzy. Lenora had been a history professor at NYU for many years, returning to Winsome a decade ago. Now she wrote scholarly articles and lorded over the Beatification Board. "And Duvall never married?"

"Never, as far as I know. Winsome and his career have been his life. That and history. He was a history buff."

"Like Lenora?"

"More of a hobbyist than Lenora, but maybe even more passionate." Clay sprinkled seeds in the last furrow, then stood straight and picked up his shovel. "Simon is—was—an odd bird, but I can't imagine who'd want him dead." He shook his head. "Things like that simply don't happen in Winsome."

Megan thought about the goats' escape and the cat inside the house. Was it possible someone had been on the property the morning of Duvall's demise? Or even the night before? The thought was unsettling.

Clay started toward the small shed they were using as makeshift storage until the police finished with the barn. When he was a few feet away, he turned around.

"You need to be careful, Meg," he said, a look of concern in his deep-set eyes. "There could be more here than meets the eye. I've lived here for fifteen years and I'm still considered a newcomer. You're a prodigal daughter returned. Hard to say who's happy to see you and who's not thrilled you're back."

"You think I've ruffled someone's feathers without realizing it?" Megan asked. She thought of King's hypothesis—*was* someone trying to set her up?

Clay shrugged. "Until King and his henchmen figure out who killed Duvall, I would watch who you trust."

Megan tilted her head, giving Clay an inquisitive nod. "And whom can I trust, Clay?"

"For now? Your grandmother, of course. And me and Clover.

And Denver Finn. But other than us?" He answered with an apologetic smile.

Megan stood still, thinking. She looked toward the barn, at the trampled grass and grimy footprints that evidenced recent police activity, and considered what Clay was saying. He was right. Winsome was a small town, but people—with all their human frailties—were, in the end, just people. Perhaps those shortcomings were better hidden in a small town out of necessity, but they still existed. Someone could feel threatened by her return. But who—and why?

"In the meantime," Clay said, "we need to figure out who will clean up the crime scene. I can do it, once King gives the okay." The look of distaste on his face told Megan what he thought about that idea.

Megan shook her head. "I've already called a crime scene cleanup crew, a firm King recommended. They'll be here later today."

"Will the police pick up the tab?"

Megan smiled. "Hardly." She nodded toward the fields. "Let's hope insurance covers it. Otherwise, we'd better sell a lot of vegetables."

Five

It was after eight when Megan finally came inside for the evening. Intent on keeping her hands—and mind—busy, she'd planted and watered and weeded and sowed until her fingers were raw and her lower back ached. More than anything, she'd dreaded the conversation she knew she had to have with Bibi. Either people were fabricating tales about Bibi or Bibi had failed to share some pretty important information. Whether it had anything to do with Simon's murder remained to be seen.

Megan placed her dirty work boots on the porch. Sadie, loyal as ever, hovered next to her, her long face pressed up against Megan's arm. She sensed Megan's angst.

"Come on, girl," Megan said. Together, they made their way into the house. In her bedroom, Megan peeled off her jeans and t-shirt. After she showered and dressed in a pair of pale green cotton pajamas, she stood in front of her bathroom mirror, applying cream under her eyes and around her mouth. At thirty-two, she already had laugh lines around her eyes. Too much sun, she thought, and vowed for the millionth time to wear hats and sunscreen. She stared into the mirror; the woman gazing back at her looked tired. She picked up a comb and ran it through her thick, dark, shoulder-length hair, struggling to get out the knots.

She turned her head from side to side, looking for gray. She didn't see any, but figured if anything would cause her to go gray prematurely like Bibi, Simon's murder would.

Simon's murder. She sighed. Bibi. The clock in her bedroom said 8:32. She'd stalled long enough.

She found Bibi in the sitting room, knitting something small and pink. When Megan walked in, Bibi looked up at her over black-rimmed reading glasses. "Rough day?"

Megan nodded. She sat across from her grandmother on a worn upholstered armchair, its thick arms covered by crocheted doilies. The arms were a dark walnut and the fabric a deep red, the color of poppies. The chair had been in this room for as long as Megan could remember, although that fact gave her no comfort now.

"Did Bobby King speak with you today, Bibi?"

Eyes firmly planted on her knitting, Bibi nodded. "For twenty of the longest minutes of my life." She looked at Megan over her glasses. "And I've had a long life."

Megan took a deep breath. She studied her grandmother's hands, still nimble despite thick, swollen knuckles. "Bobby spoke to me too."

"As you knew he would."

"Some of his questions were...well, they were ones I couldn't answer."

"You're beating around the bush." Bibi glanced up from her knitting and, seeing the pained expression on Megan's face, placed the needles in her lap, giving Megan her full attention. "What is it, Meg? What has you worried?"

"Were you planning to sell the farm to the Historical Society?"

"Oh, is that all?" Bibi picked up the needles. She shook her head. "That man is grasping at anything right now."

"You never told me you were considering selling this place."

"There's nothing to tell."

Bibi returned to her knitting, and the rhythmic *click, click, click* of the needles filled the room. Megan normally found a soothing comfort in the sound, but currently it only heightened her frustration. Bibi was hiding something. Why, Megan didn't know.

"Bibi?"

When her grandmother looked up, she appeared tired and slightly cross. "Simon did try to buy the farm on behalf of the

Society and I said no. That's all there is to it."

There was a finality to her tone that Megan chose to respect. That didn't stop her from wondering, though...what wasn't her grandmother telling her? And did it have anything to do with the body in the barn?

Megan couldn't sleep. She'd been glib with Bob King, but the truth was she had a lot of money—all her money—tied up in the farm and café. They had the house, but it had been heavily mortgaged by her father. When he'd called two years ago to announce his engagement to an Italian woman and ask Megan to take over the farm and stay with Bibi, she'd agreed. She knew it would cost her—her father was no businessman, so the farm was sure to be hurting. But things looked even bleaker than she'd anticipated. If they could make the operation into a going concern, they would be fine—a prospect that was looking less and less likely.

At quarter after midnight, tired of fighting insomnia, Megan climbed out of bed. She traded her pajamas for a pair of jeans, a thick wool sweater, and her sneakers. She walked as silently as she could through the darkened house. Sadie, confused about the change of schedule, yawned and stretched her way behind Megan.

Megan thought about going out to the greenhouse to plant some flower seedlings, but the thought of being down there alone after what happened to Simon frightened her. Instead, she'd head to the café. She could use the time alone to sort through inventory and stock shelves. It would be good to focus on something tangible, and if she stayed here, she might wake Bibi. She left Bibi a note on the kitchen table and made sure to bring her cell phone, just in case.

Outside, the night was clear, the air crisp. Stars glowed overhead, their brilliance a reminder of how small she—and her problems—really were. She opened the truck and Sadie jumped in, happy to be included in Megan's plans. Megan kept the headlights off until she was out of the driveway. She made a left and headed her way back into town.

Canal Street was empty. Megan pulled up in front of the café, turned off the car and unlocked the front door. Inside, she flipped on the lights. Normally she wouldn't have thought twice about locking the door behind her, but tonight safety was on her mind, even with Sadie beside her. She locked the door and then double-checked to make sure it was tight. Satisfied, she walked back toward the lunch counter and pulled a box of locally canned goods from underneath. Sadie ran into the kitchen area and Megan let her go. Once the café was up and running, Sadie wouldn't be allowed in the café. For now, she was fine.

Megan dragged the box toward the front of the store, then stood straight to survey the space. The store was deeper than it was wide. In the back was the small kitchen, lunch counter, and what would be a long, copper-topped wooden farmhouse table. When facing the rear of the building, the check-out counter was on the left. The right side housed refrigerated sections for farm perishables—vegetables, fruits and fresh-cut flowers—and the center sported three short rows of shelves, enough to sell local food products and a few other necessities.

Most of the store remained empty.

Not for long, Megan thought. One way or another, she'd need those permits soon. She busied herself placing jars of pickled beets, cucumbers, garlic, tomatoes, and roasted peppers along the shelves. That task completed, she moved on to canned soups, paper goods, condensed milk, and the odd item that seemed more interesting than useful. She stepped back to admire the shelves. Things were shaping up.

A noise from the back startled her. She tensed, eyes darting toward the café. Sadie came running toward her, tail wagging madly. She stopped in front of Megan, dropped something at her feet, and crouched down, ready for a game of fetch. Megan bent down to pick up the object. It was hard, but wrapped in a layer of what looked like dark red felt. Megan unwrapped it slowly. Underneath the felt was a silver flask. It was old and worn, and the initials "BP" had been carved into the front. Megan unscrewed the cap. She didn't need to sniff the opening to know what was inside: whiskey.

Must belong to one of the Dorfmans' crew, Megan thought. She screwed the cap back on and wrapped it back in the felt. Yet the Dorfmans mostly worked alone. And Megan couldn't think of a single person with the initials B.P.

She shrugged, placed the flask on the counter, and got back to work, too tired to think more about it. Maybe if she stayed with this for another hour or two she'd be able to sleep.

Megan called it quits at two in the morning. By then, Sadie was sound asleep by the front door, the counters were fully stocked, and Megan had scrubbed and polished the empty kitchen area. She needed to secure a cook. Given the mess she was in, and the questionable state of the café's permits, it felt like an act of faith to hire someone now. She needed a little faith.

She grabbed a stack of resumes from her small desk at the back of the kitchen, next to the butler's pantry, and pulled out the one she had tabbed: Jeremy Landers, a name from her school days. Megan had already offered him the job; she'd call him to confirm in the morning.

Mentally and physically spent, she snapped on Sadie's leash and opened the front door. The street lights cast a lazy glow across the cobblestones, and the stars, visible in the clear night air, shone overhead. The street was silent. A cold breeze blew up from the canal, and Megan hurried toward the truck.

Two steps from the door, Sadie stopped and growled. She tugged on the leash, her body pulling in the direction of the alleyway between Moira's Antiques and The Book Shelf. With a longing glance at the truck, Megan followed Sadie. She saw a snake of a shadow slink across the stones.

"It's a cat, Sadie," she whispered. "Come on."

But the hair standing on the back of her neck along with the niggling pull in her belly said it wasn't a cat. The shadow had been too long. Someone was watching her.

Six

It was after seven that morning when Megan finally crawled out of bed. She'd slammed down the snooze button on her alarm six times. After the seventh reprieve, Bibi finally intervened.

"Are you running a farm or a brothel?" Bibi asked. "Cause with your late hours and sleeping habits, it feels more like the latter."

Bibi stood in the doorway of Megan's room with her hands on diminutive hips, a sparkling purple "Winsome Rocks It" t-shirt draped over a white turtleneck and black pants. When Megan was little, her father had owned a souvenir shop in what would eventually be the café. The shop had earned Eddie Birch a marginal living, and had been one of a string of his promising ideas. Megan appreciated her father's vision and passion, but like his last stint on the farm, many of his projects were met with more enthusiasm than good old practical sweat equity. Bibi still wore the seemingly endless supply of leftover t-shirts from the souvenir shop days. She didn't like to see anything go to waste.

"Come on," Bibi continued, her tone kind. "Roger Becker's here. He wants to talk to you. I made both of you pancakes and coffee. Take a shower and meet us in the kitchen." She smiled. "Things pass, Megan, and this will too. You'll learn not to ride the high points or the low points for too long."

Grateful, Megan nodded. Her relatively short marriage had taught her the truth in her grandmother's words.

In fifteen minutes, Megan had showered and dressed in faded blue jeans and a navy blue "Feeling Winsome" t-shirt that Bibi had snuck into her drawer. Refreshed, she readied herself for a battle with Simon Duvall's right-hand man, town inspector Roger Becker.

To Megan's surprise, there was to be no battle.

"Megan," Roger said warmly. He'd already been seated at the kitchen table, and was cutting into a stack of thick, plate-sized blueberry pancakes. Bibi poured him coffee ("Winsome Proud" on the mug), and placed it next to Roger's plate. He smiled his thanks and Bibi nodded appreciatively. Bibi loved to feed people, and she never looked as happy as she did in the kitchen. Megan's stomach growled.

"Two or three, Megan?"

Megan eyed Roger's plate. Two would be enough, but she had a long day ahead of her. "Three," she said, and was happy to see Bibi's smile.

Megan slipped into the seat across from Roger. She forced herself to make eye contact with the man who'd been instrumental in holding back the farm and café.

"I'm sorry about Simon."

"We all are." Becker frowned. He looked down at his pancakes with a dutiful look of sorrow. "Simon loved this town. We're all in shock."

"Here too." Megan glanced away, toward the window that looked out at the barn. "How is his mother?"

"Lenora is holding up as well as can be expected."

Roger was a neatly dressed man in his fifties. Slim and balding, precise in manner and diction, he always seemed a tad reserved. He picked up the white cloth napkin Bibi had provided and touched it to his thick salt and pepper goatee before speaking further.

"I brought you this." He slid an envelope across the table. Megan stared at it a moment before picking it up.

She looked at him questioningly. "What is it?"

"Open it."

Megan tore open the top, bile rising in her throat. Another failure notice? Roger's mysterious list of to-dos? Something worse?

Annoyed, she pursed her lips. Bring it on.

But stapled together were two "Passed Inspection" notices—for the farm and the café. Megan looked up at Roger. "I don't understand. Simon said—"

Roger shook his head. "I never failed your inspections, Megan. That was Simon. I was ready to hand you the permits weeks ago." He shrugged. "Until they find a replacement, I'm the guy in charge. I was heading over to Lowry's tackle shop, and I thought I would stop here on my way." He smiled. "Don't look so surprised. I like what you're doing here, with the farm and all. When do you finally get your organic certification? Three years, right?" Megan nodded. "And that café? Please get that up and running." He patted his stomach. "Local grub isn't what it used to be. We could use another option on Canal Street."

"Well, thank you," Megan said. She heard the tentativeness in her own voice. "I appreciate the vote of confidence."

"Only doing what's right."

"About time someone did," Bibi said. She was flipping more pancakes, although Megan wasn't sure who she thought would eat them. Sadie, maybe—the dog was sitting by the stove, suddenly Bibi's new best friend.

"Bibi, come sit with us. Have some food."

"Yes, Bonnie. Sit."

But her grandmother waved away their words. "I already ate." She turned to Roger. "Any news about Simon's death?"

"Nothing so far."

"Think Lenora will make a bid for Simon's position?"

Roger shook his head slowly. "Maybe for Chair of the Historical Society—eventually. She was the one who planted that idea in Simon's head in the first place. But run for zoning commissioner? I doubt it. She's been working on some big project that has her pretty well occupied."

"Never liked that woman." Bibi slid a pancake onto a platter and poured more batter onto the old griddle.

Megan gave her grandmother a sharp look. "Tell me, Roger,"

she said. "Why *did* Simon refuse to give us the permits?"

Roger scratched his head with one pale finger. "Honestly? Not sure. Maybe because he could."

"That's an abuse of power. And it doesn't make sense. Why us and not others?"

"Who says there weren't others?"

"Were there?" Megan asked, trying to sound nonchalant.

Roger took another sip of coffee. Almost daintily, he placed his napkin across his empty plate. "That sure was good, Bonnie. Thank you for the hospitality."

He stood, reaching for his hat.

"You didn't answer me, Roger," Megan said, unwilling to let it go that easily. She watched as Roger and her grandmother exchanged a look. "Why us?"

It was Bibi who finally said, "Simon was a petty man. Probably didn't like that you have a law degree. Felt threatened by that."

Roger nodded.

"Now get back to work, Roger Becker," Bibi said. "Before I tell *your* mama that you're slacking on the job."

Back in her room, Megan called Clover to let her know the permits had come through.

Megan should have been elated, but instead a wariness had hold of her. That was too easy. After Simon's murder, she was suspecting ulterior motives everywhere.

"Whoop!" Clover yelled into the phone. She'd never been one to hide her emotions. "Awesome news."

It was awesome news. So why did Megan have that little niggling feeling in her gut?

"Can you head over to the café?" Megan asked. "Let's try to open—at least the store section—by week's end."

"And you have the cook lined up?" Clover asked.

"Sure do. He's a professional—trained in France."

"Terrific. I'll head over there today and start stocking shelves."

Megan interrupted her to tell her she'd been there last night. "You can work on the refrigerated stuff," she said. "That's still in the large cooler." Megan paused. She toyed with whether to mention the flask. Finally, she asked, "While you've been over there, have you seen anyone drinking on the job?"

"Of course not. Why?"

"It's nothing. Sadie found a flask there last night. Someone must have dropped it."

"That's curious," Clover said, although her tone said it wasn't *that* curious, not in Winsome. "I'll see you at the café?"

"Yep. I'll be there this afternoon."

Clover gave another squeal. "The café will finally open its doors. About time!"

Megan clicked off her phone. It was about time.

Dr. Denver Finn showed up two hours later. Megan had just watered the seedlings and was checking on the goats, mulling over her conversation with Roger Becker. His sudden interest in getting her those permits seemed odd. And the fact that Simon had blamed Becker concerned her. Either Simon or Becker had been lying, but which one? She couldn't very well confront a dead man—and she didn't want to antagonize Becker.

"Are you applying the antibiotic?" Denver asked, breaking her reverie.

Megan looked up from her perch on the ground, startled. She smiled when she saw the veterinarian. "I figured you'd stay clear of this place after all that's happened," she said.

"And miss more fun?" Denver sat down next to her and lifted the goat onto his lap. "How's she been?"

"A bit lethargic."

After taking the goat's temperature and giving her a thorough onceover, he shook his head. "No fever. Wound is healing. She may be recovering from the trauma. If she still seems off in a day or two, or if she gets worse, call me." He looked up, into Megan's eyes.

"Actually, call me either way."

Megan felt her face flush. She stood, brushing her hands against her mud-streaked jeans. "I will, Doctor...Denver."

The doctor, however, didn't seem inclined to move yet. He furrowed his brow. "I heard Bobby King spent most of his day here yesterday."

"Word got around that quickly?"

"Winsome's a tiny town."

"That's for sure." Megan thought about her conversations with King and his crew. "As far as I know, the police don't have any leads. King was here trying to figure out whether I had enough of a motive to kill Simon. I wish he'd focus his energy out there." Megan pointed toward the road and beyond. "It's surreal, you know? A killer in Winsome." She wrapped her arms around her chest. "A killer *here*, on the farm."

Nodding, Denver unfurled his long, muscular body. At full height, he was a good ten inches taller than Megan. With Denver this close, Megan felt small—and oddly secure. Both sensations made her feel vulnerable. She turned away, annoyed with herself. A man was murdered and she was thinking about Denver Finn.

"Are you okay, Megan?" he asked.

Rather than respond—and no, she was most definitely not okay—she said, "Wait here. I want to show you something."

Megan sprinted up to the house, retrieved the wrapped flask, and jogged back down to the goat enclosure, avoiding the yellow police tape that still cordoned off a portion of her barn.

"Do you recognize this?" she asked the veterinarian. After all, his job put him in contact with most of the pet owners in Winsome. It was worth a try.

She watched as slowly, carefully, with hands used to delicate surgical work, Denver Finn unwrapped the flask. First he examined the felt, holding it up to the light and sniffing the material. Then he turned his attention to the flask. After flipping it over and staring at the initials, his expression changed from mild curiosity to alarm.

"Where did you find this?"

"In the café. Sadie found it."

"When?"

Megan hesitated. "Last night. Late."

"Late as in..."

"Late."

Denver's eyebrows shot up. He frowned. "All things considered, that doesn't sound wise."

"I couldn't sleep."

Still frowning, Denver turned the flask over again. He traced the initials with his finger. "I know whom this belongs to. He's not someone you want to mess with." He rewrapped the flask and handed it back to Megan.

"Why? Whose is it?"

Denver sighed. "Look, the initials on that match up to Brian Porter. Brian David Porter. Do you know him?"

When Megan shook her head, Denver said, "Not surprised. Around here, people call him Brick. That's what he used to do. Brick-laying. Before."

"Before what?"

"Before Afghanistan."

"Oh." Megan thought she knew most people in town, but Brian's name was unfamiliar. And then there was the matter of the armed services. Just like Mick. "Tell me," she said softly.

Denver looked pained, his handsome, good-natured face twisted into a mask of sympathy and concern. "Brian—Brick—went over in 2013. I honestly don't know what happened, but he returned a year later and he wasn't the same man. He lives over on the other side of town now, in a small house, with his dog. I only know him because of the dog." Denver shook his head. "Brick has some anger issues. Understandable, perhaps." He pointed to the flask. "But ye don't want to be on his bad side."

"Why would his flask be in my store?"

The doctor shrugged. "Could be he was there visiting the Dorfmans. They do work at the café, right? The Dorfmans and Brick go way back. He does some odd jobs for them here and there, as I understand it. Or maybe he stopped by to see what was happening."

"And he happened to leave behind his flask?"

Denver reached out and took the flask from Megan again. His fingers brushed against hers and she felt a jolt run through her. Carefully, he unwrapped the flask again and stared at the letters. "Most likely, he visited the Dorfmans and simply forgot it."

Megan took the flask back from Denver, careful not to touch it. Once covered in its felt casing, she tucked it into her back pocket. "Thanks for the info," she said.

"You're not done with this matter, are you?"

Too many strange happenings for one small town. "How can I be?"

Seven

Megan toyed with whether to call King and tell him about the flask, but given her last conversation with him, she was afraid it would seem as though she was trying to throw suspicion elsewhere. Instead, she'd figure out whether the flask was something to be concerned about first. As a young environmental attorney for a big firm, she'd done a fair amount of investigating. Sure, it usually involved things like talking to neighbors in areas designated as "hot zones" by plaintiffs' attorneys, checking Center for Disease reports and statistics, and snapping the occasional picture of a garbage dump or an industrial site for the firm's partners, but what the heck...she figured the same principles applied.

At noon, she was raking organic hay around the newly-transplanted broccoli plants when Clay came bounding down the hill, a sheet of paper in his hand.

"I need to run out." He waved the paper. "Cops are still tying up the barn—and everything in it. We can't exactly start picking vegetables for the farmers market without these things, so I guess we need to buy them again."

"Let me talk to King."

Clay shook his head. "I already called him. He mumbled something about forensics and said the barn is off limits for at least a few more days."

"Darn," Megan said under her breath. The barn was where

they would sort and wash the vegetables for sale at the store and market. She sighed. "Why don't you give me the list. I need to go to the café. I'll stop by Merry's store and get what we need." And do some investigating of my own, she thought.

Clay nodded. "Awesome. Thanks."

Megan handed him the rake. "Don't thank me yet. That means it's your turn to spread hay."

She found Merry Chance manning the cash register, her ample bottom pressed against a tall stool behind the counter.

"It must be awful," Merry said in her sing-song voice. "A dead body? In the barn? And Simon Duvall, of all people." She *tsk-tsk*'d her way through the checkout process. "My lord in heaven, his mother must be beside herself with grief."

Megan glanced around the empty nursery, wondering if Merry's saccharine banter was a cover-up. Suddenly, everyone seemed like a suspect, even the matronly woman before her. Merry was a fixture in town. Like many people, she could trace her lineage way back. Merry, an outspoken Anglophile, claimed to be the great-great-great-niece of some English aristocrat Megan had never heard of. She proved her provenance by raising award-winning English roses, some of which lined the interior of the nursery's gift shop area and checkout counter. The scent was overpowering. Megan tried to stifle a sneeze. She was unsuccessful.

"God bless you," Merry said, barely pausing in her ramblings. "You're getting sick. A spring cold can be a doozy, you know." She shook her head. "As I was saying, Lenora must be crazy with grief."

"I imagine she is," Megan said. "Do you know when the funeral service will be?"

Merry pursed her rouged lips. Her age was hard to tell—somewhere between forty-five and sixty, Megan figured, but she dressed like the far end of that range. She had short, tightly curled auburn hair and puffy green eyes. Her most dramatic feature was her mouth: wide and thin, it lived in a state of permanent frown, making it seem as though she was always scowling. She scowled now as she said, "Lenora has decided to push a service off until this summer. The police won't release the body what with all their testing, and then there's all the mud, plus he's being cremated...well, there will be a small memorial service sometime in July."

"Won't the townspeople be upset? I'm sure they want to pay homage to one of their own sooner than that."

Merry stopped what she was doing. Her eyes narrowed. "You mean one of 'our own,' right, Megan?"

"Yes, of course."

Merry took a moment before speaking again, the disapproval still evident on her face. Megan watched Merry tear the receipt from the credit card machine, annoyed at herself for the slip.

"There was no love lost between you and Simon, I'm sure. What with his insistence on following procedure and your need for expediency." Merry shrugged. "I imagine you were pretty angry with Simon."

Megan wasn't biting. "Did Simon tell you he was withholding our permits, Merry?"

Merry frowned, furrowing the skin between her eyes. She shifted her focus, suddenly quite interested in a ladybug that was crawling across the countertop. "Not exactly. I just knew Simon. He could be prickly about certain things."

"Was it normal for him to delay?"

Merry shrugged again. "I wouldn't really know."

But Merry was a poor liar, a trait she tried to cover up with a quick shift in topic. "Lenora is devastated, I'm sure," Merry said again. But she didn't sound convinced.

She handed Megan her receipt and bag without another word.

Still thinking about Merry's lie and the possible reasons for Simon's delay tactics, Megan headed the truck toward the outskirts of town. Brian "Brick" Porter lived in a one and a half story shotgun house along a desolate stretch of highway called Curly Hill Road. A mile down the road in one direction was a gas station; two miles down the road in the other direction was Lyle Lake State Park, and on the other side of that, Jenner's solar fields. Between the park and the gas station sat only Porter's house, set close to the blacktop and buffered by chain-link fencing and densely planted conifers.

Megan pulled up in front of the house and killed the engine. An old-model Jeep Wrangler sat parked in the driveway on the other side of the fence. She took a moment to look around, noticing heavily draped windows, a neatly trimmed lawn devoid of any decoration, and a giant metal dog dish. She climbed out of the truck and walked to the gate. It was locked from the inside. She rattled the gate, then yelled "hello" in the direction of the house. No one answered. A dog barked, and, hopeful, Megan rattled the gate one more time. Still no response.

The house felt barren, empty. The sun, shining overhead back at the farm, had disappeared. A chilly breeze caused her to shiver.

As Megan was opening the door to her truck, she caught movement out of the corner of her eye. She turned as someone pulled aside a curtain in an upstairs window. A face stared at her from within: angular, pale, young. Megan waved. He didn't wave back.

Back at the house, Bibi was baking. Not simply her normal baking. Megan could smell the aromas from outside: cinnamon and cloves and the rich yeasty smell of fresh bread. When she opened the door that led from the porch to the kitchen, the first thing she saw was lightly browned loaves lined up on the counter—at least nine of them. Then she saw the pies (two), big deep-dish pastries crisscrossed with a double crust, and what looked like a homemade Danish. Her grandmother was standing by the stove, stirring something caramel-colored and syrupy, a white and black "Winsome and Lose Some" apron tied around her waist.

"Megan, have something to eat," she called when she spied her granddaughter. "I made your favorite: raspberry Danish."

"It looks like you made enough food for the entire town."

Bibi ignored her. She dipped a candy thermometer into her concoction, gave a satisfied nod, and turned off the gas burner. She set the pan aside.

"Why all the baking?" Megan asked. She placed her car keys on the table, and walked over to the loaves of bread lined up on the worn linoleum countertop like soldiers on the march.

Bibi shrugged. "Why not?"

"It smells and looks fabulous, Bibi, but I don't think there's enough room in the freezer to store it all."

"Then we'll share it."

"With all of eastern Pennsylvania?"

"Nonsense." Her grandmother whisked the contents of the pot. "Besides, we are almost out of breadcrumbs. I'll let a few loaves go stale and make some tomorrow."

"That's a lot of breadcrumbs."

"Waste not, want not."

Megan paused by the doorway. She watched her grandmother drizzle the caramel concoction on parchment paper, making an elaborate lacy pattern. Her grandmother loved to bake, but this...Bibi's face was flushed with adrenaline. Megan's mind wandered to the flask, to Simon's inert body, to King's questions about motive.

"Is Aunt Sarah back in Winsome?"

Her grandmother blinked, turned away. "Why do you want to know about Sarah?" she asked casually. Too casually.

"I've never met her."

"You have, you simply don't remember." Bibi pulled a loaf of what looked like rye bread out of the oven. After turning down the temperature, she placed the tray of lace cookies inside and closed the door. "You used to visit as a kid."

Megan couldn't picture Sarah Birch, and that bothered her. "What happened between Grandpa and Aunt Sarah?"

"They were at odds."

"Do you still have contact with her now that she's b⌐ area?"

"You know we have been estranged from Sarah for years." She looked at Megan and smiled softly. "For reasons I would rather not discuss."

And yet somehow Sarah knew about the bid on the farm—a bid that could be tied to a murder. Megan asked nonchalantly, "When was the last time you saw her?"

But Bibi was already on to other things.

With Clay working on the spring harvest and Bibi immersed in baking, Megan decided to head over to the café early. She had her new chef, Jeremy, coming by, and she could use the extra time to work on the store. She was determined to open the store tomorrow, the café next week, but as she drove through town, her mind fixated on Simon's lifeless body. His death felt like an inauspicious start to her new life. Why kill him in their barn? Who met—or followed—him there? And why was he there in the first place?

Had he been snooping? Had he come to tell her something, something related to the permit process? Then why not go to the house and knock on the door? Why go to the barn? What if someone lured him there for the specific purpose of killing him? Someone who wanted to sabotage the farm or shine a spotlight on the Birch family.

The breeze at Brick Porter's house had been a harbinger of inclement weather, and a soft drizzle fell from a sullen sky. Megan pulled onto Canal Street and parked in front of the café, forcing her mind to think about business, not murder. But as much as she hated to admit it, the two were now intertwined.

She walked inside to the sound of Clover arguing with Bob King at the café counter in the back of the store. Megan was about to call out when she caught on to the topic of their conversation.

"Let it go, Bobby," Clover was saying. "She has nothing to do with this."

"It's my job to ask questions."

"Your questions don't make sense."

"You know I have to be thorough. It's for her own good as much as anything."

"She's not involved with what happened to Simon."

"Clover Hand, you are infuriating. I am in charge of this investigation. You know that." His voice was whiny, almost petulant. "You need to stay out of this." A pause. "Please."

Megan had heard enough. She was certain they were arguing over her. Let King investigate all he wanted. She hadn't killed Simon. But someone had...and while he was busy arguing with her shop manager, that someone was getting away with murder.

She marched to the back of the store. Clover's eyes widened at the sight of her, and King looked like a man who'd bitten into an especially sour pickle.

"Bobby," Megan said with a curt nod. "Clover."

"I hope you don't get the wrong idea—" Clover started to say.

Megan help up a hand. She turned to the police chief. "Tell me what you need from me. I didn't kill Simon. My grandmother didn't kill Simon. If I can help you move this investigation along so that you can focus on the actual killer, I would view that as progress."

"It's not that simple."

"Oh, but it is. Someone killed Simon. Until you start casting a wider net, you won't know who else may have profited from his murder. Others may be in danger." She lowered her voice. "I—or my grandmother—could be in danger. So could Clover. I want to help you cast that wider net."

King looked peeved. "Let me do my job."

Megan pulled herself up and over the café counter. She scoped out the kitchen, now finished, painted and clean as a model home, and placed her hands on her hips. "I am letting you do your job. I've given you and your staff full access to the farm. I've answered your questions. But I have a meeting in thirty minutes, so I'd be thrilled to do my job." Her eyes met his. "Please?"

Bob nodded. He glanced at Clover, his eyes traveling from her khaki capris to her midriff-bearing white peasant blouse. He flushed, swallowed, and looked like he was about to say more, but instead he walked toward the front of the store, shaking his head the whole way.

When he was gone, Clover placed a hand on Megan's arm across the counter. "I'm sorry, Megan. Bobby doesn't really think you killed Simon. He's worried, and he's letting nerves get the best of him. This is his first murder investigation and he doesn't want to screw it up." She shrugged. "Besides, I don't know the last time Winsome has had a murder. Hunting accidents are about the extent of it."

"No need to apologize. But until the police nab whoever did this, we all need to be especially careful. I intend to do what I can to help the investigation, but I sure hope Bobby gets what he needs from us and moves on. He's wasting time and resources."

Clover nodded. She, too, looked about to say something else. Instead, she pulled a white rag from beneath the counter and started wiping down the surface of the already spotless countertop, not meeting Megan's gaze.

"Spit it out."

"Spit what out?"

"Whatever you're not telling me."

Clover stopped wiping. She pushed a stray dark hair back from her face and winced as though the action had hurt her. Finally, she said, "It's your grandmother. Bobby thinks you're protecting her. He found some stuff...correspondence between her and Simon. He said she's not being completely honest and it's making him wonder what she's hiding."

"Bibi?" Megan asked. "Was it about the bid?"

"I don't know. He wouldn't tell me. He was afraid I would tell you." Clover looked down, her face a shade paler. "Like I guess I just did."

"My grandmother is in her eighties. It's absolutely ridiculous to think she'd have anything to do with Simon's murder."

"I know, Megan. I know." Clover looked up. "But then why is she being so secretive?"

Eight

Megan met with her new chef later that day. Like her, Jeremy was a Winsome native who'd returned to his roots after years away—in his case, New York City, Paris, and London. Classically trained, he'd given up the hustle and bustle of the big city for small-town Pennsylvania when he needed a change. A self-proclaimed organic-food zealot, he was now trying to figure out his next move, and the challenge of getting the café off the ground was appealing.

"When can you start?" Megan asked. They were in the café's kitchen, and he was staring at the small but tidy space, wheels obviously turning.

He shrugged. "Today."

"You're sure you're okay with the salary? I know it's nowhere near what you were making in New York."

Jeremy smiled. He had a chiseled, stern face, but when he smiled, all the hard edges softened. It was a smile that gave the recipient a frisson of satisfaction because it felt hard-earned. "I'm worn out and need to make some life decisions. Plus, I love what you're trying to accomplish here. The salary is fine."

Megan studied him for a moment. She remembered him as a boy—a teen, really. Football, soccer, track—you name it, he'd played it. He'd been a grade ahead of her in school, but he'd always been handsome in an unapproachable sort of way, and even at a young age, the girls took notice. Now, his dark, wavy hair, worn short, was graying at the edges, but he still had the aristocratic nose and strong jaw that had made women—including a young Megan—swoon. Her eyes darted to his left hand. No ring. She'd heard he'd never married.

Not that it mattered. She recognized that flutter in her stomach as excitement. A classically trained cook at her café. Maybe this whole crazy idea would work after all.

"Megan?"

Megan looked up, realizing too late that he'd been talking to her.

"I'm sorry, I missed what you said."

He smiled again. "I was asking about the menu. Do you know what you want to serve?"

Megan nodded. "I'm sure you've noticed the types of food establishments that are available in and near Winsome."

"Pizza, diners...a steakhouse or two."

"Right. The people of Winsome deserve something more."

"What are you thinking?"

"Start with fresh, whole ingredients: veggies and eggs from the farm, humanely-raised chicken, pork, and beef, sustainable fish, organic tofu. Beyond that, my only requests are seasonal, simple and, where you can, an ethnic twist."

Jeremy frowned. "Sounds expensive. I'm not sure the diner-loving folks of Winsome will pay for organic chicken tikka."

Megan smiled. "They will. I've done the number crunching, Jeremy. The key is to have a limited menu with a few standbys for the meat and potatoes crowd. That way we don't over-order and we can keep it seasonal. If the menu changes weekly depending upon the farm's crops, we limit costs for perishables and we have built-in variety." She pulled a paper out of one of the folders she was carrying. "Like this."

Megan watched as he perused her sample menu. She was sure it seemed amateurish to a professional chef, but she knew the kind of place she wanted. If he couldn't go along with that...well, maybe he wasn't the best candidate after all.

Eventually, he placed the menu on the counter and affixed his eyes to hers. "This works. I'll start working on next week's menu today."

Megan held out her hand, suddenly self-conscious of her calloused fingers and short nails. But Jeremy didn't seem to notice. He shook her hand firmly. "One day we will toast the café."

Megan laughed. "With all we've been through lately, I hope that day comes sooner rather than later."

Megan was on her way home when Bibi called. "It's that cat. Mutton Chops. He's acting funny."

"Funny how?"

"Vomiting. Listless. He doesn't seem himself."

Megan's first thought was poison. "Did you call Dr. Finn?"

"I did. He said he can see him immediately, but you have to go to his office." Bibi paused. "I already boxed him up."

"He let you put him in the carrier?"

"That's how sick he is, Megan."

Megan knew her grandmother held no great love for cats. She saw them mostly as a necessity on a farm, little hunters who kept the rodent population at bay, so she was surprised to hear the concern in her grandmother's voice. Maybe she'd misjudged their friendship. Maybe she was misjudging a lot of things.

"He'll be okay," Megan said, trying to mask the worry in her voice. "I'll be there in a few minutes."

"Better hurry. He seems worse every minute."

"Well, it's not poison, at least. He's blocked. His urinary tract isn't functioning correctly." Denver had finished the exam, and was standing by the cat, stroking his fur. "He should probably stay overnight."

Dr. Finn's office was now closed and empty, except for a young and very perky assistant who was busily cleaning the other exam room.

"Wouldn't he be better off at home, with me?"

Denver shook his head. "I'll come by later and check on him. And my assistant is on duty tonight." He smiled, and Megan felt her stomach tighten. The combination of intelligent blue eyes and the dimpled smile were irresistible, only Denver seemed completely unaware of how handsome he was—part of his charm. "No need to worry. At least not about him."

"Thank you."

They were interrupted by the assistant, who poked her head in, smiled at Denver, and said, "All finished out here, Dr. Finn. Is the cat staying?"

Denver nodded. He gave the technician a rundown of meds the cat needed and said, "That means you have two overnight guests. Are you okay with that?"

The young woman nodded, reddish curls bouncing. "Of course." She sounded almost giddy, clearly affected by Denver's charm as well. To Megan, she said, "You can take care of the bill tomorrow when you pick him up, if that's okay. We were already closed for the day when you came in." Then, realizing she may have said too much, she looked at the vet apologetically. "I mean—"

But Denver dismissed her concern. "Why don't you get the cat settled and feed our other patient?" When his assistant was gone, he turned back to Megan. "It's almost eight and I'm starving. Would you like to join me for dinner?"

Megan, thinking of Bibi home alone all day, was about to decline. But Denver looked hopeful, and he'd done a great deal for her animals. A few hours wouldn't hurt. She nodded. "But I can't stay out long. Bibi's alone. Plus, we open the store tomorrow."

Denver looked surprised. "You got approval?"

"We did. Oddest thing too. Roger Becker came by and hand-delivered the approvals not long after Simon's death."

"Did he say why Simon had been sitting on them?"

Megan shrugged. "Not really. It's a mystery."

* * *

They were on their way to dinner in Denver's Forerunner when an emergency call came in. Megan watched as Denver's face tensed, his cell phone pressed to his ear. "Calm down," he said several times. "I can't understand ye. Okay...okay. We're not far. I'll be right over." He clicked off the cell, flipped on his left turn signal, and looked at Megan. "I'm afraid there's been an accident. I can take you back to your car if you'd prefer, but we're already halfway there. Besides, this is someone you wanted to meet."

Curious, Megan said, "Of course I'll come. Maybe I can help."

"Don't you want to know where we're headed?"

"Based on the direction, I'd say Porter's place."

Eyebrows arched, Denver said, "So you did go on your own after all my warnings."

"I stopped by, but he wouldn't answer the door."

"He'll answer this time."

"What happened?"

Denver sighed. "Hit and run. His dog, Sarge."

Sarge turned out to be a hundred-pound German shepherd. As Denver had predicted, Brick was standing outside, gate open, waiting for the vet. When Denver introduced Megan, Brick stared at her for an uncomfortable moment before pointing to the dog. Sarge was lying in the front yard, whimpering, a plaid wool blanket covering him. Floodlights illuminated the small yard. Megan didn't see blood.

Denver jogged over to the dog and knelt beside him, gently peeling down the blanket. The dog strained to look at him, his tail thumping against the grass. He placed one huge paw against the doctor's chest and whimpered again.

Denver examined the dog, all the while asking questions. Brick answered without taking his eyes off his companion.

"What happened?"

"Damn bastard hit him and ran off."

"Did you see who did it?"

"Nah. It was all I could do to lift him off the road. Will he be okay?"

Ignoring his last question, Denver asked, "Why was he in the road?"

"Don't know," Porter said, running a shaking hand through closely cropped hair. He was wiry and muscular. Tattoos snaked along his arms, partially hidden by a black Coors t-shirt. A day or two of stubble shadowed his face. He looked young—maybe mid to late twenties—but his reddened, old-soul eyes made Megan wonder what horrors he'd seen overseas.

Denver moved to the dog's back end, clearly the source of the animal's distress. He leaned in farther to get a better look in the dim light.

Megan ran to Denver's car and retrieved the large flashlight she'd spied earlier lying on the passenger side floor. When she returned, she flicked it on and held it over the dog's hindquarters. Denver nodded his gratitude.

Porter crept closer to his dog, his eyes darting nervously from his dog's face to the dog's rear legs to Megan. "Sarge must've heard something. I went outside to see what was going on and someone had opened the gate. He ran out. Went after an animal or something. I called and called and finally spotted him coming back. He was almost across the road when a car hit him. Car wasn't going too fast. That was the only thing saved his life, I think."

Denver manipulated the dog's rear left leg. "Did you happen to see the license plate?"

"I was too focused on getting to my dog. I only noticed it was out of state. Florida." He paused, and Megan heard the slur in his speech—a slur that had nothing to do with alcohol.

The veterinarian stood, wiping strong hands against his thighs. He stared down at the dog, brows creased. Turning to Megan, he said, "Will you stay with Sarge for a moment? I want to talk to Brian alone."

Megan nodded. Denver and Porter disappeared into the house. While she waited outside, she straightened the blanket on Sarge and knelt down beside him to stroke his head. He appeared heathy, other than the injury from the accident. Short nails, a well-cared for, healthy coat, and clear eyes. He watched her with a look of trust that made her heart ache.

She heard a crash, a yell, and a shout in quick succession. Sarge tried to get up. She placed her hand gently on his shoulder and pushed him down. After another bang, there was silence. A few minutes later, Denver came out alone.

"Do you mind coming back to the clinic with me, Meg?"

"Of course. My car's there, in any case."

"I need you to sit in the back with Sarge, if that's all right."

"I don't mind at all." She gave the dog another stroke. "Brian?"

"I'll explain in the car."

It took another ten minutes for Denver to get the dog sedated and situated on the stretcher. He was too heavy for Megan. After a few minutes of negotiation, Porter came back outside looking pissed off and smelling like a fraternity party. His eyes were bright red and watery. He knelt down and picked up one end of the stretcher, then helped Denver carry the dog to the back of the Forerunner, which Denver had decked out like a makeshift ambulance. Megan watched Porter. She noticed sinewy muscles, clenched fists, a set jaw...and the rigid, angry posture of a rage-filled kid. Her mind jumped to the flask in her store, to Simon's lifeless body. Was it possible this young man had something to do with Duvall's murder? He seemed unstable enough to carry it out, but what could possibly have been the motive? And why at her farm—she'd never even met him before.

Denver placed his hand on her shoulder and squeezed gently. "Are you sure you're okay to sit with Sarge?"

"Absolutely."

The hand squeezed again. Denver moved it from her shoulder to her chin, tilting her face upwards, towards his. "Thank you."

He looked into her eyes, searching...for what, she wasn't sure.

She took a step back, the weight of his intimacy suddenly too much. Before he could say or do anything, Megan climbed into the back of the vehicle, next to the dog.

Nine

Megan and Denver were silent for most of the drive back to the clinic. About a mile away, Megan finally asked what had happened inside of Brick's home. Denver was slow to answer.

"A temper tantrum."

"Brian was angry that you were taking Sarge?"

"He was angry that Sarge had to be taken." Denver glanced over his shoulder, and in the faint light of the SUV's interior, Megan saw him rubbing his temples. He looked tired. "Sarge has a broken leg. Other than that, I think he's fine. He'll need to be here a few days, and I think Brick's scared to be alone. That dog is all he has."

"Poor kid."

Denver nodded. "Been back for over a year. Doesn't say much about Afghanistan, but I think whatever he saw—whatever he did— haunts him."

"Post-traumatic stress disorder?"

"Would be my guess. That, and alcoholism."

"They often go hand in hand."

Denver pulled into the clinic parking lot and stopped right in front of the double doors. A light came on inside and a minute later, his assistant joined them. Her eyes looked sleepy; she was wearing light blue sweats and her curls were pulled into a messy ponytail. At the sight of the dog in the back of the Forerunner, she pushed the sleeves up to her elbows.

Together, the three of them took Sarge inside one of the

surgeries. "Can you get him prepped?" Denver asked his technician. She nodded.

Megan followed Denver back into the waiting room. She glanced at her watch: it was almost ten. "Do you want me to help?" she asked.

Denver smiled. He looked tired, and Megan resisted the urge to reach out and touch his face.

"Ta, but we'll be fine. I'm sorry about dinner. I'm afraid this wasn't much of a date."

The word "date" lingered between them, creating an uncomfortable silence. Finally Megan asked, "Can I check on Mutton Chops?"

"Of course. He's right through the double doors. I need to go wash up—will you be okay by yourself?"

Megan nodded. They stood for a moment, listening to the sounds of water running in the adjoining room. Finally, Denver spoke. "Can I get a raincheck, Megan?"

"I would love that."

"Tomorrow?"

Megan laughed. "Sure, why not." Then she remembered the store opening, and all the work that would go along with it. She apologized. "I may be busy."

"Later in the week, then."

"We can talk about it tomorrow. When I pick up Chops."

Denver nodded. "I'll have someone call you when he's ready to go home." He leaned in and kissed Megan on the mouth, surprising them both. She closed her eyes. He pulled back quickly.

"I'm sorry."

"Don't be."

"Megan, I—"

"Stop." Megan took a step, closing the gap between them. Denver smelled of Old Spice and wood chips and she fought an almost overwhelming urge to lay her head against his chest. Instead, she put her hand against his torso, feeling the warmth of his body, the hardness of his chest. "Later this week?"

Denver took a deep breath. "Yes," he said. And then he was gone.

Sleep was a stranger again that night. Around midnight, Megan wandered into the kitchen, now clean and neat after her grandmother's baking spree. Megan sliced Bibi's banana bread and popped two pieces in the toaster oven. She slathered them with butter, warmed some milk on the stove, and settled into a chair at the kitchen table. It wasn't long before she was joined by Sadie and Bibi.

"Couldn't sleep either?" her grandmother asked.

"Not a wink."

Bibi took the seat across from Megan, easing into the chair with obvious discomfort. Megan reminded herself that Bibi was in her eighties—a fact she shouldn't take for granted, no matter how spritely she seemed.

"Would you like some banana bread? Milk?" Megan asked.

"No, thank you. Well, maybe some milk."

While Megan warmed the milk, Bibi scratched circles on a piece of scratch paper that had been lying on the table. "You seem distracted," her grandmother said. "Simon's murder?"

Megan nodded. "And I'm feeling anxious about tomorrow."

"The store will be a success, Megan. So will the farm. I have no doubts."

"I wish I could share your confidence."

Bibi smiled. "Somehow, the older you get, the clearer your vision." Bibi reached down to pet Sadie. "Don't get distracted by things you can't control."

"Not always easy."

"When your father was young, he would become fixated on something—some goal, some idea, some vision. Whatever it was, it would be great. The souvenir shop was a great idea. Restoring the farm was a noble project. Even his newest pursuit—this woman, Italy—a great adventure. The problem with my Eddie? Along the way, he would become distracted, usually by setbacks. He would let them overwhelm his vision. We both know what happened then."

Megan knew all too well. Her ne'er-do-well father had always been ready to claim defeat. Megan's mixed feelings toward her father stemmed, in large part, from this lack of resolve and perseverance.

Bibi smiled. "I'm saying stick to your plan. Don't let Simon's death, or anything else, distract you. No matter how tragic."

Megan felt like there was more, things her grandmother *wasn't* saying. She felt a twist in the pit of her stomach. But sitting there in the dark, a pink fuzzy robe wrapped around thin shoulders, Bonnie Birch looked small and worn. Too small to share in Megan's worries. Too small to hide big secrets. Megan placed a cup of milk in front of Bibi, sat down, and took another sip of her milk, the banana bread untouched before her. Maybe her grandmother was right. Maybe all of these other things—the bid on the farm, the correspondence between Bibi and Simon—were foolishness.

"I'm worried that whoever killed Simon may come back. That you could be in danger."

"There is absolutely no need to worry about me."

How can you be so sure? Megan wondered. But she refused to give voice to her thoughts. Bibi was everything to her, and she had to trust her now. In the weeks after Mick was killed, Bibi had called Megan every day at seven in the morning and again at seven at night. Like clockwork. Sometimes those calls were the only thing that got Megan out of bed. Those were dark, endless days, and Bibi's voice—clear, warm and without a hint of pity—had been the single flicker of light. She was still Megan's light. Megan would hold on to that.

Finished, Megan rose. "I'm going to try and get some sleep. Are you coming?"

Bibi shook her head. "Clearer vision doesn't mean sounder sleep," she said. "You go. I think I'll sit here for a while, thinking about the past—an old lady's folly."

* * *

Megan's problems seemed less heavy in the light of day, even if that light was weighed down by sheets of unforgiving rain. Spring was holding on with a vengeance, and gloomy weather made summer feel far away. Megan rose early, powered up her laptop, and searched the internet for anything she could find about Simon's murder. The media said little more than she already knew, and thankfully neither she nor her grandmother were mentioned by name. She moved on to Brian Porter. The man seemed to have no online presence—no social media, no news mentions, no 5K results. Nothing.

A frustrated glance at her clock told her it was time to start the day. She slipped on heavy tan cargo pants, a black fitted t-shirt, and a pair of tall rain boots. After pulling her hair back into a ponytail she took a moment to stare into the mirror over her dresser, shivering in the damp morning air.

As always, her jaw seemed a little too firm, her nose a little too pert, her cheekbones a little too broad. She knew her saving graces were clear, rose-tinted skin, a gift from her Irish mother, and deep-set, long-lashed, almond-shaped brown eyes, a feature she shared with her father. Bibi called her looks classic. Perhaps, Megan thought, although she considered herself plain.

She walked away from the mirror, frustrated with her own insecurities. Since when did she care about looks? Only she knew it wasn't a *what*, but a *who*—and that who was a tall, strong, Scottish veterinarian. Stay focused, Bibi had said the night before. She surely wasn't talking about Denver—she'd be thrilled to know Megan was attracted to the vet—but her words still rang true. No time for distractions.

Megan stopped in the kitchen to grab breakfast and was surprised to find the kitchen devoid of its usual enticing scents. Bibi was nowhere to be found, unusual for this hour—but maybe she hadn't gotten back to sleep until very late. She wouldn't wake her. Megan placed coffee beans in the grinder and brewed a large pot of salvation. Once it was ready, she poured it into a thermos, took two mugs from the cabinet—one for Clay—and tucked a few slices of banana bread into a brown bag. She headed outside, grabbing a jacket on the way, Sadie alongside her.

She found Clay down by the chicken tractor. He was holding a heavily producing Plymouth they called Omelet against his chest, stroking the bird's head gently and whispering something soft and crooning. When he saw Megan, he frowned.

"Something has them riled up this morning."

"A fox?"

Clay shrugged. With one last stroke, he put the bird down on the ground and watched as she half ran, half flew across the yard toward her fellow chickens. "When I got here, they were all squawking up a storm. I thought maybe they were hungry. I came over to see what was happening. I found Omelet and a few others pacing back and forth, making lots of noise." He shrugged again, his eyes darkening. "Maybe it's time for some security, Megan."

"I'm not buying a gun, if that's what you mean."

Clay smiled. "No, I mean get a dog." He glanced at Sadie apologetically. "I mean, another dog. A guard dog. A Great Pyrenees or some other breed used to guard livestock." He cocked his head. "Could be good for protecting against other things too."

"You're worried about our safety."

"A man *was* killed on your property." He glanced at the chickens, calmer now, but still pacing. "We can't discount the possibility that someone wants to sabotage the farm."

Megan chewed on the inside of her lip, mulling over Clay's words. Of course she'd been thinking the same thing for days—or, more precisely, trying not to think the same thing.

"You think someone was on the property?"

Clay hesitated. "Sometimes I feel like I'm being watched." He took a deep breath, looking past the chickens toward the barn. Megan followed his gaze from there to the house. "I'm probably being paranoid. Chickens have brains the size of peas. Who knows what got them going? Maybe Simon's death has me more agitated than I'd thought."

Megan thought of the night at the café, the shadow slinking between the shops—the feeling of being watched. She took a hard look at her farm manager. His manner—older than his twenty-four years—made her forget that he was merely a babe. His family's lifestyle had been different, to say the least, and with that came an unusual perspective that Megan appreciated. But he was, in many ways, still a kid.

She said, "I don't think you're being paranoid. I've felt it too."

His eyes widened.

"Come on," she said, unwilling to let fear take hold. "Let's go pick spinach. I want to bundle it up to sell at the store today."

"You're going through with this?" he asked.

"Damn right," Megan said.

"I thought...with everything that happened, the ongoing police investigation..."

But Megan waved away his concern with a bravado she didn't quite feel. "If we stop now, Becker may change his mind. Besides, if someone *is* trying to sabotage the farm, there's no way I'm going to let them win. And stopping out of fear? That's akin to acknowledging defeat."

Ten

Megan and Clay were still loading packages of fresh spinach, baby lettuce, and Russian red kale into her truck when Megan's cell phone rang. It was Clover, and she was buried. "I need help," she said. "And soon."

"Are people actually buying stuff?" Megan asked. She wondered whether the good residents of Winsome really wanted organically grown goods—after all, the nearest Whole Foods was more than an hour away—or whether they were mostly after gossip about Simon's murder.

"They're buying," Clover said. "And they want to know when the lunch counter will open."

"Not until next week when Jeremy starts."

"That's what I keep saying. Hold on." Clover put down the phone and Megan could hear her ringing up a customer. After a moment, Megan heard, "Thanks for coming, Jack," before the phone was back at Clover's ear. "Anyway, come soon. Please."

"Give me thirty minutes."

Megan clicked off her cell, ignoring a niggle of disappointment. She'd have to send Clay to get the cat. That meant no running into Denver. Oh, well, she thought. Another time.

The next few hours spared Megan thoughts of murder, chickens, Denver, or her grandmother...she was way too busy. Clover had been right: Winsome wanted fresh, organic goods. Badly. By two that afternoon, the spinach, kale, and lettuce were gone, and her patrons had made a solid dent in the local canned goods—even the pickled beets—as well as the selection of local cheeses.

At two fifteen, taking advantage of a lull, Clover leaned back against the wall behind the register and pulled a Snapple from under the counter.

"Hey, that's not ours," Megan joked. "We don't sell Snapple."

Clover took three quick gulps, as though she was afraid Megan would take the bottle away. Laughing, she said, "I don't trust foods that don't contain chemicals or sugar."

"You're joking."

Clover shook her head slowly side to side. Her long hair was held captive by a pair of quaintly old-fashioned tortoiseshell barrettes. "Afraid not."

Come to think of it, Megan had never seen her eat or drink anything other than fast food and soft drinks.

"That stuff will kill you."

"Yeah, well, after years of living on the commune, eating nothing but rabbit food, I've decided I'd rather be happy and live a shorter life."

"You say that now, but I think Jeremy will make a convert out of you."

Clover smiled. "Let him try. I'm not giving up my Diet Snapple for anyone."

Megan laughed. "Just keep that drink under the counter."

Right then, the front door opened. Megan looked up, expecting to see a customer. Instead, King stood in front of her, hands on his hips. His face was set with the look of a man who had recently settled on the right answer to one of life's conundrums.

"Hey, Bob. Can I help you?" Megan asked.

"I'd like to speak with you in private." King looked around the store. "Is there somewhere we can talk?"

Clover started to say something and Megan placed a quieting hand on her elbow. "Sure. Let's head back to the kitchen. We're not using it yet."

In the kitchen, King didn't waste time getting to the point. He pulled out a black leather glove and placed it on the stainless steel prep counter. The glove was laid out flat within a thick clear plastic evidence bag, palm of the right hand up. Two fingers and a portion of the palm were darker than the rest, the material slightly wrinkled in those spots. It didn't take a law degree to recognize dried blood.

"Can you identify this?"

"It appears to be a black leather glove."

"Does it belong to you?"

"No."

King narrowed his eyes. "Are you certain?"

"Yes, of course I'm certain. I don't own black leather gloves."

"Have you seen this glove before?"

Megan let out a sigh of exasperation. "It's a black leather glove, Bobby—as common as black socks and white undershirts."

"Yet *you* don't own a pair."

"No, I don't."

King gave her a long, hard look, one that suggested Megan had her chance and blew it. He picked up the glove and started to put it back in the bag.

"Was it found near Simon's body?" Megan asked. When King didn't respond, Megan said, "It must have been. The blood. But it could have easily been planted there. It could belong to anyone. Anyone who—"

Without a word, King dug inside his police-issued duffel and selected a pair of metal tongs. Carefully, he flipped over the evidence bag and pulled the glove out. Using the tongs, he turned it over. She saw the reason for the officer's questions along a wide swath of wool cuff that rose above the cheap leather. In white machine-stitched lettering, the phrase "Stay warm in Winsome!" had been embroidered onto the fabric.

"Now you understand?" King said, not unkindly. "We both know where it came from."

"It's not mine." But even as she said the words, Megan's mind flashed to the morning of the murder, to her goat standing on the shed roof with a black glove dangling from her mouth. A black *leather* glove. A bit more quietly, she said, "And it's not Bonnie's, either."

"I'm not so sure you can say that with conviction."

"That shop was open years ago. There could be dozens of pairs of these floating around."

King shook his head slowly back and forth. "It's a tourist item. Pretty unlikely a resident of Winsome would own a pair. Other than your grandmother, that is."

"Unlikely does not equal impossible." Megan glanced at the police bag, which once again housed the offending glove. "Where did you find it?"

"I can't say more. I've already gone beyond my bounds." Regaining the reserved edge, he said, "We know Bonnie keeps all the old store stuff. Is it possible someone working for you took these gloves?"

"Possible, perhaps. Probable, absolutely not." Megan shook her head, feeling her Birch temper rising. Clay was as unlikely as Bibi to be part of this.

King frowned. "We can't ignore a possible lead. You of all people should know that. That's not how an investigation works."

Megan was about to argue, to throw out all the reasons those gloves didn't amount to evidence against anyone at the farm, to point out the holes in their process and reasoning, but realizing she would get nowhere, she held her tongue.

She said, "Did you have the blood tested?"

"Preliminary tests match it to the victim."

"Which doesn't tell you a thing about the killer."

"Other than the fact that they likely wore these gloves." King stared at Megan through impatient eyes, eyes that questioned Megan's reluctance to see the connection.

"Did you find any identifying material inside the gloves? Have you ruled out other blood at the scene? Fingerprints? Shoeprints?"

At the last part of the question, Megan saw King flinch. Nevertheless, he said, "You know I can't answer your questions."

"Why did you show me the cuff?" Megan asked finally.

King's stern features rearranged themselves into a professional veneer, one that belied the sympathy in his voice when he said, "Because I've known Bonnie since I was a kid. And if positions were reversed, I'd like to think you'd do the same."

"What did Bobby want?" Clover asked later, when King was gone.

Megan mentioned the glove, leaving out the cuff. Whatever his reason, King had showed her a professional courtesy, and although Megan trusted Clover, she doubted Clover's ability to keep her mouth shut when it came to her boyfriend.

"Sometimes that man is unbelievable." Clover removed the barrettes in her hair. It hung loose around her shoulders. She tossed it back defiantly. "Let me talk to him."

"No, please don't. Concentrate on the store. This will all work out."

Another wave of customers had entered, including Merry Chance, the owner of the local nursery. Merry wandered around the shop, peeking down aisles and in the dairy coolers.

"No meat?" she asked.

"Not yet," Megan answered.

Merry made her way toward the cash register and stood in front of it, empty-handed. "I passed Bobby King on my way in. Funny thing, seeing a police officer here. I thought maybe he was coming to see Clover—" Merry threw a pointed look in the direction of Megan's shop manager "—but perhaps he had other business?"

A line was forming behind Merry. Megan smiled politely and asked if there was anything she could help her find.

"Oh, I'm being nosy," Merry proclaimed with a self-conscious laugh. "Stopping by to see what the competition is up to and all that."

Clover stared at her. "We're hardly competition."

But Merry simply raised her over-plucked eyebrows and clucked in the direction of the organic seed display.

Megan smiled, her patience waning. "Merry, if you'd like help with something, let us know. In the meantime, I think the gentleman behind you would like to pay for his chocolate and flowers."

Indeed, the owner of Winsome's only bookstore was standing behind Merry, looking rather impatient himself. Soft, hairless white hands clutched two bars of Love's organic chocolate and a bouquet of spring flowers.

The town rumor mill said the bookseller had a penchant for online slot machines and every time his wife intercepted an American Express bill, he bought her a gift. His basket had the makings of an apology.

The man moved around Merry, who had only shuffled to the side. She seemed to be weighing her next words. Megan decided not to give her the chance to continue. "Next," she called. She'd get the next customer started while Clover finished ringing up the burnt offerings.

Denver walked up to the counter. Megan was surprised to see him. The veterinarian placed a bottle of sparkling apple cider, a loaf of wheat bread, and two cans of Aunt Lila's organic butternut squash soup near the register.

"Quite a difference," he said. "The store, I mean. It looks great."

The line extended beyond Denver, beyond the rubbernecked Merry Chance, and out between the shelves.

Megan said, "Thank you." She could see two of Winsome's most eligible single women at the rear of the line, staring at the doctor and whispering. Their gazes skimmed the back of him, clearly appreciative of the view.

"Did Clay pick up my cat?" Megan asked, not sure what else to say.

"Aye, he did. But he forgot his pills."

Their eyes locked. This time Denver was the first to look away. Clover had finished with the register and Megan slid the apple cider toward her. While Clover rang Denver up, Megan pulled a paper bag from beneath the counter.

"Is this stuff good?" Clover asked, pointing to the cider.

Denver shrugged. "I would have preferred a good lager, but I'm on call. Anyway, this is date food. I hear American women love to be wined and dined."

Clover laughed. "Maybe, but I'm not sure canned soup and cider are exactly what most women have in mind."

"Ah, but I don't plan to share this with most women. My date is with someone special."

Clover asked, "And who is the lucky gal?"

"Well, I haven't actually asked her yet, ye see." He looked at Megan. "Know anyone with a soft spot for butternut squash soup?"

Cheeks flaming, Megan said, "I may."

The store was silent, all eyes suddenly on the counter. From the corner of her eye, Megan could see the two women at the back exchange a glance. Winsome was a small town—a very small town—and the only thing less common than a handsome eligible bachelor in this part of Pennsylvania was a Michelin star-rated restaurant. Most of the good ones married young. The rest left.

Paper bag in hand, Denver was ready to leave. He slid something across the counter. "Here are our business hours. Come by for the laddie's medicine whenever it's convenient."

"Alright, everyone, nothing to see here," Clover said after Denver was gone. She flicked back her long hair with two flower-stenciled long nails and reached for her Snapple. With a guilty glance at Megan, she put the bottle back underneath the counter.

But Megan was barely paying attention. Denver had slipped her a business card. And in small, even printing, he'd written "7:00—dinner?" and his address along the bottom. She slipped the card in her pocket, unsuccessful at suppressing a grin.

Eleven

Dinner was a casual affair.

After checking in on Bibi, who was watching television and knitting, Megan took a hot shower. She changed into a simple vintage dress in a beige and berry-colored floral fabric and a pair of sandals. Sadie demanded her dinner. Megan fed her and grabbed a Danish from the freezer before locking the doors and heading toward the west side of town, where Denver lived.

Denver's house was a dark gray and white bungalow on a quiet residential street. Architecturally precise down to the low-pitched roof, broad eaves, and sturdy, square white columns, it was an attractive and tidy house, freshly painted and situated on a large trimmed lawn. The only nod to his profession was the fenced-in backyard and four dogs bounding along the fence line, barking madly at Megan, their mismatch in size making for a comedic pack.

Denver opened the front door and moved aside to allow her to come in. The front door led into a wide, deep living room with quarter sawn oak floors, white walls, built-in bookshelves, and simple, comfortable-looking Shaker-style furniture. It was a masculine house, but neat and organized. Even the dog beds were lined up neatly, smallest to largest.

Thanking her, Denver took the Danish Megan had rescued from the freezer and led Megan into the kitchen. Like the rest of the downstairs, the kitchen was simple and clean, with sturdy maple cabinets, unpolished soapstone countertops and stainless steel appliances. A pot of something fragrant was simmering on the stove and the bottle of sparkling cider was chilling in a silver ice bucket on the counter. True to his word, Denver was serving soup and cider. Megan laughed.

"I warned you." Denver smiled. Megan loved the way his eyes crinkled, warming his fair features. He had the kind of face that transformed when he smiled. He looked at her apologetically, the left dimple more pronounced than the right. "I'm afraid I can't cook a lick."

"Lucky for you, I can." She pointed to the Danish. "More accurately, my grandmother can."

"I was hoping for some of that lovely spinach today. You were out of it by the time I arrived."

"Come by the farm anytime. I'll give you all the spinach, kale, and other spring greens you could want."

Denver held up his hands. "Whoa, the word 'kale' never left my mouth."

Megan smiled. "You might be surprised."

Denver looked at her, long and hard. "Ye do have a habit of surprising me. Maybe you're right."

Megan could feel her face warming. She looked toward the stove, afraid her eyes would give her away. "Put me to work."

After a moment, Denver said, "Sure, why not? You can pour the cider while I serve the soup. Sound fair?"

"Lead the way."

Over dinner, Megan found herself sharing her odd conversation with King. For some reason, she trusted Denver. Maybe it was his candor, maybe it was his warmth. Whatever the reason, it felt good to talk about the murder with someone who could be objective.

She said, "The glove must be Bibi's—or at least it originated with her. And the police know that. So the question is, why would someone want to frame my grandmother for murder? Or, if they aren't trying to frame her, how did they get the gloves?"

"You said it was the same glove the goat had in her mouth?"

"May have been. Truth is, I'm not sure. But why in the world would the police believe an eighty-four-year-old woman is capable of murder? Someone King has known his whole life."

"Maybe they don't, which is why Bobby showed you the cuffs. The police may know that Bonnie's not capable of murder, and while they can't come out and tell you that your dear grandmother is being framed, they can let you know that something smells fishy."

"Maybe."

"Have the police made any formal moves, Meg?"

"No. And if I felt like they were sniffing around with any seriousness, I would hire a lawyer."

Megan glanced at Denver's four dogs—a Golden Retriever, a very tall Great Dane mix, some sort of Chihuahua blend, and a one-eyed Beagle—all lined up in a row about three feet from the table. She could tell they wanted some of the bread but were too well-trained to ask. She longed to share, but one look at Denver's watchful eye and she knew she'd get them in trouble.

"Quite a menagerie you have," she said instead.

"Aye, a crazy lot. I started out with no dogs. I guess you could say these pups adopted me." He put his spoon down and called the dogs. All four ran to the table and sat upright next to the doctor. "The pure-breed retriever was dumped at the clinic by her former owners when they decided her health care cost more than they cared to spend."

Denver patted the Great Dane affectionately. "This one was a stray found on the side of the road. We couldn't find him a home because of his size, so he wound up here." As though to emphasize how fine he really was with that, the dog thumped his long, skinny tail against the hardwood.

"And how about these two?" Megan asked, pointing to the Chihuahua and the Beagle.

"They came as part of a threesome." Denver reached out and rubbed each in turn, his face softening. "Their owner died and no one wanted them."

"Where's the third?"

Denver sat back up, his eyes darkening. "That would be Sarge."

"You gave Sarge to Porter?"

Denver nodded. "He'd recently returned from overseas. I could tell Sarge had lots of training. In fact, his previous owner had epilepsy, and Sarge was used to...helping."

"A therapy dog?"

"Not exactly, but close enough." He smiled. "We both know that most dogs are therapy of some sort."

Megan nodded her agreement, thinking of Sadie and the million ways that dog had kept her going after Mick's death. "And Brick was open to that? He seemed kind of...rough. Not someone who would want help."

Denver poured more cider into his wineglass, took a sip, and placed the glass down on the table. "You're absolutely right, which is why I didn't offer Sarge to help him. I appealed to Brian to help Sarge." He tilted his head, looking thoughtful. "Didn't take much convincing."

Megan thought of the scene the night before, of the boy's obvious love for the dog. "How is Sarge?"

"Recovering."

"How about Porter?"

Denver paused. "The laddie is holding his own."

Something tickled at the corners of Megan's brain. She watched as Denver raised his hand slightly and three of the four dogs laid down on the floor. Only the Golden Retriever failed to obey.

"You said Sarge came to you well-trained?" Megan asked.

"Completely trained."

"Yet he ran across the road."

"Now that you mention it, it does seem odd, doesn't it?"

"Yes, it does. Although maybe he saw a cat or a raccoon. After all the rain, the coons are active these days."

"But ye don't believe that."

It was a statement, not a question. "No, guess I don't believe that. But if the dog didn't stray, then that means—" She couldn't bring herself to finish the sentence.

"That someone let him out on purpose?"

"And perhaps enticed him away from the house." Megan frowned. "I've been to his house. The gate was latched from the inside. Unless Porter left it open, someone must have deliberately unlatched it."

"Porter is a careful sort when it comes to Sarge. He wouldna done that."

Megan glanced down at her half-full bowl, suddenly not at all hungry. "Think Sarge's escape could be related to Simon's murder?"

"You're thinking of the flask Sadie found?"

Megan nodded.

Denver frowned. "Brian is a loner here. He may not be the most stable man, but he doesn't make trouble often. People give him a wide berth."

"Is he capable of hurting someone?"

Denver's eyes narrowed. "Are ye asking whether he might have killed Simon?"

Megan sensed his disbelief, but she held her ground, giving voice to the concern that had been bothering her since she'd met Porter. "You said yourself that he's unstable. Alcohol addiction and mental illness can take a toll on people. What if he killed Simon and someone found out?"

"Brick had nothing to do with Simon's murder." When Megan only looked at him skeptically, he said, his voice softer, "Don't forget, I was with you that night, Meg. I saw Simon's body. It haunts me too."

"It wasn't on your property." As soon as the words were out of her mouth, she regretted them. Denver was kind and generous. He wasn't trying to make light of her concerns. To the contrary, he was offering her empathy and a dose of reality. She could use a smidgen of both right about now. "I'm sorry," she said. "Maybe I'm more on edge than I thought."

"Understandable." Denver stood. "This was supposed to be

relaxing and here we are talking about murder. I'm not good at this, am I?" He smiled. "Come on, let's go for a walk."

"Where are you taking me?"

"Somewhere I know you'll like."

Somewhere turned out to be across Denver's neighborhood, down a quiet country road and up a winding, tree-lined driveway. Two of Denver's dogs, the Golden Retriever and the Great Dane, accompanied them, and Denver let them off lead once they reached the driveway.

"A little farther," he said.

A little farther meant a quarter mile up the hill to a looming, pristine red barn that sat on the edge of an enclosed pasture. On the other side of the pasture, next to a stone garage, a white farmhouse sat primly against the backdrop of rolling hills and patchwork farmland. The farm was the highest point for miles around, and the view in daylight was sure to be spectacular. Even in the pressing dusk, Megan held her breath.

"Oh, Denver, this is lovely."

Denver smiled. "Ta. The house and land belongs to my aunt, Eloise Kent. Do you know Eloise?"

"Her name is familiar."

"She's the town pediatrician—or was, before she retired. Now she plays the organ for St. Marks and dotes over her animals. Come on, I'll show you."

They crossed a level, well-set stone path that led from the driveway, up a small hill, and over to the barn. A white picket fence, freshly painted, sat three feet from the path and wound around the edge of the pasture and back toward the house. Denver paused at the barn's threshold to open one of the double doors and turn on the lights. Megan felt a shiver of anxiety race the length of her spine. The last time she and Denver entered a barn together, bad things happened.

But this time, she was met with the wide-eyed, old-soul stare of a pair of horses peeking over their stalls: one sturdy Quarter Horse with a white star on his head and a beautiful Palomino.

"Watch," Denver whispered. He pointed to the Palomino.

At the sound of his voice, a second head appeared—a perfect Palomino colt. She was old enough to display the elegant confidence of a horse, but young enough that she still had the long-legged gawkiness of a baby.

"They're gorgeous." Megan rushed to the stalls. It was the Quarter Horse that met her with a spirited head nudge.

"He'll be chewing on your hair in a moment if you're not careful. Come this way." Denver led the way farther into the barn, the Great Dane trailing behind. A stall had been lined with hay bales, and in the middle, on a fluffy blanket, lay a mother cat and her kittens.

"So sweet." Megan pointed at one of the hay bales. "Mind if I sit?"

"Not at all."

Megan settled in on the edge of a bale, relishing the peace and isolation of this barn on the hill—and the company. A moment later, Denver sat beside her, his thigh pressing against hers.

"Tell me why you stay in Winsome," Megan said. "You went to Cornell for veterinary school and someone told me you had an offer from a prestigious university out west to teach and do research. Why here?"

"Aye, I've lived all over," Denver said. "California, Georgia, Wyoming. Even did some volunteer work in Guatemala and Bangladesh." Denver looked at Megan, his eyes lingering on her mouth. His lips, full and enticing, were dangerously close. "You reach a certain age, and the world narrows in the very best way possible. Winsome is home. It's the only place I've ever felt truly myself. Does that make any sense?"

It did, and Megan said so. "It's beautiful here."

Denver leaned in. Megan felt his hand caress her arm, the press of his chest against her shoulder. Time seemed to stand still. All she wanted at that moment was to be with him, here, in this spot. She closed her eyes and felt his lips gently touch her own. She kissed back and he pressed in harder. They stood, fumbling for one another in the small, darkened enclosure.

That's when Megan felt a canine nose against her backside. She jumped and Denver fell backwards, onto the hay bale, pulling Megan down on top of him. The dog lunged on them both, smothering the side of Megan's face with kisses.

"I'm sorry," Megan exclaimed, laughing. "He put his nose in...a bad spot."

"You bloody mad dog, get down." Denver was laughing too. "I'm the one who's sorry. I guess next time I should take you somewhere without an audience."

Megan started to disengage herself from Denver when she felt the veterinarian's hand against the back of her neck. Gently, he pulled her head down toward his own. Their lips met again, full of heat and urgency. Megan's pulse raced. She could feel his heart beating through the cool cotton of his shirt. She pressed her hand on his chest, over his heart, wanting badly to let it trail farther.

It wasn't to be. Footsteps echoed in the barn corridor. A soft, lightly accented voice called out, "Denver?"

Megan jumped to her feet, smoothing her dress with her hands. Denver stood also, a disappointed half-smile playing on his lips. "That would be Aunt Eloise," he whispered. "My family always has the best timing." To his aunt, he called, "In here!"

"Ah, you startled me, Denver." Eloise's eyes glanced from Megan to the dog and cats on the floor to her nephew and back to Megan. "I see you brought a guest."

Megan wished her Irish features didn't advertise her embarrassment quite so well. She hadn't been caught making out with a boy since she and Mick were dating in high school. One look at Denver told her he didn't share her shame.

"Megan Sawyer, my aunt Eloise. Megan owns Washington Acres—the farm across town—and the new café and store on Canal."

Eloise, a slender older woman with a white-blonde wedge

haircut and pencil-thin eyebrows, raised those eyebrows now. "You're Eddie's girl. I know your family quite well."

The tone of her voice left open the question of whether knowing her family "quite well" was a good thing or not.

"Pleased to meet you," Megan said. She held out her hand. Eloise took it. The other woman's touch felt bone cold. "Your farm is absolutely lovely."

"Yes, well, I'm not sure how much of it you could see from in here." She gave Denver a pointed look. "Tending to the kittens, were you?"

"I was showing Megan the animals. That's all."

Denver sounded impatient. Megan wondered what this unspoken dance was between aunt and nephew.

Eloise, composure regained, turned her attention to Megan. "As I recall, Bonnie doesn't particularly care for cats, but if you would like a kitten, please, have one. They will be ready to be weaned in two to three weeks." She looked to her nephew for confirmation. Denver nodded.

"I'll ask her. Thank you."

"Would you two like to come back to the house? For a glass of wine, perhaps?" Eloise looked hopefully at Denver. He, in turn, glanced at Megan.

"Thank you, but I should get going," Megan said.

"Very well." Eloise leaned in to give Denver a quick peck on the cheek. "Next time, Denver, let me know you're coming. There's been a murder in Winsome. I could have called the police. Or worse, come out here with a gun."

Twelve

Back at Denver's house, the intimate mood felt lost. Megan and Denver were standing on his front steps, an expanse of wood and concrete between them.

"Bibi's been home alone all day. I should check on her."

Denver nodded. "Of course. I'm sorry about that little scene with my aunt. She's up to high doh."

Megan laughed. "Come again?"

Denver smiled. "Aye, sorry. It means she's all riled up. Simon's death has everyone off-kilter."

"I'll say. She didn't sound crazy about my family either."

"She's not crazy about most people. Don't take it personally."

"Is she crazy about you, Denver?" Megan regretted the words as soon as they were out of her mouth, but if the Scot was offended, he didn't let on.

"It's complicated."

Intrigued, Megan wanted to press, but the closed look on Denver's face stopped her. Instead she said, "Well, I hope she's willing to give the Birch family a fresh try."

"She's slow to trust my judgment when it comes to women. My ex-wife was not exactly her ideal." He flashed that boyish smile. "I'm afraid the Finn family is not always so lucky when it comes to love."

"Eloise too?"

"She's had more than her share of judgment issues, if that's what you mean." He shrugged. "Again with the serious stuff. I'm sorry. This was supposed to be a fun night."

Megan moved closer. Standing on tiptoes, she reached up and touched her lips gently to his. "I had a lovely evening. Can we do it again?"

Denver smiled, and his face lit up. "When are you free?"

"Soon. I'll make you dinner this time. My grandmother has Bridge from four to seven some nights. Come early enough and we can have some time alone." She smiled. "Think of it as the early bird special of the dating world."

"I love a good early bird special," Denver said. "Especially when it's served by such a pretty lassie." His words teased, but his eyes held her own.

Megan saw Denver in her rearview mirror as she pulled away from his house. He was watching her from his front steps, his face unreadable, and his body as rigid as the columns flanking him.

Megan pulled into her driveway at nine. Her mind was still on Denver, the kiss they shared in the barn, and the feelings that overtook her when she was with him—feelings, she realized guiltily, she'd only known with Mick.

As she climbed out of the truck, Megan noticed that the lights to the back porch entryway were off. Bibi always left them on when Megan was out—a habit from Megan's youth. Megan felt the hairs on the back of her neck rise. Megan was hurrying toward the door when something caught her attention. She saw, then heard, a figure in the shrubs lining the porch steps. She was deciding whether to yell, run, or stop and confront when a voice rang from the shadows.

"Megan Sawyer?"

It took Megan a moment to place the voice as Porter's.

Megan placed her key between two fingers, the way she'd learned in self-defense class. "Come out here," she demanded. "And keep your hands in front of you."

"I'm not here to hurt you. I only want to talk." If he'd been drinking, Megan couldn't tell. His words were sharp-edged, clear.

"Then come out here, now."

The rustling continued until finally Porter was standing in front of her. Skinny and underdressed in a tank top and army fatigue cargo pants, he stood stock straight. His expression, not unlike Denver's a bit ago, was unreadable, but there was fear in his eyes—fear, and something akin to desperation. Megan understood desperation. Desperate people did stupid, reckless things, and if Porter had been the perpetrator of some desperate acts recently, she wanted no part of being the next victim. She reached for her phone, keeping her key hand in front of her as a warning, as weak as it seemed now that she was standing before a trained soldier.

"Please," Porter said. He spread his hands out in front of him. Although his posture was rigid, his eyes were as energetic as a swarm of mayflies. Finally, he settled his gaze on her. "I need to talk to you."

Megan's mind flashed to Simon's inert body. "If you try anything, I will call the police."

He looked at her incredulously. "Really—I only want to talk. That's it."

Megan hesitated. One look at Porter's emaciated form, and she knew she would follow in her grandmother's footsteps. "Come in," she said with a sigh. "I'll make you something to eat."

After assuring herself that Porter was not an immediate threat, Megan left him in Sadie's care and ran to check on her grandmother, whom she found snoozing soundly under half a dozen handmade quilts. She watched her grandmother's chest rise and fall a few times, gratitude for Bonnie's steadfast presence washing over her. Thinking of the odd conversation with Denver's aunt Eloise, Megan closed Bibi's door softly and returned to the kitchen.

While Porter sat at her kitchen table, hands cradling his shaved head, Megan assembled leftover salad, cheeses, bread and

Danish, all of which she placed in front of Porter. He eyed the food. "Not hungry," he mumbled.

"I can tell, and that may be part of your problem."

"Who says I have a problem?" His chin jutted. "Dr. Finn?"

Megan sat in the seat opposite him, taking her time to slice a piece of cheddar and place it on a slice of sourdough. "Do you usually show up at women's houses late at night, unannounced and uninvited?"

"I suppose I could ask you the same question. You came to me first."

He had a point. With a scrunch of her nose, she said, "That was you at the window. You were home, after all."

He nodded. "Why'd you come?"

"I found something of yours at my store. I wanted to return it."

His eyes narrowed. "What was it?"

"A flask."

"What was my flask doing at your store?" Puffy eyes widened to surprised orbs.

"I was hoping you could tell me."

"I want it back."

Megan weighed whether to give it to him. If he'd had something to do with Simon's murder, it could be evidence. On the other hand, a flask hardly made him a murderer.

Looking at him now in the bright lights of her kitchen, Megan saw the dragon tattoo that snaked its way up his scrawny neck. She saw the angry purse of his mouth and the shaking of his hands, hands far too young to be afflicted with palsy. With a suffocating feeling of empathy, Megan remembered the first time she saw Mick after he'd left for the Middle East. He'd been given a short leave, and she'd flown to Germany to meet him for three days of R&R. When she'd opened the door to their hotel room to greet him, she'd flown into his arms. It wasn't until they parted, until she had the time to study her husband's face, that she saw the hollows under his eyes and the emptiness in his gaze when he wasn't looking at her. She visited with Mick twice after that, and each time the shadows had grown darker, the emptiness more pronounced. Had he lived, would he have shared Porter's fate?

"Brian," Megan said, standing. "Why was your flask at my café?"

"I told you. I don't know."

"Do you remember the last time you saw it?"

He thought for a moment, eyes shifting. "No."

"You have no idea where you left it?"

"No." He looked down at his hands, which were dancing on the table top.

Megan sat forward in her chair, thinking. He was clearly lying, but she didn't know why.

Porter said, "I came here to ask *you* questions."

"Ask away."

He tapped one finger nervously on the table top. "Why were you with Dr. Finn when he came to help Sarge?"

"Because we were going to have dinner together."

"It was coincidence, then?"

"What was coincidence?"

"You coming by my house, and then you showing up again with Doc Finn." Porter sat forward, matching Megan's posture. His gaze darted from object to object in the kitchen, settling finally on Megan's face. "Did you hit my dog?"

"Brian, no! I would never hurt your dog—or any dog."

"It seemed awful coincidental, you showing up twice like that."

"I told you, the first time I came by about the flask. It was Denver—Dr. Finn—who told me it must be yours. The second time was strictly a coincidence. I happened to be with Dr. Finn when you called."

He eyed her with suspicion. "You're dating Dr. Finn?"

"No." *Maybe.* "Not that it's your business."

Porter stood abruptly. "This was a waste of time." The tendons on his neck were taut beneath reddened skin, the portion of the dragon visible a sickly green in the dim light.

In a calming voice, Megan asked, "Why are you really here?"

"I told you. You were nosing around and I wondered—"

Megan held up her hand to stop him, exhaustion and impatience suddenly raining down on her. "The truth, please?"

His head spun toward her, eyes flaming. "What are you suggesting?"

"Someone was killed here, in case you hadn't heard." Megan straightened her spine, trying hard to ignore the pounding in her chest. "A man sneaks around my property, it makes me wonder what he's up to."

His eyes narrowed to slits. "And you think I had something to do with Simon's death? Is that it?" He took a step toward Megan.

She held her ground, refusing to be cowed. Her pulse raced. She scanned the kitchen, her gaze fixating on the serrated knife she'd used to slice the bread, and mentally calculated how quickly she could reach the counter.

Silence stretched, and with it their game of mental chicken.

Finally, Porter said, "I knew Simon—everybody did—but I didn't kill the old man." His shoulders drooped, the green dragon losing its tautness.

Megan studied him, deciding whether he was playing games or being truthful. In the civil light of her grandmother's kitchen, Brian "Brick" Porter looked more boy than man.

Upstairs, a door slammed. Sadie sat up straight, ears back and tail wagging. Echoing the dog's posture, Porter bolted upright.

"Who's here? I don't need any trouble."

"Relax. It's only my grandmother."

A minute later, Bonnie walked into the kitchen. She'd taken the time to put on a pink housecoat over her gray flannel pajamas. She walked with resigned purpose—an insomniac's nod to the night.

"Hello, Brian," she said as though it were the most natural thing in the world to have him sitting in her kitchen.

"Mrs. Birch." Porter nodded.

"I guess you two know each other?"

They shared a look—fleeting, but noticeable—before Bibi said,

"It's a small town."

Megan stood to make her grandmother tea. It was a small town, all right.

Thirteen

"The spinach is starting to flower." Clay stood straight, propping his elbow on his shovel. With the back of one gloved hand, he pushed a long, lank strand of dark hair away from his eyes and glanced toward the sun. "Weather's warming up. The spinach will go crazy. We need to pull the rest." He leaned down, picked a spinach leaf, and flipped it over. "This one's clear, but I saw aphids on a few in the greenhouse and down there." He pointed to the very end of the row.

"Ladybugs," Megan said. "Aphids' natural enemy."

"No time. The aphids will spread and once they do, we'll lose the whole crop."

"They rinse off."

Clay shook his head. "It's bolting anyway, Megan. We can sell it. And what we can't sell, we can freeze." He shrugged. "You like spinach, right? It's too late to do anything else."

"Nonsense."

Megan and Clay both turned abruptly at the sound of Bonnie's voice.

"Bibi. I thought you were napping." It was after eleven. Bibi had been up half the night, so when she went to put her feet up at nine and dozed off, Megan let her sleep.

"Naps are for babies and the infirm." She waved a hand in the direction of the spinach. "Get some watering wands, take off the sprinkler, and put on a hose nozzle. Then drag the hose over here and spray the unbeliever out of the spinach. Start from the bottom, especially the underside where the little critters lay their eggs." She tapped one of the spinach plants gently with a white Keds-clad toe. "And Clay's right. The spinach is bolting. You need to pick it and sell it or soon it will be worthless."

Megan and Clay stared at Megan's grandmother open-mouthed. This was the first time she'd shown an interest in the workings of the farm.

"Close your mouths and get to work," she said. With obvious difficulty, she knelt down on the ground and started picking the healthy spinach leaves. "Clay, we need a few large, clean coolers filled with cold water. The spinach will wilt if it stays out here like this."

"We know, Bibi—" Megan started to say, alarmed. Her grandmother was in great shape considering her age, but having her kneel on damp earth to pick spinach did not seem like a fantastic idea.

Clay threw Megan a "don't bother to argue" look. "Of course, Mrs. Birch," he said with a smile. "That's what we typically do. But if you're willing to help us, perhaps you'd prefer to bag the spinach. I can get you a table and chair and set them up in the shade."

"What, and miss all the fun of watching me try to get up?" Bibi scoffed. "Stop coddling. I may be old, but I'm not dead—or useless. Let's get to work. All of us."

"What was that about?" Clay asked later. He and Megan were putting away the last of the spinach-picking supplies. While Clay rinsed out the large coolers used to store the freshly-picked leaves where they awaited bagging, Megan was storing the bagged lettuce in the large commercial refrigerator. Both of them avoided the barn.

"She's been acting odd for days now."

"It was nice to see her engaged."

"I guess." As Megan shelved the spinach bags neatly within the walk-in refrigerator, she considered her grandmother's behavior, both last night and today. Something was off, and she wondered about all the things that could have occurred before she arrived in Winsome. Small towns were microcosms, and like humanity at large, Winsome saw its share of bad and good, avarice and fear. Did whatever was underlying Bibi's behavior have its roots in something older and bigger than what she could see now?

Clay straightened. "You don't sound convinced."

"I'm worried about her."

"Talk to her."

"I've tried."

Clay's eyes traveled from Megan's face to the car that had just pulled into the long driveway. Megan followed his stare. She watched as King climbed out of the unmarked vehicle. Mirrored sunglasses hid his eyes, but even from this distance Megan could see the glower on his face. A young cop, barely out of his Little League uniform, stood beside King.

"Finish this," Megan said to Clay before walking up the slight incline to meet the police chief. "Bob," she said.

"Where's Bonnie?"

"Inside. Why?"

"We need her to come with us. We'd like to ask her some follow-up questions."

"Why can't you do it here?"

The two officers exchanged a look. "I'm really sorry, Megan, but we need her in the station."

"You can come too," the young cop said quickly, but his words were met by a sharp glance from King.

King said, "It'd be best if she came alone."

"Are you pressing charges?"

"No."

"I'm fine," Bonnie said from the doorway, her tone resolute. "I was expecting this."

Baffled, Megan looked at her grandmother and then the police. "She goes, I go."

Another exchange between the two police officers, this one less sympathetic. King shrugged finally and said, "For goodness sake, fine. Let's get going then."

Bibi refused to let Megan in the interrogation room, so Megan paced in the tiny police station waiting area, nursing her hurt and trying hard to quell the rising tide of anger, but it was downright impossible.

What in the world was her otherwise gentle, *rational* grandmother up to? She didn't want Megan, didn't want a lawyer, and kept insisting that she could explain everything. *Explain what?* Megan's head was about to explode. She toyed with calling her father, but thought better of it. There was nothing her father could do from Italy and he would only panic. She had no choice but to wait. Bonnie was more mentally with it than ninety-eight percent of the people Megan knew.

Or had been.

Almost ninety minutes later, King and Bibi came walking around the corner into the waiting area. King gave Megan a hearty smile, shook Bibi's hand and said, "Your grandmother is free to go."

"Is anyone going to tell me what happened?"

Bibi started walking toward the door as though she hadn't heard her granddaughter. King smiled and said, "She cleared some things up for us. We told her we would contact her if we have further questions."

"I'm her lawyer."

"No you're not," Bibi said over her shoulder. "I don't need a lawyer."

"Bibi," Megan hissed.

But Bibi had walked outside. Megan looked at King, eyebrows raised in a mask of exasperation. "Really? You can't tell me anything? She's my grandmother. Wouldn't you want to know?"

The police chief glanced down at his loafer-clad feet and then up at Megan again. His half-smile was apologetic. He wasn't budging. "You need to talk to her. As long as everything she told us checks out, we shouldn't have more questions."

As long as everything she told us checks out? Even my grandmother has a double life, Megan thought. What had happened to Winsome in the years since I'd been gone?

Bibi was maddeningly cheerful the entire way home.

"What happened in there?" Megan asked again.

Bibi waved her hand in a dismissive gesture that was becoming much too familiar. "Nothing worth wasting breath on."

Megan glanced at her grandmother from across the truck's bench seat. "*Something* went down in there."

"I remember that Bobby King when he was a toddler in plastic pants. He needs to feel important, so he's asking questions, most of which have nothing to do with Simon's murder, rest assured about that." She looked pointedly at Megan. "He asked and I answered is all."

They pulled up to a red light separating Canal Street from Baker Avenue. Megan shot her grandmother another look, taking advantage of the traffic stop to ask her the question that had been most on her mind. "Bibi, how'd you explain the bloody glove?"

Her grandmother stared straight ahead. "What bloody glove?"

"I know about the glove. Bobby King *told* me about the bloody glove." The light turned green and Megan inched forward, reluctantly taking her gaze off her grandmother. "'Stay Warm in Winsome'? Who else would own those gloves?"

"Plenty of people."

Megan grasped the steering wheel so hard her knuckles turned white. "Why won't you be straight with me?" she asked, softening her tone. "What's going on?"

But her grandmother only gave her a gentle smile. "I didn't kill anyone, Megan, nor did you. I have souvenir shop stuff everywhere, you know that. If someone found one of those gloves and used it to do something evil, that has nothing to do with me—or you. You have a farm to get off the ground. Stop worrying about this and get to work."

"Someone died in our barn."

"And there is not a thing on God's green earth you can do about it."

For the first time in her life, Megan felt anger—true, boiling anger—toward her grandmother. "Maybe not," she said. "But I'm not one to sit around."

"No one is asking you to sit around," Bibi said calmly. She reached across the center console and touched Megan's arm, her skin dry and feathery light. "I'm only asking you to trust me."

Megan felt her anger wane, but only for a moment. Trust was one thing—she *did* trust her grandmother, implicitly—but blind trust of the system was another. And that was really what Bibi was requesting.

They rode the rest of the way without talking. Bibi hummed "Amazing Grace" quietly to herself. For her part, Megan focused on the road and thought about the random patterns formed on blood-soaked gloves.

Fourteen

Early the next morning, Megan dressed quickly in jeans and a sweatshirt and headed outside. After tending to the animals, she selected a small shovel from the makeshift tool chest near the chicken coop, glaring at the police tape as she passed the barn. She sprayed a deep cooler with bleach solution, rinsed it thoroughly, and wiped it out with clean towels before heading to the herb garden, her favorite space on the farm. Today she would bundle up small packages of the herbs she'd grown in hoop houses over the winter: curry, cilantro, parsley, oregano, chives, and great, long sprigs of sweetly scented lavender. At $3.00 a bundle, they would sell. And whatever didn't sell, she and Bibi could dry and keep for their own use or for the café.

The sun was shining through a marshmallow fluff of clouds. Megan was kneeling on the ground in front of the curry, gently clipping off strands of the fragrant herb, when she glanced up, toward the abandoned Marshall house next door. The house was a plain rectangular Colonial, one room deep, built in the solid but sparse fashion of the eighteenth century. Its stone exterior was crumbling in spots, and what had been a broad, stately porch was now a derelict appendage hanging by one peeling railing. Despite the vagaries of age and use, the house still had good posture. Its leaded windows remained intact, and the small well house a few hundred feet from the main house was in perfect condition, at least on the outside. Someone willing to invest time and money could restore the property—and even add on to the home. It sat on at least three acres of farmable land.

Maybe she'd take a look at purchasing it. She couldn't afford it now, but she would love to add an inn to the farm. Diversification of income would be a plus, and running an inn sounded like fun.

Thinking of the old Marshall property made Megan think of her mysterious Aunt Sarah—and a possible connection to Simon's murder. She decided she'd finish up the herbs, drop them off at the store, and take a ride over to meet her great-aunt. She might be able to find her address online. She could check with Bibi, but why risk upsetting her? Besides, sometimes it was better to beg forgiveness than ask permission.

Sarah had purchased a small cottage off Briar Bush Way, about eight miles from Winsome, only a few months before. The house, as close to a thatch-roofed English Tudor as you would find in these parts, sat well off the road, smack in the middle of a circle of stately oaks, and on this warm May morning, the shade from the trees' fresh spring leaves cast lacey shadows on a thick ring of lawn. The yard itself held paisley-shaped flowerbeds spaced randomly throughout, each filled with perennials in varied states of vivid bloom, and decorative birdhouses. Glass art pieces in jeweled tones stuck up from the ground on long iron poles. An American flag waved from a post near the front door, but other than the motion of the flag's material and the gentle flutter of the tree branches overhead, the house was quiet.

Megan took a deep breath and knocked. There was no answer. She turned around, ready to head back to her car. That's when she heard a voice call out.

"Over here! If you don't mind an old woman milling about in her muckers, you can join me in the garden."

Megan glanced around. She saw a red-clad arm waving from beneath the trees, past the corner of the house, before spotting a woman kneeling on the ground beneath a great oak. Megan walked toward the older woman, careful not to tromp on any flowers along the way.

"Hello," Megan said tentatively. "Sarah?"

"Depends. Who's doing the asking?" The woman peered up at her, blocking the sun with one hand. She was in her late seventies, with sun-browned skin and long, straight steel-gray hair tamed into a thick braid that hung halfway down her back. Thin and sinewy, her lean body was draped in red fabric—a long-sleeved red shirt and an ankle-length red, black, and gray skirt that spread around her like a blanket. She appeared to be building a tiny dwelling at the base of a tree. The miniature house, made of sticks, walnut shells, and bits of feathers, hugged gnarly roots. A camera case and tripod sat on a blanket nearby.

"A fairy home," the woman said. She placed a final feather on top of the bite-sized building and then stood, wiping her hands together as she did so. "For a children's book. A fun distraction, really." She held out a hand, now mostly free of dirt. "You must be Eddie's girl, Megan. You look like Bonnie when she was younger."

They shook. Close up, Sarah had the toughened skin of a woman who'd spent much of her life outside. But her blue eyes were vibrant, inquisitive, and maybe even a touch amused. Megan searched for a flicker of a memory, an echo of recognition, but found none.

"Do you have time for some lemonade? Or maybe a cup of hot tea? I have chamomile, English Breakfast, or green." She tilted her head, waiting for Megan to answer.

"Lemonade would be wonderful. Thank you."

Her great-aunt nodded approvingly and motioned for her to follow her into the house.

The inside of the cottage was clean but cluttered. Stacks and stacks of books buried every surface, from the white countertops in the small kitchen to the floral cushions on a loveseat in the sunroom. Megan read a rainbow of titles, from mysteries and thrillers to how-to books to nonfiction treatises on such wide-ranging topics as physics and photography. White frilly curtains billowed in open windows. The walls were a plain white but covered with artwork: expensive-looking oils, watercolor prints, and matted and framed children's crayon drawings. The house smelled of vanilla and lemon. Megan glanced around, feeling off-center. She expected déjà vu; she got only a vague sense of welcome.

Sarah suggested she take the overstuffed armchair in the living room. Megan moved two coffee table books and sank down into the chair.

"Give me a minute," Sarah said. "I'd apologize for the mess, but I didn't know you were coming." She shrugged. "I'm having work done in the bedrooms. I'm afraid everything has been moved out here. Not sure it would have made a difference. I'm forty years past caring what anyone thinks." She smiled. "Make yourself at home, though. Watch out for the cat. Sammy likes to bite."

Sammy turned out to be a standoffish Siamese sitting on the white-washed windowsill. He glanced at Megan, let out one disdainful meow, and returned to staring out the bay window. Tearing her eyes away from the cat, Megan turned her attention to the rest of the room. She noticed a painting leaned up against a wall on top of a buffet by the window, a series of photographs in mismatched white frames on a slate fireplace mantel. She rose to get a better look at the pictures.

Some were of small children she didn't recognize, chubby-faced cherubs in denim and white. Here and there a face looked familiar, more because of features shared with her father, Eddie, than because she actually recognized the subject. Disappointed, she strolled the length of the mantel, taking in more pictures of strangers. The last three photographs made her pause. The woman in the photos was her great-aunt—younger, perhaps, but definitely her aunt—and in each picture she was accepting an award. An Edgar. An Agatha. A Macavity.

Why was Aunt Sarah accepting prestigious mystery book awards?

"Another life," said a voice behind her.

Megan turned abruptly. "You're an author?"

"Yes." Her aunt placed a tray down on a striped ottoman next to a pile of hardcover novels. She picked up a tall glass of lemonade and handed it to Megan. She waved toward the mantel. "A silly nod to vanity. I should have disposed of those photos ages ago."

"I don't understand."

"Do you recognize the name Sarah Estelle?"

"You're *the* Sarah Estelle?"

Her aunt nodded. Moving another stack of novels from a second overstuffed chair to the top of a coffee table, Sarah sat down, sipping her own glass of lemonade.

"Why didn't I know that?"

"That's an excellent question. One I'm not in a position to answer."

Megan sat back, thinking. Sarah Estelle was the award-winning, *New York Times* bestselling author of three mystery series, including one that had been made into a long-running television show. Megan had cut her teeth on Estelle's novels. Finding out Sarah Estelle was her aunt was like being kicked in the face and winning the lottery all at once. Her mind spun for something to say. She finally asked, "Do you know my father well?"

"Eddie?" Sarah smiled. "Well enough."

"Were you ever close?"

Sarah placed her glass on a nearby empty plant stand. "Why did you come here, Megan?"

"To talk."

"About...?"

Megan took a deep breath. The sense of imbalance, of being spun topsy turvy, increased. "About Washington Acres. About my grandmother. About why I don't remember you."

"Ah, I see."

"I'm glad one of us does."

Sarah stood. She lingered by the mantel, one tanned, thick-knuckled finger tracing the top of each frame, wiping nonexistent dust from the worn wood.

"Don't you think these are things you should discuss with Bonnie?"

"She won't tell me anything."

"But she told you I was back in Winsome."

"No, my contractors told me that. Because of...because of the murder."

She turned. "Simon."

"Yes. You knew him?"

"I may not have been here for the last twenty-four years, but I knew him. Everyone knew Simon. And, of course, his mother." She gave a wistful smile. "Simon was considerably younger than me. A precocious young man. But that was before...well, I heard he'd become rather bitter and off-putting."

Megan nodded. She hated to talk ill of the dead, but Simon Duvall had given her nothing but trouble. It was hard to think kind thoughts.

"I heard my grandmother almost sold Washington Acres to Simon."

Sarah's mouth twisted into a frown. It looked like she was deciding how much to share. Eyes narrowed, she finally said, "I doubt that's true."

Megan stood, agitation rising. Why was everyone being so circumspect? "Neil Dorfman told me."

At this, Sarah laughed. "Neil? Really, Megan—I assumed Teddy's granddaughter would have more sense than to believe a Dorfman, especially Neil. Simon was never kind to the Dorfmans, or their family. In fact, he shut down their sister's antique business before it even got off the ground. Called it an eyesore. No, he wasn't a nice man, especially in his later years." She shook her head, sending the braid flying across her back. "And you're a lawyer, from what I understand?" She smiled, her hand reaching out toward Megan. "I'm happy you came. I really am. You're a lovely girl, exactly as I imagined."

Unhappy at being dismissed easily, Megan stood firm. "Why would Neil make that up?"

"Perhaps he heard it from someone else and simply got his source wrong." She made a motion like she was sipping from a bottle. "As one of my characters would say, he has a tendency to get ripped to the giddy tits."

Neil did like to drink. Megan took another look at the award photographs, at the pictures of babies lined up across the mantel. Grandchildren. That meant Megan had cousins, cousins she didn't know. The house felt claustrophobic, the ground moved beneath her.

She turned, and she was suddenly staring at the painting on the buffet. She recognized the subject in the painting. It was the Birch farm, only as it must have looked years ago. The barn without additions, the house a plain rectangle, and a second house. The Marshall house. It had been one big parcel.

"Where did you get that painting?" Megan whispered.

"Your father. He found it on the farm."

Sarah had loved the farm enough to keep a painting of the original homestead for all of these years. Megan felt like an interloper. Her vision clouded, a vise squeezed her temples.

"I shouldn't have come."

"Nonsense. I'm glad you did."

"No—it was wrong of me." Megan backed away, toward the kitchen and the door that led outside. "I have to go."

"You're always welcome, Megan. I—"

But Megan was back in the yard, hurrying toward her car. She never heard the rest of her great-aunt's sentence.

Megan drove the truck wildly, pedal pressed to the floor. She didn't know where she was going, she just wanted to get *away*. Her mind was reeling with what she'd learned. She had a great-aunt living near Winsome. Not only that, she had cousins—baby cousins—an entire branch of family members she'd never met. And her aunt was *the* Sarah Estelle! In all those years, why wouldn't someone—her grandmother, her father—have told her that?

She flew past Winsome's small medical clinic and was approaching the elementary school when she applied the brake to slow down. Unconsciously, she had headed in the direction of the veterinary hospital. She started to pull over to turn around and thought better of it. She wanted to see Denver. Needed to see him. He'd have no answers, but that was okay. He wouldn't be hiding anything either.

Fifteen

Denver returned from an appointment at a horse farm. His arms were covered with abrasions and blood streaked down the side of his neck. He gave Megan a cheeky smile when he saw her, and continued to lather up his arms in the back room, strong hands working disinfecting soap into his tanned skin with long, firm strokes.

"The receptionist let me back here," she said. "Hope you don't mind." She eyed his arms, wincing at the sight of the scratches—now enveloped in soap. "Get into a fight with razor wire?"

Denver laughed. "Aye, might as well have." He rinsed, then began drying his arms with a clean white towel. "Lowry's filly gave birth. While I was there, he asked me to take a look at his feral cat. Last time I was there to give the lassie inoculations, we had to sedate her by drugging her food. I should have known better." He glanced at his arms and shrugged. "Hazard of the job, I suppose."

Megan reached out a hand and tentatively fingered a spot above one particularly nasty-looking scratch. "She's up to date on her shots?"

"Aye, thankfully." Denver glanced down at the finger pressed against his skin. "What brings you here?"

Megan shrugged. "A visit, I guess."

"You look troubled." He said this candidly, eyes searching her own in a way that was kind without being intrusive.

Megan found herself explaining recent revelations—her aunt, her aunt's career, the fact that she had cousins she'd never even met. She left out the questions surrounding the bid on Washington Acres. Her grandmother's reticence was too much for her to talk about, and mentioning it aloud felt disloyal.

"So you feel hurt and betrayed," Denver said. "And it seems to me you have a right to those feelings."

"That pretty well sums it up."

"I can understand." His accent made it sound like "kinna understand."

"You can, huh?" she said.

Denver, arms clean and dry now, took a step closer. "I learned a long time ago, Meg, that family can be a bit awful. But if you love your family—and it sure seems to me you do—then you can decide to trust them. Though their reasons for doing what they did may not make sense now, no doubt they made sense at some point. And likely they had naught to do with you." He smiled, his intelligent eyes crinkling at the corners. "Ask your grandmother again what happened with your aunt. But timing is everything, as you well know." He bent his head toward her, and Megan could feel his warm breath on her face. Her skin tingled; her legs felt weak. "Wait for the right moment."

Megan was no longer sure he was talking about her family. She felt herself leaning in, toward him, the desire to have him in her arms as overwhelming as her earlier feeling of claustrophobia.

The door slammed open. Denver's receptionist poked her head in, saw the two of them standing there, close enough that a ruler would not fit between them sideways, and stammered, "Deek was hit by a car."

"Again?"

The receptionist shrugged apologetically. "He's a runner— what can I say? Broken leg, by the sound of it." She glanced from the doctor to Megan, who had taken several steps back. "I'm afraid it's urgent."

Denver nodded. "When the dog arrives, get him right into x-ray. I'll join you."

With the receptionist gone, Megan said, "Thank you for the

pep talk."

"Aye, don't be thanking me so quickly," Denver said. "We gave the town a new thing to talk about. I love my assistant, but she can make gossip spread faster than a California wildfire."

Megan laughed. "So by the time news of our...talk...reaches the other side of Winsome, we will have been twisted in an intimate embrace right here on the scrub station."

Denver, hand on the knob of the door, shook his head. "Intimate embrace? Nah. More like a full-fledged orgy, with you dancing naked on the examining table." His face sobered for an instant, and he looked at her in a way that made blood rush to her face. "'Course, that's something I wouldn't mind seeing myself."

He left, leaving Megan to ponder whether he was joking. Or more specifically, whether she wanted him to be.

Megan spent the next few hours at the café alongside Clover. Business was brisk, and she couldn't keep the fresh greens, sugar snap peas, and herbs on the shelf. The milk, cheese, and canned goods were popular too, although mostly with the other shop owners who seemed relieved they didn't need to drive to the next town to go to Giant or Whole Foods for that night's dinner. The real test would be the café. Tomorrow she and Jeremy would try out the sample menu, and Monday was set as the date for the café's grand opening. She felt lucky to have nabbed a chef with Jeremy's history. He'd insisted on doing things his way, but he clearly knew better than her.

Megan had already decided she would offer free samples from eleven until one on Monday in the hopes of attracting the lunch crowd. The Dorfmans were due any time to drop off the new tables—she needed them before the grand opening. They were Megan's design and she couldn't wait to see them. She was ringing up Merry Chance's three dozen eggs (and wondering what Merry needed three dozen free range eggs for) when she heard the front door bells jingle. Clover poked her in the back.

"It's Dave," she hissed. "The tables are here."

"Quiche," Merry said perkily over red-framed readers. "In case you're wondering about the eggs. I've promised quiche for the reenactment after-party." She tilted her head. "You will be there, right?"

Reenactment? After-party?

"A week from Saturday," Merry said, continuing her uncanny ability to read Megan's mind. "We're setting up a tent. Cost is five dollars per person to watch, free if you participate. Proceeds benefit the Historical Society."

"I thought they'd cancel it after...well, after what happened to Simon," Clover said with an apologetic shrug toward Megan. "You know, the Historical Society and the reenactment were his babies."

But Merry wouldn't be deterred. "No sense ruining the things Simon loved most. Roger is managing the reenactment at the church, and Lenora is handling the Historical Society fundraiser next week. I'll be hosting." Merry pulled her glasses off and let them dangle by the gold chain around her neck. She said, "You are going to that, right?"

In truth, Megan had completely forgotten about the fundraiser, but she nodded her head in any case. The last thing she wanted to do was spend a ton of money to stand around and talk about the benefits of the Beautification Board.

"Well, that was weird," Clover said when Merry had disappeared. "But ever since her husband left, she's acted odd."

"That'll do it to a person."

"I guess." Clover was silent for a moment. "Are you going to the fundraiser?"

"With a new business? It's an opportunity for networking." And sleuthing, she thought. Bibi might be off the hook, but King was still poking around. "You?"

Clover made a face. "No way. Bobby can go alone."

"Don't blame you." Dave Dorfman, carrying a legal-size pad of paper, had been standing by the counter, waiting. "If it weren't for Amelia's pestering, I wouldn't go either. Now the Revolutionary

War reenactment? That's a different story."

"Aw Dave, you know you love quiche," Clover teased.

"I do, as a matter of fact. Especially with gruyere and bacon." He looked dreamy for a moment. "But not fake conversation and tedious speeches," he said, recovering from his food reverie. "Those things I can do without."

"I'm still surprised all of this is going despite Simon's murder," Megan said. "The man died a few days ago. Shouldn't everything be postponed?"

Dave gave Megan a long, hard look. "To what end?"

"Out of respect? To avoid further incidents? Winsome's not exactly out of the woods."

"She's right," Clover said. "It does seem peculiar."

"I don't know," Dave said. "I heard the police have a suspect. Found a shoe print by the barn that matches up to someone in town."

Now that was news. "Even so, there's the issue of respect. A mourning period."

Dave shrugged. "I guess for people to mourn for someone, they have to miss them. I'm not sure many folks miss Simon, right or not."

Megan arrived back at the farm to find Clay in the back fields with her grandmother. Bibi was standing, hands on hips, mouth upturned in a look of absolute delight. She was watching a miniature dune buggy as it made its way down a long garden bed in a lumbering fashion, trailing what looked like a rotating butter knife and leaving a pair of furrows behind it.

"Faster," she said and clapped her hands. "Make it go faster, Clay."

Clay's finger was pushing a tiny joystick. He frowned. "Bonnie, I'm trying, but I think that's as fast as it will go."

Her grandmother laughed as the buggy made its way over a small mound of dirt, laboring in a particularly soft spot. She turned her head and caught a glimpse of Megan. "Do you see this?" she asked with another clap. "There it goes. Now follow with the other."

Clay obediently pulled another vehicle from a box near the edge of the bed. This one had been reconstructed to add what looked like a small silo on the top of the car. After flipping a switch on the bottom of the buggy, he added the contents of a packet of leaf lettuce seeds to the silo. Then he put the buggy down on the edge of the same row gently, over the furrows created by the first buggy. With a "here it goes" glance at Bibi, he pushed the tiny lever with his thumb. To Bibi's delight—and his own—the seeds sprinkled out in a neat pattern along the furrow.

Smiling, Clay handed the first remote control to Bibi. With patience that reflected the goodness in his soul, he showed Bibi how to work the seed sprinkler. Once she understood, he continued with the furrow-maker while she sprinkled the seeds behind.

Megan watched in silence as two buggies completed the work along the long garden bed. When it got to one end, they started another furrow train in the opposite direction. This went on for the better part of an hour. The sun started to dip closer to the horizon, and the only sounds were the birds overhead, the occasional chicken squawk from across the field, and the gentle whir of the two machines. Hard to believe a man died here a few days ago, Megan thought. She shivered and thought about Dave's words— maybe the killer would be caught and this could all be put behind them.

About three quarters of the way through the last furrow, the seeder ran out of seeds. Clay finished the furrow and then took the remote from Bibi, who looked happy but tired.

Clay turned to Megan. "Well?"

"I love it." She smiled. "Of course, that works for leaf lettuce because you can sprinkle many seeds in one place. I don't think it will work for other vegetables, especially ones that require holes, not furrows."

Clay grabbed a hoe from the ground near the boxes that had housed the buggies and began pushing soil over the seeds in tiny, careful strokes. "You're right," he said. "But it's all about timing. For example, for broccoli, I need a buggy that digs a hole every nine inches. I need to calculate the time needed for a given vehicle to reach that distance and program it accordingly. Then the seed dispenser will need to drop one seed in the same time interval."

"That sounds complicated," Megan said.

Clay shrugged. "Not hard at all."

"How will you use it on the farm?" Bibi asked.

"These are simply prototypes. The real ones won't need remote controls. We get a bed ready, put them down, and they do the job. They won't work for everything, but let's say I'm planting leaf lettuce in early spring in the greenhouses. Once the beds have been mulched and composted, I can use these to plant the seeds while I get beds ready for spinach."

"A day saved here or there adds up," Bibi said knowingly. "Maybe if your father had had something like this, Megan, he could have made a go of the farm."

"Maybe," Megan said, but she wasn't so sure. Her father liked to have a good time, but with or without gadgets, farming was hard work. It took elbow grease, stick-to-itiveness, and more than a hint of faith, none of which were Eddie's strong suits.

"I'm also working on a portable windmill we can use at the farmers market to run a refrigeration unit. That will come in handy in the height of summer. Everyone else will have droopy cucumbers; ours will be hard and fresh."

Megan didn't have the heart to tell him that coolers of ice did a fine job of keeping things fresh. And maybe he had a point—the church lot where the market was held was windy, even on a clear day.

"Well, this was fun, Clay, but I'm pooped." Bibi wrapped her arms around her chest. "I'm going to head in."

"I'll be right behind you," Megan said. "I'll cook tonight. I have some beautiful peas. I'll make the risotto you love."

Bibi smiled. "First seed-spreading buggies, then risotto—what a day."

"Stay for dinner?" Megan asked Clay.

Clay, who had finished covering the tiny lettuce seeds and was boxing up his prototype, shook his head. "I'm having dinner with Clover and Bobby tonight." He frowned. "I'll see what I can learn about the investigation."

"Yeah, I'd be curious," Megan said. The police had finally removed the crime scene tape earlier that afternoon, but their presence was still visible in the mess they'd left behind. Bales of hay, tools, packing material...all were spread along the floor of the barn like refuse. She wrapped her own arms around her chest, a sudden chill taking hold. Overhead, a crow called three times, the sound like nails on a clay tablet. "King's called a few times, asking follow-up questions. Dave told me they have a suspect."

"Hallelujah." Clay shook the small bag that had contained their organic lettuce seeds. "That was the last of them."

"I'm out at the store too. I'll head to Merry's tomorrow and get more."

"That would be good. We go through the baby lettuces, and I'd like to plant a fresh batch every week. You'll need them at the café."

The café. The opening. "We'll need more than that." She shared her plans for the following Monday's grand opening. "I'll get you a list."

Clay smiled, looking content for the first time since the murder. "This is what it's all about, you know. Feeding people good, wholesome food. Getting back to basics." He tilted his head, his eyes probing her own. "Thank you. For taking over the farm. For giving this a chance. I know it's a far cry from big city life."

Megan smiled. Clay was right, of course. This was what it was all about. She wished she could share his easygoing optimism. More than that, she wanted Simon to leave her alone. She felt his icy fingers wrapping around her mind, deadening her enthusiasm and making her doubt her dreams, even from his place in the grave.

"It'll be okay, Megan," Clay said, reading her expression. "It'll all be fine."

Sixteen

Megan was nine minutes into stirring the risotto before she had the courage to ask about Sarah Birch. Bibi was sitting at the kitchen table, dicing spring onions with a knife as old as it was sharp on a worn wooden chopping block Megan's grandfather had made. She was quiet, concentrating intently on her task, but she looked well rested and happy, the result of some time spent outside.

Dusk had given way to night, and outside the brightly lit kitchen the farm was bathed in shadows. Megan, turning from the window to the stove to add another ladle of vegetable stock to the simmering Arborio rice, said casually over her shoulder, "I met Aunt Sarah today."

Bibi paused in her chopping but only for the smallest fraction of a second. "Oh," she said equally as casually.

"Are you curious why? Or how?"

"Not really."

Bibi's chopping increased in rhythm.

"Well, I'll tell you anyway," Megan said to the stove, thinking suddenly it was better that she not be able to see her grandmother's expression. "I found out her address and drove over unannounced."

"I know."

"How do you know?"

"She called me."

Megan stopped stirring and turned around, hands on her hips. "I thought you weren't on speaking terms."

"You're going to burn the rice," Bibi said, all stern eyes over wire-framed reading glasses.

Megan resumed her stirring, adding more vegetable broth and testing for consistency.

"Bibi, why all the sudden secrecy?" She glanced over her shoulder at her grandmother, eyes pleading. "You've never been one to hide things from me. Of all the people in our family, you were the person I could count on to be honest. Always."

Bibi stood. Slowly, she walked to the stove, peeked into the pot, and with soft, fluid movements, scraped the spring onions in with the rice. Next, she picked up a small bowl of freshly shelled peas and added them too. Taking the wooden spoon from Megan, she gave the ingredients a stir, added another ladle of warm vegetable broth, stirred again, and then stooped to sniff the risotto. Clearly not satisfied, she added a pinch of sea salt from a salt cellar next to the stove. After one last stir, she handed the spoon back to Megan.

"Lemon rind. And a splash of juice at the end. Plus some butter and parmesan. A lot of butter."

"Not too much butter. Your cholesterol."

"Nonsense. I'm almost eighty-five. Let my final years be happy ones. And you know what makes me happy? Butter." Her grandmother pulled a lemon from a basket on the table. She rinsed the knife and cutting board and then settled back on the Windsor chair. "When you were little, you were obsessed with Old Man Cambridge. Do you remember him?"

Megan had a sudden flash of a stooped body, bristly white hair, a crimson slash of mouth. An unwelcome shiver ran down her spine. "How could I forget him?"

Bibi rubbed the lemon against a grater with swift, practiced strokes that left the bitter white pith behind. "Christmas. You were nine. The nativity?"

And like that, Megan recalled the scene. Old Man Cambridge had always seemed sad to her. The neighborhood children were scared of him, and behind his back they called him names.

Sometimes, when they thought he wasn't looking, they would throw eggs at his house or stick nails on his driveway. It had bothered Megan, but when she brought it up to her father, he'd told her in an unusually harsh tone to stay away from the man.

"But they tease him," she'd insisted.

"He's mean, Meg. Stay clear." Her father had taken her face in his hands and said, "Don't cross me."

But Megan couldn't shake the sadness of the old man's lonely figure. She'd approached her grandmother about it days later. "He needs a friend."

Bibi had taken her by the shoulders. "Listen to your father," she said. "You must trust him."

"Why?"

"Trust him, Megan. Stay away from Mr. Cambridge's house."

"You couldn't stay away," Bibi said now. "You had to bring him that tiny nativity scene you made in Sunday school." She shook her head. "Look where that led."

"It felt like the right thing to do."

But it hadn't been. With the self-righteous determination of a zealot on a mission, Megan had knocked on his door the day before Christmas to bring Gerald Cambridge her small token of friendship. He'd opened the door to let her in, but with the door closed behind them, the lost look in his eyes had hardened. He'd grabbed Megan's arm, knocking the cardboard nativity to the floor of his dirty house, and started pulling on her, what Megan would later think of as a lascivious leer on his whiskered face. She had been terrified.

Panicked, Megan had tried to pull away. Old Man Cambridge had put his hand across her mouth. Megan had stomped on his foot and bit the inside of his hand all at once. He was old and slow and when he jerked away, she'd run out the door, crying all the way home. Stubborn, she'd waited two days to tell her grandmother, only giving up the information when questioned repeatedly about the thumbprint bruises on her arms. In the end, the police had been called. Cambridge had denied it, but her nativity had been found crumpled in the corner of his living room where he'd kicked it, damning him.

"A pedophile," Megan said.

Bibi scrunched her face into a frown. "A pervert, but we couldn't very well tell you that. And had you listened, you wouldn't have gone anywhere near the old fool."

Megan turned off the gas and added parmesan to the aromatic mixture in the pot. But memories of Gerald Cambridge had turned her stomach.

"I was a child then, Bibi. I'm an adult now. You can explain things to me. It's hardly the same."

Rising to taste the risotto, Bibi shook her head. "You're missing the point. What's the same is your tendency to disregard what others tell you and go your own way. What happened with Aunt Sarah isn't important anymore. Don't drudge up old hurts—it will do neither of you any good." She dipped a spoon into the risotto, tasted it, and nodded. "Much better."

"That's it? First, a man is murdered in our barn, and I find out you and he had entered into secret negotiations to sell this house. Then I discover I have an aunt who is a famous mystery author, one who reappears in Winsome after years of estrangement, and I'm supposed to stay quiet and not ask questions?"

Bibi nodded. "That's right."

Seeing the look of disbelief on Megan's face, her features softened. She put the spoon in the sink and came to where Megan was standing, on the other side of Sadie. She put a hand on Megan's arm.

"Sarah's back. Get to know her. Form your own opinions. But you have certain ideas about your grandfather—about your family— and these ideas are correct in the way one person's interpretation of art is correct. Sarah has a different view, but if I share it—if she shares it—that would be unfair. It will color your ideas about your family in a way that can't be undone, because your grandfather is no longer here to give his side."

"So you're trying to protect Grandpa?"

Bibi smiled, but only an echo reached her eyes. "I'm trying to protect you."

"I'll say it again: a man died here, Bibi. Have you thought about that?"

"Of course I have. Even more reason. Even more."

The risotto was excellent; the conversation, not so much. Megan resented her grandmother's paternalistic attitude and lack of what she saw as trust in her. Even more, she hated being angry at Bibi—the one person in her life at whom she almost never got angry.

For her part, Bibi was pleasant but quiet, which only made things worse. Had they been able to argue, Megan would have had a stronghold, something to dig her claws into.

Instead, she picked at a bowl of risotto, drank a glass of Sauvignon Blanc—resisting the desire to make it three or four glasses—and, after cleaning the kitchen in a moody silence, decided to go for a walk.

It was cool outside. A damp chill permeated the air, so Megan pulled an old cardigan over her sleeveless blouse before leaving. With Sadie beside her, she said good night to her grandmother, ignoring her pleas to be careful, and stepped into the darkness.

She walked along the perimeter of the farm, near the entrance to the woods, her eyes on the stars, her feet familiar with the rise and fall of the hilly landscape. Unlike Chicago, night was thick, the darkness a heavy blanket. Even the stars were hidden behind a thick layer of clouds.

Megan headed down the slope by the house, toward the chicken tractors. She'd tucked a flashlight into the back pocket of her jeans and as she neared the birds she pulled it out. A nightly fox inspection was a good idea. Fox, hawks, raccoons, bobcats...plenty of animals out here to raid the chickens and kill off her flock.

She was about to flip on the flashlight when she heard it: a low rumbling sound, like someone dragging a sack of flour across concrete. Sadie growled, alert beside her. Megan restrained the dog and pressed her own body against the nearest chicken tractor, willing the birds and Sadie to stay quiet and calming her irregular breathing. Her eyes, well-adjusted to the darkness, scanned the farm for movement. She focused on the barn.

Thinking of the goats, she slowly made her way toward their pen, careful not to make any sound. She saw it suddenly, the soft glow of a phone or small flashlight coming from the front of the barn. She turned her own flashlight around so that the metal base could be used as a club and fumbled in her pocket for her phone. *Bibi.* She looked back at the house and, relieved, saw her grandmother's silhouette in her bedroom window. Megan had locked the porch door when she stepped outside. She was pretty sure.

Stepping back into the shadows of the chicken tractors, Megan laid a quieting hand on Sadie, who was wound tightly beside her. "Shhh, girl," she said. Then she cupped her shaking hands around her phone in order to dial 911. Her phone rang, startling her. Megan jumped, dropping the phone before she could silence it. She watched as the light in the barn went out. A few more scrapes and then nothing. She thought she saw a figure running across to the abandoned property next door, but she couldn't be sure.

Breathing hard, she finally answered the phone. It was, of all people, the police chief himself.

"Bobby, get a patrol car out here pronto," Megan whispered. She told him what had happened, her words falling over one another in her haste to get them out.

"Someone will be on their way," King said. "Go inside. Now."

"Heading there as we speak," Megan lied.

She wanted to check on the goats before heading back up to the house. Another glance at Bibi's window assured her that her grandmother was fine.

"Megan, I'm afraid the barn's not your only problem," King said. "You've had a break-in at the café."

"What?" Megan gripped the phone harder. "When?"

"Not sure. Someone drove by and saw the front window had been smashed and the door was open."

Megan choked back a moan. "Did they...did they destroy anything?"

"Not that we could tell. But we need you to come down to the café."

Megan agreed and hung up the phone. Now at the goats' enclosure, she looked inside, probing the shadows for errant figures or anything that seemed out of place. Assured that her two Pygmies were fine and the shelter was clear, she flicked on her flashlight and looked around the entrance to the barn. She knew better than to go inside—if the intruders had been up to something she needed to preserve evidence—but if there were footprints or something incriminating, she wanted to show the police before they trampled on them. Not that she didn't have confidence in Winsome's finest...but, well, they were a young bunch.

A thorough sweep of the entrance showed nothing. She was heading back up to the house to let Bibi know what was going on when a black and white pulled into her driveway. She jogged to the car, the adrenaline produced because of the night's events giving her speed.

King climbed out the police car along with a young uniform Megan didn't recognize.

"Show me where you saw the intruder," King said without preamble.

"My grandmother—"

"Jake," King said to the young man in uniform, "go tell Bonnie what's going on and meet us down by the barn."

"I should really—"

"You should really come with me." King's voice was tight. He asked, "Did you see the intruder?"

"No. I saw a light and then my phone rang. The noise must have startled whoever it was because next thing I know, the light was off and I thought I saw a figure dashing across the yard."

"Where did this figure go?"

Megan pointed in the direction of the abandoned Marshall house. In the cover of night and the shadows born of a crescent moon, the old Colonial could give any haunted attraction a run for its money.

"Only one figure?"

Megan nodded. They'd arrived at the barn. King removed his gun from his holster and motioned for Megan to stay outside, behind the walk-in cooler. The police officer walked into the barn, gun tip up. He yelled a warning. There was a long silence followed by King's return.

"Empty."

"Anything missing?"

"Not that I can tell. Come inside. But don't touch anything."

They walked through the barn. Nothing seemed out of place.

King sighed. "I'll meet you down at Canal. Jake can finish up here and search the dump next door."

Megan felt herself bristle at the word *dump*—the home had potential, after all, and had once been part of the Washington Acres estate—but she agreed to go downtown after she checked on her grandmother. As she was heading out the door, she felt a hand on her shoulder. She spun around to see King's inquisitive eyes staring into her own under the glare of a flashlight.

"Any idea who'd want to mess around in here?"

"Kids?"

"Do you really think that?"

Meeting his gaze, Megan said honestly, "No, I don't. I think whoever killed Simon came back."

"Why?"

Megan shrugged, her mind rebelling against the thought of killers on her property. "They left something behind and don't want anyone to find it?"

"Like a glove?" King smiled sardonically.

"Like a glove. Or—" Megan arched her eyebrows. "Or they have other unfinished business at my farm."

"What do you suppose that business could be?"

"I guess that's your job to figure out," Megan said. "Because right now, I have no idea."

Seventeen

The Washington Acres Café & Larder was in better shape than Megan had feared. Nonetheless, when she pulled her truck up against the curb on Canal, behind King's unmarked, she put her head on the steering wheel and took a few deep breaths, holding back the urge to cry. The desire for Mick—for his friendship, his counsel, his steady hand, and his practical outlook—pelted her at every angle, a vicious hailstorm of grief.

But although she knew missing Mick was the most real thing in her life right now, she also knew what his advice would be. Get out there, Meg, and prove them all wrong. Figure out what you're up against and conquer it.

And so she climbed out of the truck and headed for the café, pushing her wary exhaustion aside and letting anger creep in its stead. Anger, at least, was productive.

"Did a bang-up job," King said as she approached. He was standing in front of the café, hands on his hips, while two uniforms poked around inside. "Broke your window, busted open the front door," he glanced at Megan, "and that's about the sum of it."

"No theft?"

King shrugged. "Give my boys a few more minutes and then you can go in and see for yourself."

Megan waited outside, next to Winsome's police chief. The fact that he'd called his men boys seemed funny to her. Bobby couldn't be thirty himself.

"Clover wanted to come, but I told her she had to stay back

home." King shook his head. "Good thing she wasn't born a few centuries ago. She's as able to obey as I am capable of bearing children."

"And that's what you love about her, Bobby."

The police chief crinkled his pug nose. "Yeah, I guess that's the truth."

It must be, Megan thought, because the pair had nothing in common that Megan could tell. Clover was a throwback to the seventies, a displaced, late-born hippie with a carefree attitude and enough naïve goodwill to fuel a thousand soup kitchens. Her lover was a military school graduate with a gun collection and—so she'd heard—an eye on public office. But they'd been together for more than a year. Clearly something was working.

"Any idea who did this?"

Megan shook her head.

King chewed on the inside of his lip, his eyes focused on the uniforms in the store. Looking at him here, in the milky light emanating from her café, she had to admit she may have underestimated the man. This was only a break-in. It would have been easy enough for the Chief of Police to send uniforms and call it a day. But he'd had the sense to see a possible connection to Simon's murder, and his presence here, in person, gave a clear signal to his crew: I am taking this seriously and so should you.

He turned his ruddy face in Megan's direction. "Looks like they're done. Let's go in."

Inside, the first uniform—a small, wiry man with glasses too large for his narrow face—said, "No prints, Chief. Nothing but this." He held up an evidence bag containing a large rock. "Presumably the instrument that caused the hole in the window."

"Good deduction, Lou," King said sarcastically. He took the rock. "Check the security footage?"

The uniform glanced at Megan. "There is none, sir."

King swung around toward Megan. "Is that right?"

Megan nodded. "I moved back home thinking I wouldn't need a security camera."

"Clearly you were wrong." He wrinkled his nose again, looked around the store, and focused on the window and the door. "Help Megan get the door and window secured." Turning back to Megan, he said, "Do you have cardboard and duct tape?"

Megan pointed to the storage room. "There's plastic sheeting back there too."

"I'll keep a patrol on Canal Street tonight. But I suggest you change the locks and get a security system pronto."

"I will."

King walked over to the counter that housed the cash register. He glanced from there to the stocked shelves and then over to the produce case, which was empty in anticipation of the next day's crop. "You're doing a good thing here, you know," King said softly. "For the town and for Bonnie."

With a weak smile, Megan said, "Clearly *someone* doesn't think so."

It was after eleven when Megan finally pulled into her driveway. She was surprised but happy to see Denver's SUV parked there, next to Clay's ancient, refurbished BMW. The lights in the kitchen glowed softly, and when Megan opened the door to the enclosed porch entrance, there was Sadie, waiting. The dog's tail thumped loudly and she whined at the sight of Megan, alerting Bibi and their guests to her arrival.

Denver stood and opened the door that led into the kitchen. "We were worried about you."

Behind him, Clay and Clover stood. Megan could see her grandmother behind them, still seated at the kitchen table. She wore a pale yellow robe over her nightgown. A worried expression darkened her face.

"I'm fine, the store and café are fine." Megan smiled. "How did you know?" But as soon as she said the words, she knew. Clover must have been with King when the call came through, and she would have called Clay immediately. But Denver?

"I was tending to a customer's dog and he told me. Didn't know news traveled so fast in Winsome?" He smiled warmly. "I came over as soon as I could fix up the guy's Coonhound. Got himself tangled up with a porcupine again. Six times now—you would think the dang dog would've learned."

"They never do," Megan said.

"Aye. They never do."

Denver held her gaze a few beats too long and she felt like they were sharing a joke. He stepped aside to let Megan in the kitchen, and her arm brushed against his chest. She glanced up into his face. He smiled.

Behind him, Bibi cleared her throat.

"Do they know who broke in?" Bibi asked.

Megan shook her head. "Someone threw a rock in the window and used the opening to unlatch the door. No evidence and nothing seemed to be missing."

"Kids?" Clover asked.

"Could be. But I don't think so."

"Because of the barn?" Clay asked. He looked as troubled as Bibi, his aquiline features pulled into a pained frown.

Megan nodded. She looked around the kitchen, noting the coffee cake and teacups on the counter. They must have been here a while, keeping Bibi company. A surge of gratitude for their friendship washed over Megan and she sat down in a chair, suddenly exhausted.

"We should go," Clay said. "Now that we know you're okay." He glanced at Clover. "I'll be bringing salad greens and sugar snap peas by the store tomorrow. Do you have room in the cooler?"

"We sold out today." Clover glanced over at Bibi. "Mrs. Birch, your cakes are delicious. Have you considered selling them?"

Bibi shook her head, but she looked pleased. "I'm too old for baking with any purpose other than enjoyment," she said.

"Besides," Megan said, "we can't sell what we bake here." Megan looked pointedly down at Sadie, who was now stretched out on the floor, sound asleep. "No dogs in a commercial kitchen."

Clover pouted. "Ah, that's too bad."

Denver had been silent this whole time, but he reached down and stroked Sadie behind the ears. She opened one eye, thumped her tail, and returned to her slumber. Clay and Clover rose to leave.

"If you need me, call," Clay said. He glanced at Bibi and then added, "Unless you want me to stay?"

Megan smiled. The thought of Clay as their protector was sweet, but not necessary. "Thank you, but I think we'll be okay."

With a skeptical look at the dozing Sadie, he shrugged. "I'll have my phone by the bed. Call."

"Promise."

Megan walked Clay and Clover to the porch entrance, and with a hug for each, watched them go. She was all too aware of Denver's tall, broad presence behind her. When the Hands' taillights were only red dots at the end of her driveway, Denver whispered, "Walk me to my car?"

Megan nodded.

"Goodnight," Bibi called.

"Goodnight," Megan and Denver said in unison.

Outside, the air was chill and crisp, the sky still starless. Megan wrapped her sweater tightly around her shoulders. She shivered.

"Are you cold, then?" Denver asked.

"I'm not cold, no."

"Are you scared? Do you need me to stay?"

"So many men offering to stay, you'd think we were helpless." The thought of Bibi waking up to find the deliciously disheveled Dr. Finn in their kitchen made Megan laugh. "No, honestly, we'll be fine. Besides, we have Sadie."

"Well, now, that's part of what I wanted to talk to you about."

Denver leaned against his Toyota, his lean, muscular body looking quite James Dean in the soft glow of the outside lights. But his expression was serious. On impulse, Megan reached out a hand and traced her fingertips lightly down the sharp angles of his handsome face. He lifted his own hand to hers, pressing her finger into the whiskered skin of his cheeks, his eyes questioning.

Megan stretched up on tiptoe and pressed her lips against his. She felt his body react. Strong arms encircled her, pulling her close. His hips moved against her own. She gasped.

"Did I hurt ye?" he asked, his voice husky.

"No, no...I'm fine."

"I have a proposition," Denver whispered into her ear. His day-old beard tickled her skin.

"Does it involve more of this?" Megan kissed him again, frightened and startled by the hunger she felt—hunger that had been absent the last few years.

Denver smiled through the kiss. She felt one large hand engulf hers, fingers intertwining with her own.

She could feel his hardness pressed against her belly. "Denver," is all she said before pulling away. She wanted him, there was no denying that. But she was like a kid living at home. She couldn't invite him to stay, and she couldn't leave.

Under different circumstances, she might have suggested the barn, but that seemed, well...improper, all things considered. And downright creepy.

"I really do have a proposition for you, Counselor," he said, moving backward himself. "You need some protection here, Megan, and that sweet dog of yours loves you, clearly, but I don't think she's up for the job of farm dog. Too much of a city life before now."

"What do you suggest?"

"Can you come by tomorrow? The clinic is closed for surgeries in the afternoon. Maybe stop by around three? I should be done by then. I will explain it all when you come."

Megan nodded, curious. "Okay."

With obvious reluctance, Denver opened his car door. "Go inside, then. I want to watch you lock the door." He smiled sheepishly. "For my own peace of mind."

Megan was about to argue—she could take care of herself and Bibi, after all—but stopped herself. Denver looked genuinely concerned, and it had been a while since a man had regarded her that way.

He climbed in the car, door still open. She bent low, fitting herself in the space between the door and the driver's seat, and kissed him again, gently. Before she could change her mind, she went back inside.

Eighteen

The next day, Megan pulled open the door of the clinic expecting to see Denver's receptionist, but instead Denver met her in the lobby. He wore a gray Colorado State University t-shirt and a pair of hospital scrub pants. His hair, normally combed neatly back from a high forehead, fell around his face in tousled reddish-brown waves. The stubble that was barely noticeable last night was now a light growth of beard. His blue eyes, normally bright and amused, were ringed with dark circles. He looked like he hadn't slept all night.

"Hi," Megan said, feeling suddenly worried. "Are you okay?"

"Aye, I'm fine." His accent sounded heavier today. "Ta. Appreciate you asking."

Megan stood, clutching her purse. "You don't look so good. I mean...you look fine, it's just—"

Denver held up his hand. "It's okay. I dinna have a good evening after I left you." It came out "guid eenin," taking Megan a moment to decipher what he said.

"What happened?"

But Denver only shook his head and turned away, back toward the surgery. Megan followed him through a narrow hallway, past the immaculate operating room and toward the ruckus that sounded like an entire pack of dogs barking.

"Sarge still here?"

"No, he went home this morning."

The words appeared to trouble him, and Megan put her hand on his arm. He froze under her touch.

"What's the matter? You don't seem yourself."

He rubbed his temples, his eyes locked on her own. He pulled himself up a degree taller, taking her measure, while he made up his mind about something. Finally, he said, "It's Porter. I think he's the one who broke into your store yesterday."

"Porter? But why?"

"Because when he came in this morning to get his dog, his right arm was covered with deep scratches—the kind you'd get when reaching your hand into a broken pane of glass to unlock a door." He bit his lower lip. "Doesn't take a medical degree to figure that out."

"I meant why would he do that?"

"That's just it. I don't know. He may have simply been a drunken fool, looking for trouble."

A thought occurred to her, one she was sure had occurred to Denver as well. "Do you think he went from there to the farm?"

"I guess it's possible, though the laddie denied it."

"And it could have been him who—"

Denver shook his head vehemently. "I've known Porter since before he joined the service. There's no way that boy is a murderer. A vandal—maybe. A thief? Even that's a stretch. But not a killer."

"Did you tell the police?"

"No."

Denver said that one word with heaviness so absolute it told her of the struggle he was battling within himself. She decided to let the subject go for now.

She said, "I heard the police have a suspect. I don't know if it's true, but if it is, this may get cleared up soon."

Denver looked like he'd swallowed a horse pill and it didn't quite go down. "Let's hope it's not Porter. He's had enough trauma in his life."

Megan decided a change of topic was in order. "What was that proposition?" she asked, pointing to the door that led to the kennels.

"Not a 'what' but a 'who.' The pup's name is Gunther, and he needs a home." Denver placed a hand under Megan's chin and raised her face to meet his gaze. "And the way I figure it, you could use some company a bit more discouraging of trouble than that sweet-natured lassie of yours, whether the police have a suspect or not."

"Thanks for thinking of me, Denver, but I don't want another dog. See, I kind of have my hands full, and the last thing I need—"

But Denver wasn't listening. He'd entered the kennel and walked past two little Yorkshire Terriers yapping from the safety of a small pen, past a Rottweiler laying on his side in a cage, his right front leg in a cast, looking downright glum, and past a Vizsla with a shaved belly and an IV who clearly wasn't letting a small thing like surgery cause her to stop barking. He paused by the largest pen and turned around.

"Ah, but he needs you, Megan."

The seriousness in his tone stopped her. She walked closer until she could see inside the cage. Her breath caught in her throat. He—Gunther—was a veritable giant of a dog. Thin to the point of emaciation, with a thick white coat—or what might have been a white coat had it not been full of burrs and caked with mud—and a black nose and lips. But most arresting of all were the dog's eyes: kind and gentle and wise, they burned like two embers of coal in the pathetic body.

"He's not a *wee laddie*," Megan whispered. "But someone has not been kind to him."

"You are right about that."

"Who is he? What happened?"

Denver knelt down and motioned for her to do the same. Slowly, he opened the cage. Pulling a dog treat from the pocket of his scrubs, he held it level on the palm of his hand. The dog stood with some effort and, studying Denver with those intelligent dark eyes, took the treat gently.

"Your turn."

Denver handed Megan a treat and she echoed his motions. The dog sat before her and took the treat from her hand. She reached out to pet him. He pulled back slightly, then let her. His matted fur was silky—underneath the filth.

"Is he a Great Pyrenees? A white Newfoundland?" That's what he looked like to Megan, with his great head and his thick jowls. A white Newfoundland, if there was such a thing, or maybe a giant Golden Retriever.

"He's a Polish Tatra Sheepdog, and a good one. They're rare, but they're known for protecting livestock." He cast a sharp eye Megan's way. "And their families."

"How did you get him?"

"From a local," Denver said matter-of-factly. "And not without a bit of a struggle, I'm afraid."

"I don't understand."

"You know Carl Sauer?"

"The farmer up Morton Road, off of Glen Dwyer Street?"

"That's him. He uses me for his cows now and again when he can't get someone else. I hate going there because he treats those animals poorly, like they're nothing but chattel." Denver rubbed his beard. "Which I guess to him, they are. Anyway, he knows I feel that way and I'm not quiet about it, so we don't see each other often. Not exactly the romantic picture I had of being a large animal vet when I was a laddie myself, you know?"

Megan knew Carl. When she was deciding what to grow, she'd visited his farm. She didn't want to create a hostile environment with the locals by infringing on their turf. She needn't have worried. Unlike her own tiny farm, the Sauers were running a huge operation. Fifteen minutes on Carl's land and she left disliking the man and his dour-faced wife.

"I've been there."

Denver nodded. "Then you understand. I went to the farm earlier this week because one of his cows was having a difficult birth and I asked about that puppy, Gunther. I had given the wee dog his first set of inoculations awhile back but I hadn't seen him since, you see. I figured Carl had taken the dog elsewhere, or maybe the pup hadn't made it. Carl mumbled something about that dog not living up to its breed's reputation and that was it. When I was leaving, I saw a flash of white in the distance. I walked up the hill, past the barn and found him tied to a tree. He looked like this. Had no water, no food, and no shelter." Denver shook his head. "Bloody bastard."

"So you took him?"

"I went back down to the house and Carl and I had a wee chat. Then I took the dog."

Megan smiled. "A wee chat, huh?"

"Aye," Denver said, smiling. "I'm a pretty persuasive fellow when I want to be."

"What's to stop him from claiming you stole Gunther?"

"Nothing to worry about. I quoted him section four-six-seven of local code seven-seventeen. It's Winsome's animal cruelty law. I was in my rights to pull the dog, and I took pictures of Gunther's condition before I left." He gave Megan a sly smile. "I sent them to King in case Carl tries to make trouble."

Gunther had crawled across the floor until his head was close to Megan's hand. She sat on the floor, legs crossed, and rubbed the dog's ears. He placed his head in her lap.

"I've never heard of a Polish Tatra Sheepdog."

"Not surprising. Carl wanted one for the novelty, I think, and because he'd heard they were fierce guard dogs. I helped him locate the pup." He watched as the dog's eyes closed with contentment. "He's still a babe at heart, but what Carl didn't understand is that they're fiercely loyal dogs—gentle beasts, really. They want to be with their family, not shut outside and left to their own devices." He frowned. "Bloody bastard," he said again. "He likes you, Megan."

Indeed, the dog seemed at peace. But another dog, another responsibility...now?

"I was trying to figure out what to do with the laddie when I realized you needed him as much as he needs you. He'll be a good watchdog. These dogs guard livestock, and they can be awake at night. I will get him cleaned up for you. With some basic training, he'll be a good addition to your farm."

As though on cue, Gunther opened his soulful eyes and stared into her own. He was skinny and dirty and had clearly been neglected, but he didn't seem aggressive or overly shy. He could be a striking dog.

Who was she kidding? Gunther had her the moment he put his head on her lap.

"Fine," Megan said.

Denver grinned. "I'll bring him by one day next week. We can work with him together. Get him used to the goats and the chickens and that wee sweet dog of yours."

"And Bibi."

"Leave your grandmother to me. I'll work my charm on her too."

"Charm, huh?" Megan laughed.

"Aye, I can't help it if the lassies love me."

"They do, do they?"

Denver leaned over to kiss her. He teased, "Yes. It's my Scottish brogue. Even the older ladies can't resist."

Megan went from the veterinary clinic to the café and then to Merry Chance's nursery to buy more lettuce seeds. She'd forgotten all about the lettuce, but three texts from Clay served as a reminder. She didn't mind. She was hoping Merry could clue her in on who the police had in their sights for Simon's murder. If anyone would know, it would be Merry.

It was there, in aisle B of Merry's crowded seed section, where Megan ran into Lenora Duvall, Simon's mother. She'd only met the woman on a few occasions, but Lenora was a celebrity in Winsome—the closest the small town had to royalty. Other than, perhaps, Aunt Sarah. But it seemed most people didn't know about Sarah.

"Megan," Lenora said coldly.

"Lenora, how are you?" Megan stood up and turned around— her backside had been unattractively facing Lenora while she bent over to find the right variety of organic seeds—and gave Lenora a friendly nod. Lenora responded with a tight smile.

"As well as can be expected under the circumstances."

"I'm sorry about Simon."

"It was a shock."

An attractive woman in her late seventies, with skin so tight it looked like Saran Wrap, Lenora had the kind of prim confidence that made people want her to like them. Megan found her to be judgmental. She always *looked* like she wanted to tell you exactly what she thought of you but *knew* it would be poor manners.

"Yes, well..." Megan searched for a reason to end this conversation quickly. Awkward was not her specialty, and the longer she stood in front of the impeccably dressed Lenora Duvall while wearing jeans and a cream peasant blouse she'd found in a Chicago thrift shop, the longer she felt like a student in the principal's office awaiting a reprimand.

"I trust you will be at the Historical Society dinner next week?" Lenora asked. Her tone had gone from cold to scolding. "Your farm will be up for discussion at this month's session. It may behoove you to attend and spend some time with the officers from the Beautification Board."

"Up for discussion?"

"George Washington stayed there." When Megan graced her with a blank stare, Lenora said, "That is the reason for the name, right?"

"Right, but what does that have to do with anything? Anyway, it's only a legend."

"You know I'm a historian. I did quite a bit of research on the area, and the old stories are true. The Birch family farm should be rezoned."

"Rezoned?"

"As a historical asset." She smiled. "It could be the first home to be added to the historical preservation project."

Alarmed, Megan said, "With all due respect, what exactly does that mean?"

"You need me to explain what historical preservation means?" Lenora put a hand on her hip. She was wearing wide-legged cream linen pants and a deep brown linen tunic embroidered with small vines in matching brown thread. Her hair, cropped close to her head, was a beautiful silvery-white, and all of her jewelry was understated gold. Her only nod to color consisted of a pair of vibrant aqua reading glasses, which hung from her neck by an aqua, cream, and fuchsia cord. She fingered the cord now with her free hand, wrapping the material around one slender finger until it was tight enough to cause the skin of her finger to pale underneath.

"I know what historical preservation means, Lenora. I'd like to know what it means for the farm."

Lenora waved the hand that had been on her hip. "That's what the Historical Society needs to determine." She shrugged. "In any case, I'm sure you feel as strongly as I do about the importance of keeping our history alive. If my research is correct—and it usually is, dear—that farm of yours is a treasure. The aspects of it that make it special should be preserved."

Could that be why Simon had wanted it? "I know they can't change the zoning rules without public notice and a hearing."

"Ah, but they had one, Megan. It's a shame you didn't come."

Puzzled, Megan said, "You met? When?"

Lenora pulled claw-like fingers through her thinning white hair. "May first." She smiled apologetically. "You know how it is. Zoning officials are volunteers. Sometimes they have to get together when they can, no matter how inconvenient for the larger group."

Megan bristled internally. Awfully convenient—all of it.

Clearly enjoying the look of shock on Megan's face, Lenora said, "You can find the full transcript online, I'm sure. In the future, you might want to pay a bit more attention to the local happenings so you don't get caught unawares." She put her glasses on, then studied Megan from over the aqua rims. "My son had his foibles, certainly. But he was a kind man at heart. He wanted what was best for Winsome, and documenting Washington's stay at Bonnie's farm...well, you know what they say. What's good for the goose—"

Could kill the gander, Megan thought. Before she could say another word, she walked away, forgetting all about the lettuce seeds and any other reason she had for coming to Merry's store in the first place.

Nineteen

"Bastards," Clay said to Megan later, echoing Denver's words from earlier in the day. "Damn bloody fools."

"I guess no one told you either."

"Damn right." He looked up from the weed trimmer he was fixing and gave her a hangdog grin. "I'm sorry, Megan. Had I known about the research or the meeting, I would have told you." He shook his head. "I knew Simon wasn't to be trusted, but people generally respect Lenora. I thought...well, I guess I was beguiled by her professional reputation."

Megan tugged on the hem of her hiking pants and sat on the floor of the barn, next to Clay. She watched as dexterous fingers wound string around the motor. He didn't even glance down as he worked.

"Don't worry about it. How could you have known?"

"I had more interaction with Simon than you did. Should've realized they were in cahoots."

Megan smiled at Clay's choice of words. For a young man, he had an old soul...and an old vocabulary. "There're a few things about this that are troubling. One, the fact that certain people in Winsome seem to be collaborating behind our backs to get to the farm. Whether it's ownership they seek or simply some type of preservation hold on the property, clearly they want access to it. Why, I don't know."

Clay looked thoughtful. "Maybe it's as simple as Lenora said.

Maybe they really want to have that claim to fame made official."

"That can be done without the zoning change."

"Ah, but you could decide to sell the farm to a developer or a strip mall owner. Or you could come to hate old, crotchety homes with expensive-to-fix slate roofs and drafty lead glass windows and remodel the place into something modern and hideous." He sat back on his heels, looking intently at her in the way of his. "You could put in a *pool*."

He said the last word with such utter disgust that it made Megan laugh. "I suppose you have a point."

He wiped his hands with a clean rag and stood, reaching a hand out to help her up. She shook her head and stood, glancing around the cavernous barn. It looked far less ominous in the light of day.

"Look, let me see what I can find out. If the zoning board hasn't made any decisions, then you can still fight this."

"It's their underhanded approach that bothers me most. I checked the town's website. They announced the meeting the day before and then held it at eleven at night."

Clay's eyes widened. "Is that even legal?"

"I'm afraid it is—for urgent matters, at least." Megan made air quotes around the word urgent. "In this case, the justification was the Historical Society fundraiser. They wanted it on the agenda for the general meeting and that was the only way they claimed they could do it."

"So it happened right before Simon's murder."

Megan nodded. "I think there's a connection."

Finished with the weed trimmer, Clay hung it neatly on a hook on the wall. He stared at the structure for a moment, then followed a crack in one large stone with the tip of his finger.

"What bothers me," he said, still turned away from Megan, "is that I see these people all the time. Merry Chance, Amelia Dorfman, Roger Becker. Even Lenora." He shook his head, turning around. "I can't see them going behind your back that way. And certainly not behind Bonnie's back. Maybe I don't know them as well as I thought I did," he continued, looking glum. "Group-think can be a powerful thing."

"There's another possibility," Megan said quietly. "What if they were convinced they were doing the right thing? By someone who had something at stake."

"And what stake would that be?"

Megan shrugged. "Hell if I know. Whatever it was, they believed it was worth taking a life." She stared at the barn walls, thinking. "Maybe it's time to do more digging of my own."

Megan spent the evening on her computer, in the tiny parlor off the kitchen that doubled as an office. It was an old room full of old things. An antique dresser, its hard walnut edges worn smooth from years of use, served as a printer stand; Megan's grandfather's ancient rolltop desk housed her computer. Built-in curio shelves, lacquered with high-gloss white oil paint by her father when Megan was only a girl, now stored books—sideways, upside down and every which way, their multicolored spines the only real color in the otherwise timeless room.

For Megan, the parlor held special meaning. It was the last place her mother hugged her before she went away, and keeping it the way it had been all those years ago somehow gave her comfort.

Megan had been eight when Charlotte Birch left, carrying a hard, red suitcase, a shoulder bag, and a basket of fruit for the drive. Her mother had been sick of small-town life and of her father—or so Eddie later explained. Megan was never sure of the truth because the history of Charlotte Hoffman Birch had been rewritten many times. Family and friends couldn't even agree on whether the leaving was her fault.

To some, her mother was a saint, tied to the irresponsible and fun-loving Eddie Birch in nuptials forced upon them by an unplanned pregnancy, outdated social mores, and overly strict parents. Others painted Charlotte as a harlot—a tight-skirted, big-busted brunette with ivory skin and Hollywood dreams that overrode any common sense. Megan's grandfather had been in this camp, and quite vocal about his opinions. Yet another reason Eddie had been a failure in his father's eyes. Even his choice of wife and mother didn't work out.

But back then, her mother had been a larger-than-life figure: beautiful in a fragile way, with a warm smile and distant eyes. Megan remembered her with a mixture of fondness and awe, the way one might think about a sophisticated but aloof aunt who drifts in and out of your life.

Only Charlotte had drifted out and never drifted back.

Sitting at the rolltop now, computer on and a search engine looking for links between her farm and George Washington, Megan thought about her mother. Megan missed the thought of having a mother, but her grandmother had always been the real maternal figure in her life, and Bonnie never left. Megan realized that any ache she felt over her mother's abandonment had been soothed by her grandmother over the years. Bonnie Birch was both friend and mother.

So why was she being secretive now?

Megan's search was turning up nothing. Yes, George Washington had been rumored to have stayed in Winsome, but that wasn't news. There had only been a few houses in Winsome back then, and Washington Acres, with its large size by yesteryear's standards, would have been the practical choice: room for Washington's men, fresh hay and shelter for their horses. Plus, with its location near the canal, Winsome would have been a handy spot to refresh supplies. Still, all that supposition didn't amount to fact.

So what *had* Lenora found? And how was it connected to Simon's death—if it was at all?

Clearly the former professor had better resources than an internet search engine and limited research skills. Frustrated, Megan stood and pushed her chair back more violently than she'd intended. It was then that she saw her grandmother standing in the doorway, watching her, an odd expression on her weathered face.

"Bibi, I didn't know you were there."

"What are you doing, Megan?" Her voice sounded wary, resigned.

"I got a surprise today." Megan described her conversation with Lenora Duvall. "I don't need to tell you that a zoning change could be disastrous, at least depending upon what restrictions they place on the farm."

Bibi sank into the room's only armchair, a faded gold brocade with Queen Anne legs and rounded wooded armrests. "Oh, that man."

Megan frowned. "Simon?"

"Roger Becker."

"What does Roger Becker have to do with anything?" But even as she spoke, she recalled the zoning official's pancake breakfast at their house not long ago. His willingness to push everything through seemed odd then. "He did make things happen awfully easily."

Bibi nodded. Bright green eyes shone from her frazzled face, and in that moment she looked every one of her eight-four years. "Lenora's doing, no doubt. The Historical Association wants their claws in this farm. Simon was desperate—" Bibi clasped a hand over her mouth.

Megan arched her eyebrows. "You were saying?"

Her grandmother simply stared, weighing her next words.

"Bibi, please. I'm an adult. Tell me what's been going on."

Finally, Bibi nodded. "After all that happened yesterday, I was going to tell you."

"Tell me what?"

Bibi sighed. "A story."

"As far as your grandfather knew, this house was built in 1764, not too long before the beginning of the Revolutionary War. The first owner was Paul Caldbeck, a gentleman farmer and landowner from England. He and his wife Elizabeth sold the property in the 1780s to a neighbor, whose family then owned it for years."

"I know all this, Bibi." She'd heard it so many times as a kid she could recite the home's history by heart. What did any of it have to do with Simon's murder?

"Patience, Megan, because I'm going to tell you something I haven't shared before." She breathed in deeply, contemplating her granddaughter with a heavy look. "In 1856, when your great-great-grandfather Jeremiah Birch bought the farm, it consisted of a rundown house and a dilapidated barn—the oldest sections of the current barn.

"Now, Jeremiah Birch was a good farmer, but he came from a poor family. He and his wife had four children, two boys and two girls, one of whom was your great-grandfather, Jeremiah Birch the second. His brother, Adam, was what they called simple-minded back in the day. The two women married local men and moved into their husband's houses. So as was typical in the day, Jeremiah senior left the entire farm to his son, Jeremiah junior."

Bibi grew silent. She closed her eyes for a moment before continuing. "Jeremiah junior had three children: your grandfather Theodore, your Uncle Samuel, and Aunt Sarah. Jeremiah's wife, my mother-in-law and your great-grandmother, was a deeply religious woman, and very traditional. She would no more question her husband's judgment than she would run for president. So when Jeremiah decided to leave his farm to his eldest son, Samuel, she let him do it—even though Samuel was a no-good drunkard with less sense for farming than your father."

Bibi pointed to the brocade ottoman that matched the armchair. "I need to rest my feet, Megan. Would you mind pushing that over here?"

Megan pulled the ottoman over and helped her grandmother to lift her swollen feet onto the cushion. "I'll get you some ice water."

But Bibi shook her head. "Let me finish. I know it's a lot to follow, but I'm almost there."

Megan sat back down on the desk chair and waited. The cuckoo clock in the dining room rang ten. Sadie, on the floor between her and her grandmother, let out a low snore followed by a loud yelp. Megan reach down and stroked her with her toe, rousing her from her doggie nightmare.

"Uncle Samuel died young and childless," Megan said, trying to help her grandmother along. This much of the family history she knew.

"Yes, he did. And everyone expected that he would leave the farm to his siblings, Sarah and Teddy."

"He didn't?"

"No, he didn't. To our surprise, he left the entire estate—what was left of it—to your grandfather only. Sarah and Teddy had been very close and Sarah loved the farm—the history, the animals, the reality of farming. She was the true farmer in the family. Samuel was too soft for farming; Teddy too hard.

"When we found out that Samuel had left your grandfather the farm, I thought for sure he would say no. We were living on Bentley Road back then, on a smaller farm where we grew vegetables for our family and had a few chickens. With only Eddie, who showed almost no interest in farming, I knew taking on this place would be tough for Teddy. He was working at the steel plant up in Bethlehem at the time. He was a foreman, and the money was decent." Bibi shook her head. "But he wanted the farm."

"And he gave Aunt Sarah her fair share?"

Her silence was answer enough.

"So Grandpa accepted the farm and she got nothing—again."

"I'm afraid so."

"When she came back to town, you offered her the farm to make up for old wrongs? Is that it?"

"Yes, Megan. I...when Eddie met Giada, I knew he was leaving. I could feel his restlessness building. And the farm was...well, you saw what it looked like when you came, before you and the Dorfmans started fixing everything up." She looked up and Megan saw tears in her eyes. "It's not easy being an old woman. Your mind wants control. Sometimes, your body doesn't cooperate. I didn't want to leave, but if I had to go, I wanted Sarah to have the house."

"But she refused."

Bibi nodded.

"So you approached Simon."

Bibi's eyes widened in surprise. "Oh, no. He approached me."

"Sarah told him you were looking for a buyer?"

"I honestly don't know how he knew. But he offered me a good price. I almost accepted, thinking it was for the Historical Society and the house and farm would be looked after, but then I had a change of heart." She smiled apologetically at Megan. "When I heard you were coming."

"Oh, Bibi, why didn't you tell me?" The thought of her grandmother feeling alone, thinking she had to leave her home because she could no longer manage and there was no one to help her, was almost unbearable. "I would have come sooner."

"If you were to come back, I wanted it to be for you, not for me."

"*You're* my family, Bibi. You've been a mother to me most of my life."

A shadow passed over Bibi's face. She sat forward in her chair and placed her hands on the armrests, her signal that she was getting up.

But Megan wasn't willing to end the conversation yet. "All these years, Sarah never spoke to Grandpa because of the farm?"

"No. It was your grandfather who refused to speak to Sarah. He cut her out of his life—our lives—altogether."

"I don't get it. Why would Grandpa be angry at Aunt Sarah? Shouldn't it be the reverse?"

Bibi sank back into the chair. "This is the part I didn't want to tell you. Your grandfather stopped speaking to Sarah because she's the one who convinced your mother to leave. And she helped Charlotte do it."

Twenty

Megan sat forward in her chair, arms wrapped around her torso. Her grandmother's words were a punch to the gut.

"So that's why you didn't want to tell me," Megan said. "It wasn't about Simon at all."

"No, it wasn't. This has always been about you, I'm afraid."

"Why did...why would Aunt Sarah do that?"

"You'll have to speak with her, Megan. I can't answer that. All I know is that Charlotte was an unhappy girl—and let me be clear, at that time, your mother was still a girl, mentally if not physically—and Sarah thought she was helping. Although Teddy didn't see it that way."

"He thought she was getting back at him for the farm?"

Bibi, eyes still closed, nodded. "He wouldn't budge on the farm, despite her pleads and protests. I wanted him to give it to her. She wasn't the well-known author she is today and she didn't have any money back then. I told Teddy we could have her pay us half the farm's worth over time. Work something out. But he was Birch-stubborn and insisted it was what his father meant to happen." Bibi scowled. "As though his father had had some grand plan."

"When my mother left, Grandpa took it out on Sarah."

Bibi's eyes flew open. "Make no mistake, Sarah had a hand in your mother's leaving. And to her credit, she never tried to hide it. She helped arrange for a job in New York. She even drove Charlotte to the train station."

That day in the parlor, her mother's tailored suit and stiff goodbye. Sarah had been waiting to drive her to her new life. One that didn't include a little girl.

"I lost a mother and an aunt that day." Megan thought about the pictures in her aunt's house, the babies with their fat cheeks and innocent smiles. "And cousins—family I have never met."

A tear trekked down Bibi's face. "Your aunt never married."

"Then who are all of the children on her mantel, if not Aunt Sarah's grandchildren?" But Megan knew the answer by the glaze of despair in her grandmother's eyes. "My mother's grandchildren?"

"Yes." Bibi held a hand out, as though in supplication, the tears making streak marks on her skin. "She remarried and had two more kids. Sarah never lost touch with her. Those pictures? Your nieces and nephews."

Friday was blessedly dry. Megan, still reeling from her conversation with Bibi two nights prior, was happy to spend the day in the fields, picking lettuce, sugar snap peas, kale, and mustard greens for Saturday's farmers market. Clover was holding down the fort at the café, and Jeremy, the new chef, was there with her, finalizing the menu for Monday's café grand opening. If they were going to have enough vegetables for the farmers market, the store, and the café's needs, Megan would have to pick almost all weekend, a task that suited her fine.

The local high school had sent over two volunteers—students in the vocational technical program—and Megan could see them down by the barn, washing lettuce in giant tubs of fresh water, their young backs bending in ways hers no longer could withstand for long.

"I still can't believe it," Clay said. He was on his knees, pulling tender sugar snap peas off the vines and tossing them efficiently into a large basket he'd strapped around his neck. Every once in a while, he'd pop one into his mouth. "And your grandmother has known all this time?"

"About Sarah? Yes. About my mother's other family?" Megan shook her head. "She told me she learned about them when she visited Aunt Sarah. My father doesn't know either, and Bibi made me swear not to tell him."

Clay paused to examine a pod, holding it up to the sun. With a squinty frown, he tossed the snap pea in another pile, one meant for compost. "You don't sound terribly upset."

"I feel numb, like I heard news that was disturbing, but about someone else. Does that make sense?"

Clay nodded. "That's how I felt when my father died. We hadn't really known him—he and my mother never married, and he lived hours away. I was sad for all that could have been. Less so for the man himself."

"Yes, that's exactly it," Megan said. "I was young when my mother left. And truthfully, she was more like a kindly aunt than a mother. Bibi was always my mother, at least in my mind."

Megan heard a shout followed by a squeal. She glanced toward the barn in time to see the students squirting each other with the hose. They caught Megan watching and quickly returned to their chore.

"Kids," Clay said, smiling.

"Kids."

"Speaking of kids, will you make contact with your mother?"

Clay asked this nonchalantly, as though he was inquiring about the taste of a new brand of butter. Knowing he was keeping any trace of sympathy out of his voice lest it be mistaken for pity, Megan smiled at her friend. It was nice to have someone to confide in, and Clay, for all his youth, was a good listener.

"I don't know. Right now, I'd say no. Maybe that will change." Megan looked up, keeping an eye on a series of darker clouds edging in from the southwest. Rain this weekend would be a problem. It would make working outdoors unpleasant, and the farmers market could get canceled. "I'd like to talk with Sarah again." She smiled, though her heart wasn't in it. "Once I have the emotional fortitude."

Clay dumped the overflowing basket of peas into a larger bin attached to a wheelbarrow. He covered the larger bin, protecting its contents from the harsh midday sun, and moved on to a new row.

"Do you think Simon's bid for the farm is somehow connected to his murder?"

"My gut says yes. He wanted this property—that much we know. And when he couldn't buy it, he became part of the zoning initiative. Then there's the Washington connection."

"But what would any of that have to do with a motive for killing him?"

"That's just it. On its face, the person with the most to lose is me. The permits, the rezoning."

"Then there is a motive we're missing."

"There's Porter." Megan shared Denver's hypothesis that Brian Porter had broken into her store.

"I don't know." Clay looked troubled. "It's possible Porter had a beef with Simon that we know nothing about. One that was unrelated to the farm. The setting of the murder could have been coincidental. Porter—anyone—could easily have followed him here."

Megan considered this. "What about the other night? The intruder, and the break-in at the store? Your theory would make sense if Simon's death was the end of it."

"I know, I know," Clay said. "And that scares me more than anything. I worry for your safety."

Clay's mention of safety reminded her about the dog, Gunther. She described their new addition to her farm manager.

"A Polish Tatra Sheepdog? Never heard of the breed."

"Kind of looks like a Great Pyrenees. Or a large Golden Retriever. Or a white Newfoundland."

"You're really painting a picture."

"Yeah, well." Megan wiped her hand across her sweating brow and then replaced the glove. "Between the dog, the café opening, and the Historical Society fundraiser, next week is promising to be a busy one."

"Don't forget the farmers market."

"That too," Megan said, returning to her chore. She glanced toward her high school volunteers, pleased to see them washing the lettuce exactly as she had instructed. "The first one of the season is always a treat."

Denver called Megan at four o'clock that afternoon. His voice, normally cheerful, held ominous undertones that caused Megan's hands to tense around her mobile phone.

"They've questioned Porter," he said. "About your store...and about Simon's murder. And they searched his house."

"Today?"

"Aye. Brian called me earlier. Sarge was his excuse, but it was clear the laddie had been drinking."

Megan was quiet for a moment. "Denver, why are you telling me?"

"Because maybe you can talk to the police on his behalf." When Megan didn't respond, he said, "Look, perhaps I understand Porter better than I'd like to admit. He's got a hot head and some nasty demons chasing his skinny arse and it wasn't that long ago that I was in the same boat."

"What would you like me to say to the police?"

"That he needs some help, yes, but that he's not a killer."

"But we don't know that."

"The boy is not a murderer."

Megan rubbed her temple, massaging the tension away with strong fingers. There it was again: that question of trust. Did she trust Denver enough to do this for him—on the basis of his request alone? What did she feel about Porter deep down in her own gut? Did it matter?

"I'll talk to King," Megan said. "Not that it will do any good. I think he half believes I'm involved."

"He'll be looking to see whether you want to press charges against Porter for your store. I think you should."

"But you just said—"

"I said the boy's not a killer. He admitted to the break-in to me. Maybe a good scare will help set him on the path to usefulness."

Megan sighed. Since when was farming so damn complicated? "Okay."

"That's it? *Okay*?"

"You'll owe me another dinner."

"So it's dinner ye want, is it?"

"Dinner...and maybe dessert."

Brian Porter's house was quiet. Megan pulled alongside the closed gate—unlocked this time—climbed out of her truck, and rapped on the door. Not surprising, Porter didn't answer. His Jeep was there. He may be sleeping one off, she thought, and kept pounding, her hand aching from the effort.

Denver would be angry if he knew she was here—it was King he wanted her to talk to, not Brian. But she wanted to see the man for herself, judge whether he was simply a messed-up kid with anger management issues or something worse. She felt unbalanced from the last few weeks, and she realized that the person she wasn't trusting right now was herself. She needed to see Porter. She wanted to make her own determination.

"Brian, I'm not going away. I'll camp out here if that's what it takes." She knocked again. "Brian! Open up the damn door!"

Megan put her ear to the white wooden entrance. She heard shuffling on the other side and pounded again. "Brian! Open up!"

Her hand was raised to give it another go when the door swung open. Off-balance, she stumbled against Porter, who was standing in the doorway looking disheveled, ill, and rather angry.

He righted Megan with a touch more force than was needed. She stood straight, pulling her blouse down and checking that all the buttons were in the right place, and scowled at the man in front of her.

"We need to talk."

Reddened eyes narrowed. "We have nothing to talk about." His words slurred together like verbal finger paint and his breath stunk of beer and cigarettes. Naked from the waist up, the green, brown, and blue dragon tattoo she'd only glimpsed before bared its fangs from beneath his armpits.

"You're drunk," Megan said.

"Who made you my mother?"

"Yeah, well, you could do with some mothering." Megan glanced around. "Invite me in. And go put a shirt on."

Porter, eyes narrowed to menacing slits, looked about ready to argue. Pulling her spine straighter, she said, "Go. Straight away."

Straight away? Where had that come from? But Porter lowered his head and backed away from the doorframe. Not exactly a welcome, but at least he let her pass. Without a word, he disappeared into a darkened hallway.

Megan looked around, trying to get a feel for Porter's life. The living room was stark: old plaid sofa, beat-up coffee table, charcoal gray dog bed next to it, flat-screen television on a stand by the wall. A line of empty Coors cans ran along the floor, aluminum soldiers marching in vain against madness. Like the man, the house smelled of cigarettes and beer.

Megan sat down on the couch, sinking deep into worn-out springs, and edged forward until she was perching on the frame. Another look around underscored his poverty and his aloneness. Porter's dog tags, hung from a lampshade along with a set of ivory rosary beads, were his only nod to anything personal.

"My grandmother. She prayed for me every day I was overseas—using those." Porter returned wearing an army green t-shirt along with the khaki shorts. The shirt hugged his torso and accentuated his biceps, but at least Megan wasn't staring at that dragon anymore.

He tossed a curt nod toward the rosary beads. "Died right after I got back," he said without emotion.

"I'm sorry. About your grandmother."

Porter shrugged. "What do you want?"

"Why did you break into my store?"

Porter's jaw clenched.

"Don't you have anything to say about that?"

Stony silence.

"Look, Brian, I'm not sure what game you're playing with me, but I need you to stop." Megan used her attorney voice, the one she saved for recalcitrant witnesses. Porter's eyes were like daggers and it was everything Megan could do to maintain eye contact. "I know King pulled you in today. And by now I'm sure you realize they're not merely investigating a break-in."

"What are you saying?"

"Murder, Brian."

"I didn't kill anyone."

Genuine emotion, but Megan saw the slight shift of his eyes to the right. Back in her deposition days, that would signal a witness who was likely lying. But lying about what?

"Think about it. The cops have you pinged for a hothead. Winsome's a small town." Megan met angry stare for angry stare, then shrugged. "Suspects are limited, and as far as possibilities go, you look pretty damn good."

Porter leaned against the wall, studying her. A fine sheen of sweat covered his face; his hands shook. "You should go."

"You should tell me why you broke into my store."

Through gritted teeth, Porter said, "Please go."

Megan stood, then sidled toward the door, remembering his reaction the night Sarge was hit. She watched the end of the dragon's tail rattle as Porter's arm trembled.

At the door, she stopped, her hand on the doorknob. "There's a certain veterinarian in town who believes you're innocent. He may be the only friend you have, and right now, you're making him look like a fool."

Brian Porter shook his head slowly, back and forth. His eyes were dead black orbs. "Then maybe he is a fool," Porter said before slamming the door in Megan's face.

* * *

Megan stopped by the police station on her way home. With a heavy heart, she signed the papers against Porter for breaking into her store. He was a man who needed help, she saw that clearly, and maybe Denver was right—having the police sniffing around for breaking into her store would put the fear of God in him. Only Megan couldn't shake the parallels to Mick. What atrocities had her husband witnessed those weeks before his death? Could he have come home as broken as Brian Porter had he lived? Whatever Porter's sins, Megan didn't think him a murderer.

When King told her they were investigating Brian for the murder of Simon Duvall and asked whether it could have been Porter at her farm the evening of the break-in, Megan simply shrugged, another frisson of guilt coursing through her.

"He has a record," King told her.

"For what?"

"Aggravated assault. Bar fights, mostly." King pursed his lips. "But crime is a slippery slope, Megan. You know that. Kids start small, go big. Aggravated assault to murder? Not a hard leap to make."

She knew King was right. Once certain boundaries were crossed, it was hard to turn back.

She thought about sharing her theory about the flask, her belief that Porter's stony silence had more to do with fear than guilt. But when she looked again at King and saw the impatience on his face, she decided to save her theories for another day, when she had more proof. For now, Porter needed to cool off. And maybe having him behind bars—if it came to that—would cause someone else to get comfortable and show their hand.

Twenty-One

The Winsome Farmers Market was small by national standards. Tucked into the parking lot of the Eternal Life Episcopal Church, it boasted thirteen vendors selling wares under a shady line of maple trees. More like a craft fair than a true farmers market, only five of the vendors sold food products. In addition to Megan's vegetables and flowers, locals sold free-range chicken and pastured pork, apple products, canned fruit, fruit pies, and fruit jellies. Megan walked past a blueberry crumb pie that made her stomach growl so loudly she had to cross her hands over her midriff to soften the sound.

"Morning," Megan said to Merry.

Merry nodded in return. Merry was selling her award-winning roses from the tent next to Megan's. She'd forgone a large table, and instead had pots containing young rose plants surrounding a small foldable bistro table on which she'd placed her cashbox and calculator. Two large coolers held bunches of roses for sale and their fragrant scents perfumed the air between the two tents. Megan couldn't complain about the scent—the heady flowers were more welcome in the outdoor setting—or the added business. Merry's roses were always a hit, and inevitably customers who stopped to see Merry would drift over to pick up some vegetables afterwards, as was the case with Lenora Duvall.

Lenora perused Megan's table, taking in the vegetable selection. She paused by the kohlrabi, picked up two, and placed them in a plastic bag.

"Can I assume these won't be fibrous?" she asked Megan.

Clay, who was bent over behind the table, sorting through the eggs and organizing them according to size, smiled so that only Megan could see him.

"We grow a hybrid that's supposed to remain tender, even as the weather gets warmer," Megan said. "Try them. If you don't like them, I'll refund your money."

Lenora frowned. "Simon used to make kohlrabi fritters, but that's far too much work for me. How do you prepare them?"

"I like them steamed with butter."

Another frown, as though Megan had said something distasteful. "I'll take these two. And a bunch of your basil. Oh, and Clay, hand me a dozen of those eggs. The smallest you have."

Megan packaged the kohlrabi and basil in a small bag while Clay grabbed the eggs. The day, which had started out chilly and overcast, had warmed quickly as the clouds gave way to sun, and now sweat trickled down the back of Megan's linen shirt and between her breasts. A breeze blew through the lot, offering some relief. She wiped her forehead with the back of her wrist before handing Lenora her change. She noticed that the other woman looked pale. Dark circles smudged her eyes, and her normally impeccable clothes seemed rumpled.

"Lenora," Megan said casually. "That research you mentioned, about Washington's stay in Winsome? Fascinating stuff. I would love to see it."

A crowd was gathering at the market, and the large parking lot was filling up quickly with cars, people, and dogs. Two small boys darted across the market square, heading for the comic book table. Lenora was watching their progress, a deep frown on her face. Megan shifted her gaze in that direction and saw Porter. He looked better today, although his eyes were hooded and distrustful. He carried a camera and was busily snapping photos of the market. He glanced in the direction of Megan's tent, saw the two women watching him, and snapped a photo before heading off toward Annie's Alpacas.

Megan said, "Wonder what he's doing here?"

Lenora said, "Someone must have hired him to take pictures for the local column."

"I didn't even realize we had a local column."

Lenora, still frowning, shifted her attention back to Megan. "You were asking—?"

"Yes, about Washington's visit to our farm."

"You'll see the information this summer," she said half-heartedly. "When my article is finished. *Journal of Revolutionary Times* bought it for their August edition. It provides a whole new spin on the town—and Washington."

"That's exciting, Lenora, but maybe it would be possible to see some of your research beforehand? The part related to our farm?"

Lenora clutched the bag to her body as three more locals entered the tent. "I'm afraid not. A lot of effort went into that research, and not merely by me. I'm planning pieces for several other magazines, and if I share, well...you understand."

A condescending half-smile from Lenora was coupled with, "Do you have any spinach?" from a tall, lean man wearing a bowler hat.

Megan pointed to the large basket of spinach packages at the end of the table and said, "Is this related to Caldbeck, the original owner, Lenora?"

A shadow passed across Lenora's face. Her lips turned downward. "Wait for the article, Megan." She raised the carton of eggs and waved. "I have to go."

"Ah, that woman," Megan said under her breath to Clay after Lenora was out of her sight. Clay was standing next to her, shaking his own head.

"She's difficult," he agreed.

"Did she seem distracted to you?"

Clay shrugged. "Eccentric, as always. Perhaps more tired than usual. Why?"

"I don't know. She lost her son recently. Maybe I'm sensing grief." Megan shrugged. "She just seems off."

But there was little time for ruminating over Lenora's state of mind. The crowd was migrating from Tanya's Handmade Soaps, at the farthest end, toward Megan's tent. A few stragglers were already ogling Merry's roses. Megan quickly straightened the vegetables, put a few more bouquets of early wildflowers into the bin of cold water, and waited.

"Will you and Clay watch my tent for a moment?" Merry leaned over and asked after the last of her customers had moved on. She motioned daintily toward the church with one polyester-clad shoulder, indicating her need to use the ladies' room. "I'll be back in a jiffy."

"Sure."

Fifteen minutes later, Merry was back and Megan had four customers, all crowded around the table. A banner day.

The Dorfmans arrived a little past eleven. "Can I come by next week and finish the barn?" Neil asked.

"That's fine," Megan said. "It will be good to have it finished."

Dave, who was sorting through bunches of kale and Swiss chard, finally decided on a bundle of Red Russian. Megan refused to ring him up. "After all the work you and Neil have done, the least I can give you is some kale."

Dave's face reddened. "That's awfully nice, Megan, but we can pay." He placed three crumpled dollar bills on the table.

"Suit yourself." Megan took the dollars and was in the process of straightening them out when she caught another glimpse of Porter. This time, he was moving between the comic book table and the soap seller, his camera now tucked back in its bag.

"Hey, Dave," she said quietly to the elder of the two brothers. "You've hired Porter in the past. What did you think of him?"

The skin on Dave's face turned a darker crimson. "You know I don't like to say anything bad about people, Megan—"

"But?"

"But he's unreliable," Neil piped in. "Sometimes you can trust him to do fine work, and sometimes he'll fail to keep his word for days on end." Neil grimaced under his bushy red mustache. "Hard to give work to someone like that.

"You're being hard on the boy," Dave protested. "He's more of a—"

But Dave's words were cut off by the next round of customers, who formed a line around the front of the table and out into the lot. The market was livening up. The smells of Bernie's BBQ filled the air, as did the steady murmur of the crowd, all of which was accompanied by the musical sounds of a small jazz band set up under a tent by Tanya's Handmade Soaps.

And so they continued for the next hour: answering questions, bagging vegetables, handing out Bibi's recipe cards, and filling the cashbox with much-needed revenue. The eggs went first—their small flock could only produce a limited number and Megan needed some for the store and the café—followed by the lettuce and the broccoli. She jotted notes about other vegetables people asked for, determined to grow what she could in the greenhouse and hoop houses over the winter so she could have a fuller bounty come next spring.

"Pretty decent haul," Clay said.

She nodded. It was more than enough to cover Clay's time and the expense of hauling the tent, coolers, and vegetables the six miles to the market, but that was about it. No one was going to get rich selling vegetables locally, that was for sure.

"Next year we'll start the CSA," Megan said. "And then people will come to us."

"And pay ahead of time."

"That would be nice." Megan hoped the new zoning rules, if they passed, wouldn't preclude the community supported agriculture model, or CSA, as it was called, from being employed on her property. Having customers order shares of a harvest ahead of time would mean capital for maintaining and expanding the farm. Plus, she would offer customers a choice of full price or a discount if they volunteered hours on the farm. She could use the help, and the more people who understood how their food was produced, the better. That disconnection from the environment was one reason she left the law practice; she hoped like hell the Historical Society and its grand notions of making Winsome the best place to visit wouldn't impede that vision.

A young college student, a rosebush in hand, stood in front of the table and opened her mouth to ask a question. At the same time, a high-pitched scream erupted from somewhere in the sea of cars on the other side of the parking lot. Megan, surprised by the unexpected wailing, thought for a moment the scream was coming from the student. It took a second to realize people were running toward a spot near the shadiest portion of the church lot.

"Woman down!" one man yelled. "Call 911!"

"She's dead!" another shouted.

Neil Dorfman went flying past. Megan grabbed his arm. "What's happening?" she asked.

"Lenora," he whispered. "Someone killed her."

"But she was here only a few hours ago."

Neil's eyes widened. He shrugged.

Megan could hear a siren's wail.

"Clay, stay here, okay?" she asked. Her companion nodded, his face stricken.

Megan put her hand lightly on his arm before turning toward the gathering crowd. She scanned the parking lot for a sign of Porter, but the young man was nowhere to be found.

Twenty-Two

"Everybody get back now. *Please.*" An officer held up her hands and motioned for everyone to move to the side. "Let the paramedics do their job."

Megan, on tiptoe, watched as two paramedics started an IV while rushing a limp and lifeless-looking Lenora into the ambulance. Blood pooled around the base of the gurney and trailed behind, a house of horrors indication of what had happened. Megan, feeling numb, was in awe, as she always was, at the hurried ease with which the paramedics worked. To be the barrier between life and death for another human being was unthinkable to her; to do that daily—terrifying.

"She's alive," she heard someone say.

"Just barely," said another. "Knife wound. Bad one."

Within minutes, the ambulance was off and the police got to work. They cordoned off the area and made an announcement that no one was to leave the premises. "Vendors, please go back to your tents and remain there," the female officer called to the agitated crowd. "I repeat: everyone should remain at the market until we have had a chance to speak with you."

Megan lingered for a moment before going back to their booth. She caught herself wondering about Porter's checkered past. Had any of those bar brawls included knives? It took an especially callous—or desperate—person to thrust a knife into another, to feel flesh rip and dig deeply enough to cut through sinew and cartilage.

Was Porter capable of such an act?

Just a day ago, her answer would have been a firm "no." Now she wasn't so sure.

"He was a soldier," Clay said later, giving voice to the fact that had been bothering Megan all along. A trained soldier, like Mick. Had Mick ever killed anyone in the line of duty? She never asked him. She should have asked him.

"I know." Megan sighed. They were sitting in the goat pen, attending to Dimples and Heidi. Dimples had recovered nicely, and her sprightly little body was up to its old antics. Just this morning she had eaten one of Megan's galoshes. "He's ornery and ill-tempered, and perhaps he's capable of taking another life, but why would he go after Simon and now Lenora?" She shook her head. "It makes no sense."

"Maybe they owed him money. Maybe he didn't like them. Or maybe he is paranoid, thinks they were somehow out to get him and wanted to get to them first." Clay knelt on the ground to pet Heidi, rubbing his fingers between her ears and down the slope of her nose. She rewarded him by chewing on his fingers with her tiny, strong jaws. "Alcoholics can become paranoid."

Megan grunted. "I think motive is key. Who would want Simon and Lenora out of the picture?"

"Besides you?"

Megan stuck her tongue out at Clay. "Yes, besides me."

"The cops did seem to grill you for an unnecessarily long time."

Megan nodded. "I think they had moved on from Bibi and me after Simon, but now Lenora's death raises questions again. Of course, it didn't help that Merry Chance told the police she overheard Lenora and I having a 'heated discussion.'"

"Nosy cow."

Megan laughed. "I hadn't left the tent, though—but she had."

"You could have hired someone to go after Lenora."

"Thanks, Clay." Megan waved a white rag playfully in his

direction. "I thought you were on my side."

"I am, but you have to be ready to face down any and all accusations." He looked out at the goats, reaching absentmindedly for Heidi. "Aside from Porter, I can't imagine who it would be. Simon's relationship with most people in town was strained. And then there's your aunt and her sudden return to Winsome."

"Sarah? You think Aunt Sarah killed Simon and attacked Lenora? She's close to eighty. Why not blame Jeremy, while you're at it? And Merry too."

"Told you, Megan. You have the most to lose."

She shook her head. "We don't know who else stood to gain by Simon's death." She thought about the morning Simon was killed, the open goat gate, Mutton Chops in the house. The blood-soaked glove. "Whatever the motive, I'm convinced it involves Washington Acres." She allowed herself a frustrated shrug. "But why?"

"And we may never know." Clay stood and walked toward the gate. His jeans hung loosely around skinny hips. He'd been working at the farm nearly nonstop. He also had a tendency to lock himself up in his room, studying or working on some invention, forgetting to eat. "I'm going to feed the chickens, water the tomatoes in the greenhouse, and then I'm out of here. I'll be back tomorrow to pick for Monday's café opening. Is that okay?"

"That would be great." Megan stood, following him out. Dimples trailed behind. "You need to stay here, little girl."

"You have a date tonight?" Clay asked, a twinkle in his brown eyes.

"No," she said, thinking of Denver—and the fact that he hadn't called. "I'm going to finish up a few things, then head in for an early night. It's been an eventful day."

"Suit yourself. Just keep an eye out for anything unusual. Not that we even know what normal is anymore."

Megan planned a quiet evening with Bibi: a dinner of lentil stew, a field green salad, and Bibi's crusty bread, followed by a glass of

Sauvignon Blanc and some mindless television. But first she needed to clear her mind. After Clay left, she made her way past the barn and down the other side of the hill. The field of flowers she had planted last year—a sign of faith that things would work out—were in bloom, and Megan watched a dozen honeybees buzz from flower to flower, their presence reassuring. One wonderful thing—and there were many—about farming organically was the host of living creatures that made the fields their home. Megan noticed that with organic seeds, the plants seemed to have better natural resistance to harmful pests, and without all of the pesticides, she saw an influx of ladybugs, honeybees, and hummingbirds. A good reminder to keep her eye on her larger goal: bringing sustainable, wholesome food to Winsome.

Feeling a little lighter, she meandered through the fenced-in corn fields, past the garlic beds and out toward the perimeter of their property. It had been a long day. To get to the market by eight with fresh vegetables, she and Clay had been up and working since four, but rather than tired, Megan felt antsy and restless. She kept seeing Lenora's body lying on the pavement not long after they'd spoken. The police believed she'd been stabbed in the back while walking toward her vehicle, her body hidden between two SUVs until the unfortunate owner of one of them returned to her car.

When she had told Clay she believed motive to be key, she meant it. Her gut still told her Porter hadn't killed Simon, but his presence today had given her pause. What could Porter's motive be? She wondered again whether the Duvall attacks could have had something to do with the Historical Society.

The sun sat low in the sky, an orange orb ribboned with swaths of gauzy haze. Taking advantage of the remaining daylight, Megan crossed the shaggy border of long grass that separated her farm from the abandoned Marshall property next door, her leather boots sinking into the soft ground.

When she was a kid, the Marshall house had been owned by an absentee landlord and rented to a young couple with two kids. Megan had played with their daughter, a small bird-like girl with hazel eyes and a soft voice. When Megan's mother left home, the girl's parents stopped inviting her over. She'd missed her friend, but Bibi had told her it was for the best. The family moved out when Megan was eleven.

Megan hadn't been inside since.

In fact, it'd been so long since she'd been over here that Megan felt as though she was trespassing on hallowed ground. A bird called from one of the oak trees in the yard and another one answered from some distance. The field surrounding the house—once a manicured yard with a small swing set—buzzed with grasshoppers and bumblebees and industrious white moths. An ant crawled up her arm and Megan flicked it away. She scanned the play area, now an overgrown mass of weeds and detritus, including the rusting swing set frame. Megan's heart ached—for the family who lost their home, for her own runaway mother, or for the broken Duvall family, she wasn't sure.

At the edge of the house itself, Megan paused, listening. The house was quiet as a bomb site. Up close, she could see the impact of time and neglect. The stone needed repointing, the porch, once a grand structure spanning the face of the house, lay in disrepair. Paint peeled in strips off white window frames and missing roof shingles left patches like bald spots on the aging roof.

Megan strained to see inside one of the windows. Three of the upper panes were shattered, and the lower panes were thick with grime. All that was visible inside was a shadowy glimpse into what had been the living room.

Megan left the porch and walked carefully around the back of the house, mindful of the holes and debris in the high grass around the foundation. The cellar doors, which opened from the ground directly into the basement below, were secured with a rusty chain and new-looking steel padlock. On the other side of the cellar doors was a covered patio, its concrete base cracked and buckled. Megan climbed over a discarded picnic bench and tried to see inside. One window was boarded; the other, which looked directly into the kitchen, was filthy. Only a corner of a stove was visible.

The house would need major renovations—and major money.

A bat swooped overhead, diving down toward the grass and then upward again in a graceful arc. Megan followed its movements, wondering whether bats were living in the attic...bats, mice, and who knew what else.

She turned to leave, the thought of crawling creatures urging her home, when she noticed the footprints on the edge of the patio. To Megan's untrained eye, it looked like several sets of boot prints. Her mind flashed to the new cellar lock. Workmen, here to do repairs? A real estate agent? Or her trespasser—or trespassers?

Megan hurried home, scuttling creatures less of a concern than other things that could lurk here in the dark.

After dinner, Megan sat at her computer in the parlor and looked up the Marshall house. It didn't take long to find it on a half dozen foreclosure sites. The house was selling for cheap; but even cheap surpassed her budget. She skimmed through the details about the house, which were very limited, and opened the photos attached to the link. There were only two: one of the front of the house, one of the back. Both were slightly out of focus, as though the photographer had been unskilled, or in a rush. At the bottom of both photos was a timestamp, notable only because the date reflected was the same date Simon Duvall was murdered.

Fifteen minutes of internet research later, Megan found the bank that was selling the Marshall house. She made note of the bank's phone number. Tomorrow she'd call. Someone had hired that photographer. There had to be a trail. And that photographer may have seen something related to Simon's murder.

Later that night, her father called, his voice sounding raspy and sad.

"Hey, Dad," Megan said. She tried to picture her father in his apartment in Turin but couldn't. "It's very late there."

"I wanted to hear your voice," he said. "See how things are going on the farm, and with Bibi."

"Bibi's fine. The café opens Monday, and today was the first farmers market." Megan went on to describe their crops and the heavy sales volume. She found that she couldn't mention the murder, or today's attack on Lenora—nor did her father bring it up. Perhaps he didn't know. Why would he, living all those miles away? She had a hunch that even if he did know, he'd prefer not to talk about it.

"So you're doing well then?" he asked.

"I am. You?"

He paused, and Megan could hear the hushed murmurings of a British television show on low volume. "Doing great," he said finally, and the lie rang loud and clear.

Megan could have said many things in that moment. She could have told him about the murder. She could have inquired about George Washington, the Caldbeck family, and the history of the house. She could have asked him what was wrong. She could have mentioned Aunt Sarah. Instead, she said "I love you," and hung up the phone, an anxious feeling lingering.

Twenty-Three

Chef Jeremy was already at the café when Megan arrived early Monday morning. Clover, dressed in a long tie-dyed skirt and a midriff-baring peasant blouse tied right above her tanned, pierced navel, had driven to the farm early to help Megan bring vegetables and eggs to the café for the day's open house. Together with Clay and Bibi, they'd loaded vegetables from Jeremy's list, placing them into coolers and then the large coolers into the truck.

Once at the café, she, Jeremy, and Clover unloaded the truck. Megan was happy to see the window had been fixed, and Clover had come in late on Sunday to clean the store and polish the copper-topped tables and the bar. Everything gleamed, ready for show time.

The trio worked without talking, listening instead to Clover's The Cat Empire CD, each focused on their own task. Clover stocked the small produce section of the store, carefully stacking the vegetables in the small glass-front refrigerator. Megan acted as sous chef, washing and chopping vegetables, rolling out dough, cutting bread—whatever tasks Jeremy requested. And Jeremy created little bits of edible art.

By eleven, when the open house was set to start, trays of cold appetizers had been set out along the lunch counter. Megan and Clover stepped back to admire the presentation. There were beet and goat cheese toasts, deviled eggs with chives and country ham, Caesar salad spears, mini goat cheese and spinach quiches, vegetable tortes, finger sandwiches, and crudités with homemade buttermilk ranch dressing. In the kitchen, Jeremy was putting the finishing touches on his hot offerings—spanakopita triangles stuffed with spinach and tender kale, mushroom tartlets with garlic and gruyere, and tiny empanadas filled with fragrant grass-fed meat, vegetables, and cheese. The store was rich with the smells of roasted vegetables, beef, and garlic.

Megan took a step back. "Do you think it's too much, especially given everything that's happened in Winsome over the last few weeks?"

Clover, eyes wide with excitement, shook her head. "I think it's incredible. Everyone will love it. Don't worry."

"Tartlets, salad spears, empanadas—" Megan rubbed her temples, thinking of the hard-working men and women of their small town, many of whom grew up on meat and potatoes, quite literally. "Will our customers be willing to *try* these things?"

"Give them some credit," Jeremy said. He walked into the seating area of the café carrying a small sampling of today's menu and held the tray out to each of them in turn. Megan took a mushroom tartlet; Clover ate three empanadas and stole a quiche off the counter.

"Amazing," they said in unison.

"Why would you want to work in a hole like Winsome," Clover asked, her mouth full, "when you can make magic like this anywhere?"

Jeremy, dark, brooding eyes suddenly stormy, gave her a tepid smile. "*Anywhere* is not what it's cracked up to be."

True, Megan thought, and remembered Denver had said something similar. But she didn't have time to comment before the bell on the front door alerted them to customers. Looking up, Megan saw the Dorfman brothers, Dave and Neil. Dave was dressed in his Sunday finest; Neil, as usual, looked like he'd just rolled out of bed—stained jeans, a ragged t-shirt and sneakers worn through in two spots.

"Smells great," Neil said. He ambled back toward the table,

broad shoulders balanced by equally broad hips, and smiled. "I'll have one of everything."

Dave reached a hand toward a quiche and Clover slapped it back. "Not yet. Wait until the doors open."

"They are open," Dave said.

"I mean until the party officially begins." Clover pulled a chair over and plopped down, hiking her long skirt up above her knees. "I know Bobby will be here soon. He texted me from the hospital."

"Is he with Lenora?" Dave asked.

"Yes. He's been there since early this morning."

"How is she?" Neil asked.

Clover shrugged. "He doesn't tell me anything. I know she lost a lot of blood. I mean *a lot*." She gestured with her green-manicured fingers, indicating copious amounts of something. "She's still alive. I guess that's good."

"The attack is in the Philadelphia paper," Jeremy said quietly. "Simon's murder too."

"Imagine that," Neil said. "Little Winsome in the big city paper."

"Well, that's not exactly what we want to be known for. The Historical Society and Beautification Board are trying to make Winsome a place tourists want to visit, not a place to be scared of. Forget 'Win Back Winsome.' They'll start calling us Gruesome Winsome or something like that. You know how the media are." Clover reached up and stole a Caesar salad spear. Jeremy shot her a withering glance.

"Hey, I thought you said they were for the guests," Dave joked. He looked at Jeremy, appraising the chef in that unsettling, steadfast way both Dorfmans were known for, and added, "Nice to see you back in town."

Megan smiled. "Chef Jeremy, I guess you know Neil and Dave Dorfman, the craftsmen behind the remodeling of The Washington Acres Café and Larder and the farm."

The men shook hands.

Megan clapped her hands. "Okay, ten minutes until the open

house officially begins." She looked at Clover. "Balloons and banner?"

"Balloons—check." Clover pointed toward the front window, where a bouquet of helium balloons floated above the cobblestone pavers. "And here's the banner." She pulled a roll of neon-pink paper from her bag. "Take an end," she said to Neil, who obliged. Unrolled, "Grand Opening of the Washington Acres Farm Café & Lardey" was written in bold black letters. Someone had crossed out the "y" and written "r" above it with black Sharpie. "I may have made a small error." She brightened. "But I fixed it! And now if one of you gentlemen would be kind enough to help me hang it out front, we'll be good to go."

Dave and Neil looked at each other, communicating in brotherly shorthand. Dave nodded reluctantly. "Fine, Clover. It's always something with you women. Let's go."

Clover rolled her eyes dramatically but followed Dave outside.

The rest watched them leave. "Ready, Chef?" Megan asked Jeremy. "This is the big test to see whether Winsome is ready for some winsome grub." She smiled at her own corny wit.

"They will love it," Jeremy said with a confidence only someone who hasn't experienced failure can muster. "Every last bite will be gone. I guarantee it."

Jeremy was half right: every last bite was eaten. As soon as the banner went up, Winsome's residents began wandering into the store.

"Where's the beef?" Dave Dorfman teased as he popped four tartlets in his mouth at once.

"Oh, look at these adorable mini turnovers," Merry exclaimed.

"Those are empanadas," Clover said dryly.

"Is that Indian? I despise curry." Merry scrunched her nose and put the empanada back. Megan tossed it in the garbage when she wasn't looking.

"I love curry." Dave ate an empanada, frowned, and said,

"That's very bland. I like my curry spicy."

Jeremy and Megan locked eyes. He gave her a half smile and winked. "We'll remember that for next time," Jeremy said.

"And who is this?" Lydia asked, looking pointedly at Jeremy. A regular, Lydia was tall and curvy. A black pencil skirt accentuated a heart-shaped bottom, and the top three buttons of her pale yellow blouse were open, giving everyone a glimpse of the lacy white bra she wore underneath. Megan watched her walk on four-inch stilettos, surprised she hadn't fallen on the cobblestones on her way in.

Jeremy reached his hand out, lightly touching her arm. She smiled demurely, showing him her whitened teeth, and bent low over the table, showing him something else altogether.

Neil Dorfman, who was quietly eating a pile of cookies in the corner of the store, had his eyes firmly affixed to Lydia's ample bottom. His brother had his eyes affixed on Jeremy.

The front door opened and more people poured in, including Bobby King.

"Megan," he said, nodding. "Seems like a different place."

Looking around, Megan had to agree. When she'd first taken over the store, the kitchen was used for storage and the counter to display newspapers and gum. The walls had been a dirty white, the floor chipped linoleum, and most of the items for sale were nearing their expiration date. Eddie Birch may have had great ideas, but execution was not his strength.

"Thank you, Bobby." She moved closer to the police chief and lowered her voice. "How is Lenora?"

"Still in critical condition."

"Was she able to identify her attacker?"

Bobby hesitated before answering—just long enough for Megan to understand that he still didn't trust her completely. "No," he said finally. "He or she came from the back and caught her by surprise."

"How about the knife? Did the attacker leave that behind?"

Bobby hitched up his pants. "Now you're treading where I

can't go, Megan. You know that."

"It was worth a try." But the mention of tread reminded her of the footprints by the Marshall house. Quietly, she told King about the footprints she'd seen near the back entrance.

"Sheesh, Megan, they could belong to anyone. I'm sure that house has seen its share of teen partiers and dog walkers in the last several years."

"These prints were newer. I know you're checking every angle." She told him about the foreclosure photos, about the tiny date and time stamped in the corner. "Whoever took those pictures may have seen something, Bobby. It was within the timeframe of Duvall's murder, and we both know that house has a direct view to the back of the barn."

King nodded. "I'll send someone over to have a look around."

"Thank you," Megan said. She doubted he would follow through, but she wasn't going to push it. Not here, not now. "Go have some food," she said instead. "Clover says you love fancy eats." Megan smiled.

"As a matter of fact, I do. The more frou-frou, the better." King laughed in a way that made Megan like him—a little bit. "Sure smells good."

"Eat up."

Twenty-Four

By the time Bibi and Clay arrived, only a skeleton of the original table setting was left. Bibi stood in the front of the store and looked around at the twenty-plus people milling about. "Winsome Smiles" was emblazoned on the front of her light blue sweatshirt, but she had worn her best pants—she called them slacks—for the café opening, along with a light blue, butter yellow, and pink scarf that she had tied in a fashionable knot around her neck. Looking at her, Megan felt a stab of pride. Her grandmother's eyes shone with intelligence, her posture stayed erect. Bonnie "Bibi" Birch was still one cool lady.

"Well, I haven't seen this many people in this place since the day Elvis died and we had the only working television on Canal Street." She honed in on Neil Dorfman. "And there's Neil Dorfman. Now I *know* Megan must be giving away free food."

Everybody laughed, including Neil.

"Come on in, Mrs. Birch," Clover said. "I'll get you a root beer."

Megan watched her grandmother greet and entertain their guests, some of whom she'd known her whole life. She had a sophisticated ease with people, an ease that belied the fact that she'd lived solely in one location her entire life. She seemed to be enjoying herself today. She hadn't been out other than to church and Bridge in weeks, and Megan was happy to see her this social.

"Will we see you Wednesday at the Historical Society fundraiser?" Merry was asking Bibi. Both women were dipping carrot sticks in Jeremy's homemade dressing, but Merry's eyes were on Jeremy; Bibi was watching Roger Becker, who was, in turn, talking to Clover and Lydia.

"Will that still go on in Lenora's absence?" Bibi asked, clearly surprised.

"Oh, yes," Merry said. Her head bobbed up and down for emphasis. "Lenora would want it that way. Both the Historical Society and the Beautification Board need the funds. There will be a silent auction, and dinner, of course." She glanced over at the lunch counter, scrunching her features into a look of distaste as she did so. "Normal food."

"Of course," Bibi said. Megan caught the sarcasm, but she doubted Merry did. "And will you still be voting on the new preservation rules?"

Merry, still looking at Jeremy—he *was* rather good-looking, in an urban-sophisticate sort of way, Megan had to admit—shook her well-sprayed head. "Lenora was supposed to present her findings during her talk. Apparently *George Washington* stayed at your farm," she whispered loudly, clarifying that it was George and not some other Washington who had resided there. "Imagine that. Lenora says she found historical records that *prove* he was there. What a boon for Winsome!"

Megan sidled closer to Bibi and Merry. She busied her hands with a rag, wiping nonexistent crumbs off the copper-topped table, and strained to listen.

Bibi, playing at casual, said, "Oh, dear, that is exciting."

"It is, indeed. The Historical Society has toyed for some time with applying for historic district status with Pennsylvania for Canal Street, but first we must have a local preservation ordinance. Frankly, Lenora's findings gave us the push we needed to get moving."

Coolly, Bibi said, "It's really the downtown area you want designated."

"Oh, no. We want to nominate Washington Acres. We can do that if we have a local ordinance and can show the significance of your farm." She beamed. "Wouldn't that be wonderful? Your house would be a timeless treasure in our small town. And then if we can get the downtown area designated a preservation district, we can advertise that to tourists. Just think, we may even be able to get on the national register."

Clenching the rag tightly, Megan bit her lip to stop from interrupting. It was one thing to nominate the downtown area—but their farm? Megan was familiar with the preservation rules; she'd looked them up after her conversation with Lenora at Merry's nursery. While she and Bibi could make repairs and take basic restorative actions, she would have to ask for permission from the town's to-be-created preservation board for any improvements or changes to the older buildings on the property. More red tape, and the possibility that the local board members could make decisions that would impact the farm. Even something as simple as a new outbuilding or a change to the home's front porch—which needed paint and windows—would be subject to a vote. Like her grandmother, Megan had little patience for bureaucratic nonsense. Wasn't that part of the reason she'd moved back to the country in the first place?

"Merry, do you have a say in this?" Bibi asked. Clover had handed Bibi another glass of root beer and she was using the cup to hide the growing scowl on her face.

"Of course."

"Well, this sounds lovely. Truly. I wonder who else might be deciding how to proceed?"

Merry, oblivious to Bibi's true feelings on the subject, said blithely, "There are a number of us. Roger, of course. Lenora, God-willing she make it. Eloise. Sarah Birch—"

"Sarah?" Bibi looked startled. "My sister-in-law? Since when is she a member of the Historical Society's board?"

Bibi's cool was slipping. Megan wondered whether it was time to interrupt.

"She's not," Merry said. She grabbed one of the few remaining empanadas and popped it into her mouth, chewing slowly. Finally she said, "But she has pledged a great deal of money to the Society

Wendy Tyson

and our cause. You asked who the influencers are. She will definitely be an influencer."

Megan saw Bibi's neck turn red. To her credit, her voice remained steady. "Is that it?"

"And then there's Jeremy."

Megan and her grandmother both shot glances in the direction of the chef. "But he's new to Winsome."

"Ah, but he is a native. And he has very strong opinions," Merry said, smiling. "Like me, he envisions a prettified Winsome, a place with wonderful gardens, well-preserved historical sites, and glorious restaurants."

Is that so, Megan thought. She was pressing hard on the table and her fingertips were numb.

Roger interrupted Merry's chatter, and Bibi wandered off to speak with Bobby King. Megan, full of spit and fire, marched back to where her chef was standing, chatting up a very flirtatious Lydia.

"I need you."

"Honey, don't we all need someone like Jeremy?" Lydia smiled.

Megan couldn't help it—her eyes rolled, nearly to the back of her head. "Kitchen. Now."

Clearly not used to being ordered around, Jeremy looked indecisive about whether to comply. Finally he nodded at Lydia and said, "Duty calls."

Megan walked to the large walk-in pantry at the back of the kitchen. She opened the door and motioned for Jeremy to follow. He raised his well-groomed eyebrows but complied.

"What the hell, Jeremy? Were you going to tell me about your work on the historical preservation project?"

Jeremy looked momentarily nonplussed, but he quickly regained his composure. "What are you talking about?"

"You know exactly what I'm talking about," Megan hissed. "Your vision for a prettier Winsome? Your desire to see preservation ordinances enacted?"

"Oh, that."

"*Oh, that?* That's all you can say?"

"Megan, calm down."

"Don't you dare tell me to calm down in *my* store." Her head felt like it was going to explode, all of the angst and turmoil of the last weeks skipping like stones on the inside of her skull. Her peripheral vision dimmed and all she could see was Jeremy's aristocratic face, pinched in a look of haughty amusement. "Meanwhile, you are colluding to nominate my farm for historical prescrvation status?"

"I'm not colluding on anything. I happen to think Winsome could be a quaint little town of some significance, if—"

"If?" She was shouting, and she willed herself to take a deep breath. Jeremy had a right to his own opinions. She realized she felt betrayed by her new chef, a thought that was unsettling. She barely knew him, at least the grown-up version, and she certainly had no right to control his extracurricular activities. But she did expect a degree of loyalty as his employer, and the fact that he would be part of a movement affecting her farm without so much as a mention...well, that she felt she had a right to be upset about.

"Did you know that Lenora and the Historical Society members want to nominate my farm for preservation?"

Jeremy's eyes darted from the white, heavily stocked shelves to the door behind Megan, as though he was planning his escape. The room smelled heavily of garlic and cumin. "Yes," he said finally.

"And have you been advocating for that too?"

"Yes."

Hands clenched by her side, short fingernails digging into soft palms, Megan said, "Why?"

"Because it's right for Winsome."

"Right for Winsome, or right for you?"

"I have no idea what you're talking about. You are obviously stressed and not in control of yourself." He used a placating tone that only increased Megan's ire.

"Oh, I am in complete control," Megan said slowly, understanding dawning. "You're using me and the café."

"What on earth for?"

"To get a sense of the market in Winsome. To determine what works food-wise. To build a following." She met his gaze, despising the arrogant smirk on his face. "You never intended to stay at the café. All that stuff about wanting to do something good? BS. You want to invest in Winsome, yes—with your own restaurant. And only after you use the café as a guinea pig and raise the town's status through the Historical Society."

Jeremy stared at her, that smirk still on his face—the confident smirk Megan remembered from high school. The one girls lusted over. The pantry was tight, a six-by-eight space lined on two sides with white metal shelves. Tight—and warm. Jeremy took a step toward her, his eyes bright, his shoulders squared. When he was inches from her, he looked down and shook his head slowly, back and forth.

He said, "So what?"

"So what? *So what?*" Megan closed her eyes. "You really haven't changed, have you? Winsome isn't some crappy town you can come into, remake to suit your needs, and then walk away from, counting the cash as you leave. Winsome is home to these people. To me." She opened her eyes. "This café and the farm? Right now, it's my *life.*"

Jeremy leaned in, his face inches from hers. "Megan—"

She placed her hands on his chest to push him away when the pantry door opened.

A surprised voice said, "Megan?"

Megan froze, hands on Jeremy's chest, Jeremy's face inches above her own. She took a step back, away from Jeremy, all too aware of how this looked.

"Denver," she said.

"I need to talk to you," he said coolly. "When you're *finished.*"

"We were just..."

But Denver was already gone.

"Back to the party, then?" Jeremy asked, that smirk still on his face.

"We're not finished with this discussion."

Jeremy smiled. "I should hope not."

Twenty-Five

Back in the café, Denver stood, arms crossed, watching the festivities from a distance. When he saw Megan, he walked briskly toward her.

"Can we talk outside? I only need a bit of your time." He wouldn't meet her gaze.

Megan nodded, aware of eyes on the two of them. She passed Bibi, who seemed deep in conversation with Merry again, but who nevertheless watched her walk to the front entrance.

Out on Canal Street, Megan said, "Back there with Jeremy, it wasn't...it wasn't what it looked like."

"And what did it look like, exactly?"

Denver's hair was damp, and his auburn waves hung in his eyes. Two days' worth of shadow defined his strong jaw. He'd been outside, and the bronze skin on his face and arms held a reddish sheen. His eyes looked wounded. Wounded and angry. Megan had the urge to kiss him—or slap him. She wasn't sure which.

"You know exactly what I mean," she said. "Jeremy is my chef, and we had an argument."

"An argument? Is that what you call it here in the States?"

Megan closed her eyes. When she opened them again, Denver's expression had softened. She was sure it had looked bad in there—but what happened to trust? She was meeting him halfway; he could do the same for her.

She said, "What do you need, Denver?"

Denver pulled a piece of lined paper out of the pocket of his khakis. "Take a look at this."

It was a note, scribbled in the awkward, backwards slant of someone rusty at writing. "Need to go. Take care of Sarge," Megan read aloud. The note was signed simply "Brick." She looked up a Denver, who looked worried.

"This will look bad," he said.

"You need to tell King."

Denver's expression tightened. "He'll think the worst."

"Denver, one person is dead and another in critical condition. Things like that don't happen in Winsome. If he's innocent, he needs to cooperate with the police. Porter's a hothead—I saw that for myself."

Denver glanced at her sharply. "When?"

"Last week. The day before the farmers market." She looked away, realizing how foolish her actions were. "At his home."

"You went to his house alone?"

Megan frowned. "If he's innocent, why would that concern you?"

Denver sighed. He glanced across the street to the canal beyond and Megan followed his stare. A pair of teenage girls were walking along the canal path. Identical haircuts, both dressed in black yoga pants and tank tops. One turned, said something to the other, and laughed. The sun shone down, haloing them in golden light.

"He's unpredictable. I wouldn't want to see ye get hurt, is all. He wouldna mean anything by it, mind ye, but, well...he's got some problems. But then, ye know that."

Megan shook her head. Out of the corner of her eye, she saw the crowd in the café shifting, people shaking hands, saying their goodbyes. Soon they would be moving toward the front door, herd-like. The party was winding down. She needed to get back inside, and she said so to Denver.

"I need your help," Denver said. "I can watch Sarge, sure, but Porter...he's got no one. If you see him, if he contacts you, will you let me know? Don't deal with him yourself, Megan. I want to talk to him before he goes and does something stupid. I will convince him to go to King."

Megan studied Denver's face, looking, perhaps, for some sign that he knew more than he was sharing. She saw only a sincere desire to help someone else.

She nodded. "But only if you agree to share that note with the police."

Denver nodded his assent. Hands in his pockets, broad shoulders slumped, he started to walk away. Megan reached out and grabbed his arm.

"In there, it really was nothing. It's important to me that you understand that."

Denver's eyes met hers, his gaze intense. "Aye, I hear you. But I know what I saw. I've been around enough to know heat when I feel it, and that in there—" he motioned toward the café "—that was heat. You might think it was nothing, Meg. It may have even been an argument to you, but I'm not sure that man in there would agree."

"You're being ridiculous. Any heat you felt was anger."

"Don't forget about the dog on Tuesday, lassie," he said, as though she hadn't spoken. "He's ready for a home. And Porter. If you spot Brian, don't go near him. Call me."

Megan didn't hear from Porter, but she did hear back from the bank that was foreclosing upon the Marshalls' property. It was a small, local branch run by loquacious local people. It only took a few minutes of chummy banter to learn that it was the appraiser who was charged with responsibility for taking pictures, and only a few more minutes to find out the name of that appraiser. Megan hoped the appraiser could tell her who had taken the pictures of the Marshall house. She was pretty sure she knew. But she needed confirmation.

"Samantha Ginger," said the foreclosure manager. "Call her if you're looking for a good appraiser. She's freelance. We love her work."

Megan stepped out back, into the alley behind the store, and called the appraiser. Samantha Ginger was less friendly but no less talkative than her counterparts at the bank. She was happy to share with Megan her thoughts about the photographer who'd taken those pictures. "Brian Porter. You're looking for a reference? Don't ask me for one, that's for sure. That boy hasn't responded to a single call in days. And I have five properties needing pictures. *Five.*"

"When was the last time Brian Porter turned something in?"

Samantha told her: the day after Simon was murdered.

At nine o'clock that evening, Megan pulled a check from her pocket and handed it to Jeremy. "Your pay for today and yesterday, plus two weeks' severance."

He looked at her blankly. "What's this for?"

"Your services are no longer needed at the café."

They had just put away the last of the dishes, and he and Clover were getting ready to leave. Clover, her wide eyes tired and puffy, glanced at Megan with surprise, but she didn't say anything.

"You're making a mistake, Megan," Jeremy said. "You need me."

When Megan didn't respond, the chef slammed his hand down on the counter. He picked up his white uniform, scowled, and said, "Merry was right about you. You'll never make a go of this place. You're just like your father."

Megan watched him leave. His words stung, but she wasn't about to let him get to her. She had other things on her mind.

"What was that about?"

"He hadn't been completely honest."

"About?"

"He was using us to plan his own restaurant. And he is one of the folks planning to nominate the farm for historic preservation."

Clover chewed on her bottom lip. "But isn't that a good thing?"

"Maybe for the rest of Winsome. For us, right now, it would be another thing holding us back." She looked around the empty store, her eyes falling on the copper-topped tables, their surface still bright and hopeful. "And we have more pressing problems. Like a café without a chef."

"I can do it," Clover said. She smiled. "I make a mean grilled cheese."

Megan had been the recipient of one of Clover's grilled cheeses. It was certainly mean, but not in the way Clover meant. "I...uh...was thinking of someone with some training."

"Hmm." Clover leaned against the door. She stretched her hands over her head, baring her belly, and twisted back and forth, stretching. "I know," she said suddenly. "Alvaro."

"The cook from the commune?"

Clover nodded, her face alight with excitement. "He's back in the area. Want me to call him?"

Megan hated to dampen Clover's enthusiasm, but she was pretty sure Alvaro, the cook Clover and Clay spoke highly of, wasn't the type of cook the café needed.

But the longer she hesitated, the more Clover's face fell, until finally Megan said, "Fine. Call him. See if he can come by tomorrow for an interview."

Clover clapped. "You will love Alvaro. He makes the best jalapeno cornbread I have ever tasted. And chitins that melt in your mouth."

"Cornbread, okay. Chitins? I don't think so."

"Never say never. Bet you'd never thought you'd be a farmer."

The girl had a point. Never say never.

Megan arrived home to find Bibi in the kitchen. She was stewing prunes and reading a large-print copy of Agatha Christie's *And Then There Were None*.

"Studying how to solve a murder?" Megan asked. She leaned

down to kiss her grandmother's cheek, Sadie lapping at her heels.

"You must admit, there are similarities," Bibi said, smiling. "Winsome may not be an island, but someone here seems determined to lessen our numbers."

"Perhaps." Megan pulled some cheese out of the refrigerator and sawed off a few pieces of Bibi's home-baked sourdough bread. She sliced a tomato, added some mustard, and sat at the table to share her sandwich with Sadie, who preferred the cheese to the bread. "So tell me, what did you learn today? I saw you chatting up the café's guests."

"I learned that my granddaughter has an admirer." Bibi turned and looked at Megan knowingly. "That Dr. Finn is a handsome man. Don't go for the other one. I don't much care for him."

"The other one?"

"The chef."

"Oh, him." Megan picked at her sandwich, appetite suddenly gone. "I let him go."

"Did he get fresh with you?" Bibi looked alarmed.

Megan laughed. "No, Bibi. I overheard your conversation with Merry—"

"Yes, about that—your eavesdropping skills are wanting, Meg. Please don't take up a career as a private investigator or try to join the FBI. You're as subtle as a politician at a fundraising event."

"Gee, thanks."

"I'm your grandmother. It's my duty to help you make good choices."

"Anyway," Megan said, amused, "what did you learn?"

Bibi poured her prunes into a bowl, pulled a spoon from the drawer, and took her spot at the table. "Old body, old bowels," she said. "And those fancy food things at the café—which looked absolutely beautiful, Megan—didn't help."

"Merry, Bibi."

Bibi waved her hand. "I'm getting to that. I learned that your aunt is helping the Historical Society." Bibi scowled. "Beyond that, I didn't learn much more than what we knew before. There are a group of folks who want to see Winsome listed as a Pennsylvania historic district. They think this farm should be the first property nominated because Lenora found all that stuff about Washington, and she and Simon were working on that paper."

"Simon? I thought he and his mother didn't get along."

"They are—were, I guess—competitive sorts, true, but Roger told me Simon helped with the research. I was surprised too. Caused a fight between Simon and Lenora in the end."

"A fight?" Megan recalled that Lenora had told her multiple people helped with that research. She wondered if it was only the two of them—and what the fight was about.

"Not sure what about, and not sure it matters," Bibi continued. "Lenora was focused on her article. It was Simon's idea to introduce the historical preservation ordinance. Roger said Lenora agreed to back Simon's idea, but she cut him out of the paper. Wanted the glory for herself."

"True maternal love." As soon as she said it, Megan regretted the words. But it was too late. Bibi looked at her sharply.

"Being a mother doesn't make you any less human, with all the defects any person put on this Earth by the good Lord would have. Lenora's passion in life has always been her research and her teaching. When that university let her go, she was devastated. I don't have a great deal of respect for her, you know that as well as anyone, but I understand the need to feel useful."

Was she also talking about herself? Megan watched her grandmother slice the prunes with a knife and fork and pop a piece into her mouth. Somehow she even made stewed prunes look appealing. I need to give her more to do around here, Megan thought. Make sure she feels needed.

"Well," Megan said, standing. "Both researchers have been targeted by someone. Who else besides us wouldn't want that historic preservation ordinance to go through?"

"Or that article to be published," Bibi said.

"Good point. I guess we know why Simon was so interested in this house. Knowing what he and his mother found out meant he knew what a gem it would be for the Historical Society."

"That's the funny thing. Roger didn't know anything about Simon trying to buy this house, and he's knee-deep in the Society too. Does all those reenactments, dressing up like a Patriot and traipsing around town like he's back in the 1700s." The look on her face told Megan exactly what she thought about grown men traipsing about town in Colonial costumes. "He's going to one Saturday, in fact."

Hmm, Megan thought. She wondered who else would be there. "So we know the Duvalls were competing over research on the house and that Lenora had cut Simon out of the paper. We know Simon tried to buy the house after you offered it to Sarah. And now Brian Porter is missing." She told her grandmother about Brian's note—leaving out the details about the pantry closet and Denver's obsession with the younger man.

"Brian is a troubled boy," Bibi said. "Steer clear of him, Megan."

"How do you know him?"

"His parents lived in Winsome for a while, tenants in the Marshall house. When they moved, they left Brian with his grandmother. Good woman, but a pussycat. Couldn't control the boy." Bibi finished the last bite of prunes, wiped her mouth with a linen napkin, and placed her fork and knife in the bowl. "His father was a tyrant. Preferred the belt to talking, if you know what I mean. Eddie and I hired him here a few times, before he went into the armed services. Eddie thought he could help. Didn't do much good, I'm afraid."

Megan thought of the rage-filled, drunken man she'd visited last week. "Do you think he's capable of murder?"

Bibi looked thoughtful. "Sometimes, a person who is hurting that much can't see through their own pain to recognize another's."

"But what about a motive?"

Bibi smiled. "I think most people are capable, Meg. Under the right circumstances. A mother protecting her child, a husband avenging his wife...not too hard to imagine any of us doing that. But those motives make sense to most people. When reasons for killing get muddy, when perceptions are based in paranoia or a twisted view of reality, well, that is another story. One person's 'motive' may not make sense to normal people. That could be Brian." Bibi looked at Megan with tired, sad eyes. "If Brian thought the Duvalls did something to him, even if it's not a motive we can understand, he may have acted on his feelings."

A soldier. A trained killer. Megan thought about that foreclosure photograph, the date stamped at the bottom. She remembered Brian at the farmers market with his camera, and she wondered. But what about Denver...what about his insistence that Porter was like him, once upon a time?

"What do you know about Dr. Finn?" Megan asked.

"I know he's what you young people call a catch."

Megan and her grandmother both burst out laughing. "How about a short-term cooking position at the café?" Megan asked. "Just until I fill Jeremy's spot?"

Bibi glanced at Megan. "I can't make all those sophisticated dishes."

"You can make a soup and a big salad, and maybe we can offer paninis. Clover and I can help you. It'll only be for a day or two. Clay can hold down the farm with the help of the students.'"

"I guess I can do that," Bibi said. She smiled. She placed her dish in the dishwasher and then stood tall to kiss her granddaughter.

Megan swore Bibi walked more briskly on her way to bed.

Twenty-Six

Alvaro Hernandez was a five-foot-eight package of iron will, unpopular opinions, and Sharpei-like wrinkles, but he could make basic ingredients sing. His interview consisted of ten minutes of questioning, most of which he answered with salty brusqueness, preferring one-word answers when he could get away with it, followed by a cooking demonstration. It was after the lunch crowd—all nine people—had left, and only the few stragglers who still sat at the copper-topped tables drinking coffee and reading a paper got to sample his culinary delights.

With Bibi acting as his reluctant sous chef and a delighted Clover hovering nearby, Alvaro chopped and seared and baked his way through the interview.

"Here," he said unceremoniously, placing a plate in front of her. Megan saw what looked like corn tortillas stuffed with something, a green sauce on top, and a small salad of Washington Acres Farm vegetables and strips of jicama.

Megan looked down. "Can you tell me what it is?"

"Lunch."

Behind him, Bibi stood with her arms crossed over her chest, blocking the "Winsome" in her pale pink "Everyone wins in Winsome" shirt. Clover, a look of utter adoration stamped on her face, waited anxiously for Megan to take a bite.

Megan lifted fork and knife, cut into the corn tortillas, and placed the concoction in her mouth. She was hit with a symphony of flavors—smoky chicken, musky cheese, citrusy cilantro, earthy black beans, and sweet mango. The salad was a crisp, refreshing counterpoint to the heavier folded enchiladas.

"What do you think?" Clover asked.

Megan held the plate out, offering tastes to Clover and Bibi.

"Just like when I was young," Clover exclaimed to Alvaro.

"Not bad," Bibi said. "Needs more salt."

The truth was, it was delicious. Not only was the dish simple and tasty, but it highlighted the food from the farm, which is exactly what she wanted.

"What else can you make?" Megan asked.

"I can make anything," Alvaro said, chin raised high. "You tell me what you want to serve and I make it." His white hair contrasted sharply with the muddy tones of his skin. His mouth was set in a firm, unforgiving line, but his eyes danced with intelligence and energy. He was, indeed, a man of contrasts—just like his dish.

"Well, I'll have more of this, for starters."

Ned Carter and Tony Weiss were seated at the long table, sipping coffee and sharing one copy of *The Wall Street Journal*. Ned looked up and caught Megan's eye. "Sure smells good," he said.

"Want a plate?"

Ned nodded. So did Tony.

"Two more, Alvaro."

"He's hired?" Clover asked.

Megan glanced at her grandmother, who had begun cleaning up the kitchen.

"If you want the job, Alvaro, it's yours. But you may need some help, and I'm hoping Bonnie here will come in a few days a week."

Alvaro grunted what sounded like consent.

Bibi looked up from her washing. "If you need help, I can be here," her grandmother said. "As long as it doesn't interfere with Bridge. Or *Days of Our Lives*."

Denver was due at the farm with Gunther by three. Megan almost called him to reschedule—or cancel—but then she pictured that poor dog living in a cage after already having had such a rough life. Plus, she hated to admit it, but she'd feel better about Bibi being here alone if they had a more effective watchdog. She loved Sadie with all her heart, but Cujo she was not.

The day was as bright as the Egyptian sun. Megan wore a sleeveless, button-down Coolmax blouse and shorts. Instead of feeling oppressive, the unrelenting sun felt freeing. There were no shadows on such a luminous day.

She'd started weeding the flower garden, using a hoe to gently pull the tiny weeds from between the wild flowers. While she worked, she thought of the article she'd read about this Saturday's reenactment. They were holding it at the same church where the farmers market was held. In fact, it was to start directly after this week's market, and there was going to be an organizational meeting this evening at Otto Vance's brewery—open to the public.

Megan was almost finished in the flower garden when Denver arrived, Gunther beside him on a short lead. The dog looked resplendent, nothing like the sad creature she'd seen at the clinic. His white fur had been washed and brushed until it gleamed. His eyes were clear, his gait energetic. He even looked a bit heavier, his ribs no longer protruding like the frame of an old canoe.

"Wow," Megan said, wiping her hands on the back of her shorts. She pushed a stray dark hair from her eyes with the back of one hand, hoping she didn't look too much of a mess. "He looks like a different dog."

"Aye, it's a wonder what a wee bit of sound nutrition and a good scrubbin' can do for a dog."

And some love and nurturing, Megan thought. She squatted down in front of Gunther and allowed him to sniff her hand. He contemplated her for a moment, ears back, before that great tail started wagging back and forth, tentatively at first, and then with more gusto.

"He remembers you," Denver said. "And he likes you. Here, take his lead. Let's walk him around the perimeter of the property a few times. Get him used to the place." Denver looked around. "And we can let Sadie out afterwards. They can get acquainted once he's better situated."

"She's not a territorial dog," Megan said. "I think they'll be fine."

"One male and one female?" Denver smiled. "Aye, they'll be fine. Eventually. These Polish Tatra dogs are good with people and other animals. Their instinct is to protect but not attack—unless provoked."

The trio walked in companionable silence, Gunther intent on exploring his new surroundings.

"About yesterday," Megan began. "There really wasn't anything—"

Denver shook his head. "You have no explaining to do. It was not my business. And if you say it was an argument, then I believe you."

"It was nothing."

"Then it was nothing. And I'm sorry for making a deal about it. I felt...well, I overreacted."

Megan smiled. "It's okay."

At the hill, by the edge of the forest that marked the edge of their property, Gunther pulled, intent on something deep in the woods.

"Pull him back sternly," Denver said. "You must establish the boundaries."

Megan tugged. Denver shook his head.

"Like this." He walked around the back of her and placed his hands on hers, his stomach pressed against her back. With his right hand, he pulled sharply. "No," he said. The dog pulled harder, nearly dragging both of them with him into the trees.

"Is that how it's done?" Megan asked, laughing.

"Yeah, well, he's a stubborn bugger. It may take more than a leisurely walk around this gentleman's farm to get him to stay."

"Gentleman's farm?"

Denver disengaged, relinquishing the leash back to Megan. "What work is going on here, I ask you? All I see are some damn happy chickens, a hippie farm manager, a few teenage miscreants, and a pretty lassie with mud streaked across her forehead." He took his thumb, licked it, and wiped it across her face, rubbing gently at the offending dirt. "There, that's better now."

"Is it?"

"The truth is, you look damn pretty even with some dirt on your forehead."

"Pretty enough to kiss?"

Denver pressed his lips against hers. She submitted, leaning in to his embrace. A low whine from Gunther made her spring back.

Denver laughed. "Jealous already, are you, pup?"

Megan looked down at Gunther, who was staring intently at Denver, ears back.

"He's protecting you, but he wouldn't hurt a fly. That's what we want—guard behavior. Next, we'll let him meet Sadie, Bonnie, and everyone else at the farm. I won't leave until you feel comfortable with him."

Megan leaned over to pat the dog, the feel of Denver's lips a ghost on her skin.

"And if I need help later?"

"We can talk about that over dinner tonight."

Megan was about to agree, but then she remembered the reenactment meeting. "I have somewhere I need to be. But only for a short time." She explained her interest in scoping out the reenactment enthusiasts. "I have a feeling the Historical Society is at the root of Simon's murder. Maybe tonight will give me some clues as to what's going on."

"I'll go too, if you don't mind the company. I always wanted to dress like a Tory. Maybe now I'll have my chance."

Twenty-Seven

By five o'clock that evening, Gunther and Sadie were the best of friends, just as Denver had predicted. Bibi had been taken with the dog's sweet personality and had let him in the house with a stern, "You'd better behave or you'll live in the barn." The dog looked at her knowingly, wagged his tail, and then proceeded to steal a roll of toilet paper from the bathroom.

"Give me that," Megan said, taking the roll and picking up the shreds of paper on the floor. Sadie looked on innocently, clearly letting Megan know that she would never do such a thing. "Yeah, well, you'll *both* find yourselves in the barn with the goats if you're not careful. You know how Bibi can be about the house."

They pranced off together, in search of more trouble.

Megan headed to her bedroom. She stared at the interior of her closet, feeling hopeless. After Mick died, she didn't care much about what she wore, preferring plain suits for work and jeans and her vintage blouses. At the farm, the need for fashion was even less; neither the goats nor the chickens much cared whether she wore Marc Jacobs or Target. Tonight she found herself caring.

Finally, she pulled a vintage sixties sundress out of the back of the closet. It was made of pale yellow cotton and inset with small applique flowers, also pale yellow. Simple, comfortable—and not jeans. She slipped on sandals, ran a comb through her hair, and dabbed some lip gloss on her lips.

"Okay, don't blow it," she said to her reflection in the mirror.

When she got downstairs, she heard voices coming from the living room. As she neared the wide doorway into the room, she was surprised to see her Aunt Sarah's reflection in the mirror over the sideboard.

Sarah was perched on the edge of the couch, her eyes on someone—Bibi—who must have been sitting cattycorner to her. Sarah wore a long multicolored skirt, a black tank top, and a red silk shawl wrapped around her shoulders. Her hair was braided again and the braid was coiled around her head like a snake. Megan paused outside the door, listening.

"I'm involved for one reason and one reason only," she was saying. "Megan."

"You're siding with Lenora against Megan...for Megan?"

Megan couldn't see Bibi, but she assumed her grandmother was sitting on the loveseat, which sat up against the wall next to the piano. The same furniture still graced much of the house that had graced it when Megan was growing up. It wasn't so much that Bibi loved the furniture, or that it held sentimental worth. Rather, Bonnie Birch was frugal. If something worked just fine—like the drawers full of Winsome novelty clothes—why mess with it?

"I'm not siding against Megan, Bonnie. I'm your eyes and ears in that group. Why do you think I'm here?"

"To ruin my granddaughter's life yet again?"

"You're being dramatic."

It was unlike Bibi to be vindictive, and Megan was sure Sarah knew that. More softly, so that Megan had to strain to hear, Sarah said, "They want me in that group because they like the idea of having a mystery author amongst their ranks. When Simon and his mother got this notion up their arses to go after the farm, I decided to take them up on the invitation. I have no interest in owning this farm, nor do I want to see it made into a tourist attraction. Unless that's what Megan wants."

Megan pressed herself against the wall, mindful of her grandmother's warning that she was a horrible eavesdropper. She wanted to know more about the Historical Society, but also about

Sarah, about her career, her choices...and her connection with her mother. Maybe she'd learn something. She didn't think she'd have the courage to ask herself. Not just yet.

"Megan wants this to be a thriving organic farm. She wants to make a go of that café, to do something good for Winsome. She doesn't want to get caught up in local politics."

"I'm not sure that evil can be avoided."

"Perhaps not. But if you hadn't told Simon the farm was for sale, this never would have happened."

"Is that what you think?" Sarah said, her voice raised. "That I told Simon to get in there and make a bid for your *home*?"

"What else could I think? No one knew I'd offered the farm to you except for you, and you were never one for thinking about other people's feelings, Sarah."

Sarah rose, her face pinched with anger. Megan hurried down the hall, away from the living room, in an attempt to escape being seen. She never heard Sarah's reply.

Denver picked her up at fifteen minutes before seven. Megan was waiting in the kitchen, still trying to avoid her aunt, and went outside to meet him. Denver's hair was neatly combed back from his smoothly shaven face. He wore European-cut suit pants and a button-down blue shirt with the sleeves rolled up. Both hugged the hard angles of his body. He smiled when he saw Megan, crinkling the corners of his vibrant blue eyes. She blushed.

"How's the wee pup, then?" he asked her while they got into the Toyota.

"Making trouble with Sadie."

"You have him in the house?"

"Of course."

Denver shook his head. "The whole idea of a dog like Gunther is to let him roam so he can protect the farm—and you."

"Someone might steal him, or he might run away." Megan shrugged. "He doesn't know the boundaries yet."

"You could keep him with the goats or in the barn. He'll alert you to trouble."

Megan smiled. She appreciated his concern. "He's where he should be—with Bibi."

Denver didn't argue further. He started his vehicle, which had been cleaned, smelling now like Pine-Sol rather than wet dog, and pulled out of her driveway. The brewery was only a few miles from the farm, and they arrived shortly after the meeting had begun.

Denver led Megan around to the back of the brewery. She was surprised by the size of the crowd. Dozens of men and adolescent boys, plus a few women—including Merry—had collected to discuss the dress rehearsal and Saturday's event. Roger Becker, wearing street clothes and a tricorne, was addressing the group. He explained times, rules and costume requirements, pausing only to answer a few questions.

"Tell me again why we're here?" Denver whispered. "Ye want a bloke who likes to dress up?"

Megan smiled. "I'm simply curious. Someone wanted the Duvalls dead for a reason. I'm convinced it has something to do with Lenora's research and the article she was writing."

Roger Becker stopped talking and stared back toward Megan and Denver. "Do you have a question, Megan?"

Megan felt the heat rise to her face. "No."

"Okay then." Roger continued talking, but he kept a stern eye on them.

The lights in the brewery were dimmed and Megan couldn't get a good look at faces from the rear of the restaurant. She thought she saw Neil Dorfman slumped on a bar stool toward the front, and next to him sat Oliver Craft, the local cheesemaker, nursing a beer. Ned Carter was standing by the front, near Roger, looking bored.

"Other questions?" Roger asked.

A smallish woman with long red hair and a beaked nose stood and raised her hand. "When do we get our roles?"

Dave Dorfman emerged from the shadow of the bar. "Remember, this is not battle specific. Because it's simply a commemorative event—a generic battle—you can wear what you want. We won't be assigning roles."

The woman sat, looking disappointed.

Dave fell back into the shadows. It was then that Megan saw he was sitting with his wife, Amelia, a woman she'd met a few times at the nursery or in the local grocery aisles. Amelia, a well-dressed, plush woman in her mid-forties, was staring at Dave in a way that was anything but loving. He turned to her and whispered something. She scowled.

"Not wedded bliss?" Denver whispered in Megan's ear. He placed his hand on the bare skin of her back, sending a jolt down her spine.

"Apparently not. A tiff, perhaps?"

"Or someone doesn't like being dragged to reenactment events." Denver's hand dipped lower.

Roger Becker closed the meeting. Everyone clapped. A minute later, Becker was by their side.

"Dr. Finn," he said heartily. "Will you be joining us Saturday?"

Amusement glinted in Denver's crooked smile. "Oh, no, Roger. It's the lassie who wants a go at this. She'd like to be a Patriot soldier."

Roger looked confused. "She's a woman."

"Ta, I can see that plainly enough."

Megan dug her elbow subtly into Denver's side.

"Is she planning to masquerade as a man? We have heard that women did that, at least during the Civil War."

"I dinna think so." To Megan, he said, "Is that what you were planning, Meg?"

"You could ask me directly, Roger. I am sitting right here."

Roger shifted uncomfortably. Clearly, he had not had a woman request something as controversial as portraying a soldier during one of their reenactments. Part of Megan wanted to continue the charade in order to irk him. She settled for honesty.

"I won't be dressing up, Roger. Just showing up as plain old me."

Roger still looked uncomfortable. He nodded, and with a sympathetic look at Denver, walked away.

Denver laughed when he was gone. "I think you should dress up if only to spite him."

"Nah," Megan said, her stare fixed on a group standing in the corner. "These folks live for these events. I don't want to take anything away from them, fair or not." She nodded toward the cluster of gathered townspeople. "Interesting lot. Wonder what they're whispering about."

Denver followed her gaze. Merry was at the center, surrounded by Roger, both Dorfmans and Oliver Craft. Dave's wife was still at the bar, staring into her drink.

"You, Meg," Denver said, eyes dark. "I'm pretty sure they're talking about you."

Twenty-Eight

Denver had made reservations at The Wildflower Inn, a restaurant two towns over, but after the visit to the brewery, he and Megan decided to do something more casual: take-out at Denver's house. Megan didn't want to be far from Bibi, and neither was sure how Gunther would do his first night at the house. Leaving Bibi to handle whatever came up didn't sound right. So they ordered Chinese food from Ming's, the only Asian shop in town, and settled in his living room to eat.

"Why 'Denver'?" Megan asked between bites. She'd ordered broccoli with garlic sauce and was picking out the flaccid slices of celery that had been added to the dish. "How did you get the nickname?"

Denver placed his plate on his lap and sat back on the couch. The lights in the room were dim. He'd put the dogs outside, and the interior was quiet such that Megan could hear the gentle hum of the refrigerator in the next room.

"That's a long story."

"I'm all ears."

"Are ye now?" He gave her a wistful smile. "I told you that I had a lot in common with Porter."

"Were you in the army?"

"No, not like that. But I didn't much care for rules." He paused, eyes far away. "My father liked the drink more than he liked work—or us. My Aunt Eloise—you met her, remember?—she decided to take charge after my fourth tussle with the local police.

She'd been living in the States. Paid for me to go to boarding school in Colorado—Denver. I was sixteen. My friends back home, even my sister, they started calling me Denver." He shrugged, smiled. "It stuck."

"That must have been hard. Being that far from home."

"Aye, but so was living with my da."

"Your mom? Sister? Were they okay with your father?"

"My sister is older than me. She's the one who told Eloise what was going on. My father mostly ignored my sister. It was me and my ma who took the brunt of it. He never hit my mother, but in retrospect, he mentally abused her." He rubbed his forearm absentmindedly. "He was a hard man."

Megan nodded, trying to reconcile the man she knew now with the troubled kid he once was.

"Don't concern yourself with it, Megan. I'm not that person anymore. You asked a question and I told you. But I was given opportunities to better myself, and I took them. Eventually. Not everyone is fortunate enough to have people who care, or the wherewithal to grab opportunity by the bullocks when it comes knocking."

He was thinking of Porter, she knew. And this explained the blind spot he had when it came to Brick. "Did your mom leave...eventually?"

"She didn't have the chance. My folks were killed in a car accident when I was seventeen."

"I'm sorry."

Denver shrugged. Clearly he believed he had come to terms with his past long ago. It was only Megan who was struggling. She believed his youth and all its vagaries had a huge effect on the man he was today, in the same way her own childhood had affected her.

Denver took a bite of Kung Pao chicken and washed it down with a gulp of lager. "Ta. But truly, I've moved on. Animals saved me, quite literally. The school in Denver had horses. I found myself sneaking down to the barn so often the school finally offered me a job." He grinned. "Paid me with hours in the saddle. I had an instructor there who taught me the ropes. He was a big brother figure. I learned a lot."

Megan tried to picture a young, roguish Dr. Finn sneaking down to the stables to visit the horses. It wasn't hard to visualize.

"And the school inspired you to become a veterinarian?"

Denver nodded. "For a long time, it's the only thing I wanted." He looked at her, blue eyes piercing her own. "Now, maybe I want more."

Megan felt her face grow hot—again. She put her fork down and stood. "If you're finished, I'll put the plates in the kitchen—"

Denver placed his own plate on the coffee table. Then he took hers and put it down too. He grabbed her wrists gently and pulled her toward him. She felt the hardness of his torso, the gentle pressure of strong fingers. He kissed her. "I can clean up," he whispered, and kissed her again. "Will ye stay, Megan?" he asked, his voice husky.

She wanted to. Every part of her—even the deepest recesses of her heart, where loyalty to Mick overran any other desires—wanted to succumb to this man. But she shook her head and pulled back reluctantly.

"I can't."

"Is it Bonnie?"

It would be easy to say yes, that it was Bonnie. And her grandmother *was* part of it. She didn't want to leave her alone, not with a new dog and a killer lurking in Winsome. But it was more than that. She'd only ever known Mick, and to have another man now, even someone like Denver...she just wasn't ready.

"It's okay," Denver said. He pushed the hair back from Megan's face and leaned in for another kiss, this one sweeter, less urgent. "You don't owe me an explanation. In time, if it's right, you will know."

Megan nodded, grateful for his understanding. "I should go."

"Aye, it's late."

But despite the hour, neither was quick to move.

Twenty-Nine

"Megan, you can't wear that." Bibi looked at Megan's plain blue skirt and vintage peasant blouse and wrinkled her nose. "It's not that it's not pretty—it is—but it says 'soft flower,' not 'tough cookie.' You want the people on the Board to see you as a threat."

"What do you suggest I wear?" Megan asked, a smile playing on the edges of her lips. Her grandmother was standing before her in a pale green floral knit dress, her white church shoes, and a tan cloth handbag with "Happiness is Winsome" embroidered in white stitching across the front. Not exactly a power suit.

"Something you would have worn at the law firm. A suit with shoulder pads. A tie."

Megan laughed. They were in her bedroom and Bibi was sitting on the edge of the bed, ready to leave for the Historical Society fundraiser. "No one wears shoulder pads or ties anymore." Megan sorted through her closet. She finally found what she was looking for: a slim charcoal pantsuit with a fitted jacket. It had been her go-to outfit for court hearings. Serious, but feminine. She held it up.

"Better?"

"Better." Bibi looked down at her own frilly dress. "And I know what you're thinking, Meg. But what I wear doesn't matter. They already think of me as a harmless old lady. Let them underestimate me. It works to our advantage."

Gunther was laying at her grandmother's feet, his head resting on her shoe. The dog picked his head up and Bibi patted it fondly. "Change and we'll go."

"About the other day. I know Sarah was here." Megan didn't want to admit that she'd eavesdropped on their conversation, but if Sarah was going to be there tonight, it would be best to have things out in the open.

"You heard us." Her grandmother smiled. "I saw you, of course. Maybe *you* should be reading more Agatha Christie."

Megan laughed, embarrassed and relieved at the same time. "Did Sarah tell Simon about the offer?"

A shadow passed across her grandmother's face. Outside, thunder rumbled in the distance, promising late spring storms. "She says no."

"Do you believe her?"

After a moment, Bibi nodded. "Sarah is a lot of things, but I have never known her to be an outright liar. Unless she is part of some grand conspiracy, what gain would she have in seeing Simon, or the Society, buy the farm?" Bibi's expression softened. "And I believe she feels genuinely bad about her part in your mother's departure. Someday, when you're ready, you should go talk to her."

When you're ready. Unknowingly, her grandmother had echoed Denver's message from the night before. Being with a new man. Forgiving her aunt. Forgiving her mother. Would she ever be ready?

Merry Chance lived in a massive square home with a mansard-style roof. The house was perched in the middle of a double lot on the edge of town, across from the farthest end of the canal walking path. White and black, broad and imposing, the building was a stark contrast to the rosy woman who lived within. A white picket fence marked the boundary of her rose gardens. Rain threatened, but for now, the scent of the roses, heady and fragrant, perfumed the humid air outside. For tonight's fundraiser, Merry had set up a grand tent attached to the back of the house, into the kitchen. Black and white-clad wait staff handed out flutes of champagne and passed around hors d'oeuvres on silver platters.

"Fancy dancy," Bibi whispered as they made their way to the entrance. She handed Neil Dorfman their tickets and said, "Better be good for a hundred and fifty dollars a head," under her breath.

"You paid that much? You don't even like the Historical Society."

"And miss all the action?" Bibi shook her head. "Just watch. You'll learn more about Winsome in the next three hours than you will the rest of the year."

Megan was about to tell her grandmother she wasn't sure she wanted to know that much about Winsome when Roger swung by and took Megan's arm. "Your table is over here," he said. He led them through the crowd congregating by the makeshift bar and over to a round table set for ten. "You get your pick of seats."

"Which ones are gold-plated?" Bibi asked.

Becker only smiled. "Money for the Society is for the good of all of us, Bonnie. Rising tides raise all boats."

"Yeah, yeah, Roger," Bibi said. "Or the swell wipes out everyone in its wake."

Roger's smile faded. "You ladies let me know if you need anything. There's champagne and wine at the bar, and staff are passing around Jeremy's wonderful creations."

Megan swallowed. "Jeremy's?"

"Oh, yes. Such a food artist, isn't he? He's catering the event." He must have seen the look of surprise on her face, because he said quickly, "We would have used the café, of course, but, well, you weren't up and running yet. Anyway, Merry booked him weeks ago."

Megan bristled—she'd had no idea he'd been moonlighting as a caterer. When the first tray came around, Megan saw mushroom tartlets and empanadas—the same items he'd prepared for the café's grand opening. So much for Merry's *normal* food. She glanced around the room, hoping to see Denver.

Disappointed, she asked her grandmother, who was already seated, whether she'd like a drink.

"Club soda."

Megan left to stand at the bar. The inside of the white tent was spacious, decorated with green plants in large ornate containers and hundreds of tiny lights. A photo of George Washington sat on an easel on one side of the tent. The tables were set with white linens, and on each was a bouquet of mixed white flowers in a crystal vase.

"It's like a damn wedding," someone whispered into her ear from behind. "Or a funeral."

Megan had to agree. She turned to find Dave Dorfman behind her. He was dressed for the occasion—his finest church suit, navy blue, vintage 1970—and his breath reeked of Scotch.

"It's quite something," Megan agreed. The line moved and she took a step forward, acutely aware of Dave's heavy breathing behind her.

"Neil did a great job of setting up."

Surprised, Megan said, "Neil did this?"

"With some help from me. I told Merry not to use all white. White, white, white...like a damn wedding."

Dave sounded as though he'd been celebrating a wedding most of the night. "I didn't realize you and Neil were this interested in history."

"We're into getting paid," Dave said. He pitched forward, his drink sloshing over the rim of his plastic glass. "Money's money."

Megan wasn't quite following Dave's intoxicated train of thought. No matter, it was her turn to order. She asked for champagne for herself, club soda for Bibi, and said goodbye to Dave.

"Yep," he said, already on to other thoughts.

Bibi wasn't at the table. The son of the local judge had been hired as the DJ, and he was blaring a Taylor Swift tune from a table in the corner of the tent. A small dance floor had been set up near the DJ's table. Megan's eyes scanned the tent for her grandmother. She spotted her two tables over, talking with an older woman Megan didn't recognize.

Before she could make her way over there, she felt a hand on her elbow. It was Roger again. "Megan, I didn't know you were interested in reenactments."

"Oh," Megan said, her mind spinning for some response. "I've been curious about them for some time."

"I was thinking about your desire to be a Patriot soldier. I think that can be arranged. What's one cross-gender soldier?" He smiled, his teeth biting down on his lower lip in a distinctly feline gesture. "And your house will be perfect for reenactments. That barn, that old house...perfect. We don't even need to wait for the preservation ordinance or the nomination. If you wanted to get started sooner—"

"Roger, I would absolutely love to, but I have—"

"She has a farm to run."

Megan looked up to see who her savior was. Jeremy was staring at her from a spot to her left. He was wearing his chef jacket, but he held a half-empty glass of champagne in one hand, a pen in the other.

"Isn't that right, Megan? No time for things like Revolutionary War reenactments and fun. It's all business, all the time."

Megan held his gaze. He was still angry and was baiting her—and she knew it. She summoned her brightest smile, bestowing it upon Jeremy, then Roger. "Oh, I don't know. Parties and fun sound just fine. Eventually. But I think you would both agree that it's best for Winsome if Washington Acres gets off the ground first."

"I'm sure that makes the most sense." Jeremy returned her smile. "What's best for the farm is best for Winsome."

"I'm glad we agree."

"You're a tough woman. And a hard worker." His eyes narrowed, not unkindly. "You'll need that resolve. That house has a whole history of women who have struggled to maintain it. Your grandmother and you are not alone."

Megan tilted her head questioningly.

"The original owner's husband deserted her, and she had to carry on alone." Jeremy's tone was flat, but his mouth never lost that hint of a smile. "Quite a legacy."

Elizabeth Caldbeck's husband? He deserted her? "What's behind your sudden interest in local history, Jeremy?" Megan asked.

"Jeremy is a history buff, aren't you?" Roger looked at Jeremy with such an earnest interest that Megan felt badly for participating in Jeremy's passive-aggressive game.

"I find the local lore fascinating."

Becker nearly glowed with admiration. "In fact, he's considering buying a piece of it himself."

Now Becker had Megan's attention. "Really?" She looked at Jeremy. "And where would that be?"

Jeremy's smile had disappeared. He glared at Roger.

Roger, a few drinks in and oblivious to Jeremy's anger, said, "Right next door to you, Megan. The old Marshall place. Isn't that right, Jeremy?"

But Jeremy had decided it was time to get back to work. He mumbled something and marched off in the direction of the kitchen.

"Busy man," Becker said when he was gone. He still seemed nonplussed over Jeremy's reaction. "Great ideas, though. He'll be good for Winsome."

"What kind of ideas?" Megan asked casually. The DJ had lowered the music and guests were starting to wander to their tables. Dinner would be served soon.

"He's thinking of making the old Marshall house into an inn, for starters. With your farm and his inn both preserved properties, they'll be part of the Winsome historical trail. Downtown—the buildings along Canal Street—would be next."

Megan's mind was busy processing this news in the context of all that had happened over the last few weeks. "How did he know my house had any historical significance?"

Becker shrugged. "Lenora, I would assume."

Lenora...or Simon? "Has he placed a bid yet, Roger?"

"Don't know. You'll have to ask him yourself."

Just then, Merry sauntered over, her blue dress swishing

around her knees. "Roger, it's almost time for speeches." She eyed Megan's suit and said, "Seats, Megan. We're about to get started. Perhaps you can collect Bonnie too."

"In a moment, Merry. Where are the restrooms?"

"We have port-o-johns outside," Becker said.

Merry waved her hand in the direction of the kitchen. "Don't be silly. There is a loo on the ground floor." To Becker, she said, "Come on. Everyone is anxious to get started."

Megan made her way to the back of the tent, through the opening, and into Merry's spacious and bustling kitchen. Rain had begun to pelt down on the thick white plastic and Megan wondered if the seams would hold.

Despite the storm outside, the kitchen was warm and dry and fragrant. Jeremy was there, barking orders at a young, uniformed assistant. When he saw Megan, he turned away quickly and continued his task.

Two others were waiting in line for the bathrooms: a woman she didn't recognize and Amelia Dorfman. Amelia, who had been engaged in conversation with the unknown woman, nodded cordially at Megan as she approached. Amelia was wearing a simple, well-cut black dress and a diamond pendant, and her hair was pulled back into a neat chignon. A sheer layer of makeup covered, but didn't hide, a generous sprinkling of freckles on her nose. She looked nice, and Megan told her so.

"Thank you," Amelia said. "You do as well."

Megan had only spoken with Dave's wife a few times since returning to Winsome. Unlike Dave, Amelia was not a Winsome native. Her family was from Philadelphia, but Amelia had lived in California before she and Dave got married. Megan found her hard to warm up to. While Amelia was polite enough, there was a steely reserve underneath the sophisticated clothes, one that seemed hard to penetrate.

"Enjoying the party?" Megan asked.

"Sure," Amelia said, but the pinched expression on her face said otherwise. She turned toward the bathroom door, letting

Megan know she didn't want to make small talk—or any talk.

Bob King, at the fundraiser alone because Clover refused to attend, joined the line.

Happy for a friendlier face, Megan turned to him. "How's Lenora?"

The bathroom door opened. The town postmaster came out and the unknown woman bolted inside.

"Not well."

"Will she make it?" Megan asked. She watched the postmaster walk through the kitchen and out into the tent.

"We don't know. Whoever stabbed her knew what he or she was doing. They went low on the back, straight through the ribs. Another fraction of an inch and they would have pierced her kidneys." King held Megan's gaze. "Instant death."

But Megan was thinking about what King said. Whoever did it knew what they were doing. A former soldier would know where to stab someone in order to kill them.

"So whoever did it meant to kill Lenora, not simply warn her?"

King shrugged. "Stabbing someone is not as easy as you would think. It takes knowledge and precision, especially if you only have one shot at it."

"And during the busy farmers market, whoever stabbed her would have wanted to act quickly. Get in, get out. Multiple wounds would have meant time for Lenora to struggle and scream."

King nodded, looking impressed. "I guess they teach you something useful in law school?"

"Nah, learned it on television."

King laughed. A door opened, the woman came out, and Amelia entered the bathroom.

King said, "See you, Susan." The woman, a petite blond in her thirties, smiled and passed into the kitchen.

"Who is that?" Megan asked.

"Susan Dorfman, Neil and Dave's younger sister."

Interesting, Megan thought. "I've never met her."

"She's been kind of a hermit since her business closed. I dated her, once upon a time. Can you imagine?" King smiled, and when he did so, his whole face changed. "No more waiting. I'm going to head to the john outside, rain or no rain." He nodded to Megan before also disappearing into the kitchen.

Megan considered Susan, the Dorfmans' sister. It had been Simon who closed her business down—Aunt Sarah had mentioned that. She didn't have time to dwell. A few seconds later, from behind her, a woman's voice said, "I didn't expect to see you here."

Megan turned to find herself face to face with Eloise Kent, Denver's aunt. This evening, she wore a floor-length red sequined dress. Flashy but elegant. It was a dress meant to make a statement, and after Megan's conversation with Eloise's nephew, Megan knew Eloise Kent was a woman not afraid to make a statement.

"Eloise." Megan flashed a welcoming smile. "So nice to see you again. I was hoping to see Denver here."

Eloise smiled back. She had tiny white teeth and extra-long canines. "I'm afraid he couldn't make it. I asked about you. He said you've been busy getting the café going."

"The café and the farm, yes. It's been a lot of work, but we're almost there."

"Interesting choice for a lawyer. Farming, that is. And didn't you work for a big firm in Chicago? A very prestigious firm?"

She waited, obviously hoping Megan would explain why in the world she would leave the glamorous big city for a pit stop like Winsome. Amelia took that moment to step out of the restroom, and Megan seized her opportunity to use the facilities.

As Megan was entering the bathroom, Eloise's arm shot out and she touched Megan above the elbow. "Denver hasn't had an easy life," she said quietly.

Megan froze, muscles tensed. "I know, he told me."

Eloise let go. She gave Megan a sad, apologetic smile. "I don't want my nephew to be a casualty when you tire of small-town life, as you will inevitably do."

"You don't even know me."

"I know Eddie."

"Is Denver like *his* father?"

Eloise shook her head. "Of course not. He's nothing like him."

"We're not all replicas of our parents."

Megan closed the door of the restroom. She put her back against the wood and breathed. She wasn't like her father—or her mother. She was in Winsome to stay. For better or worse.

Thirty

"This should be entertaining," Bibi whispered when Megan sat down next to her. "A lot of hot air, if you ask me."

Merry was up at the podium, welcoming everyone to her home. Near her, the other members of the Historical Society were standing in a row, waiting for their turn to speak.

"Where were you?"

"Restroom," Megan whispered back. "Miss anything good?"

"Not yet, and you probably won't, even if you left for the evening." Bibi took a sip of club soda, her gaze on Merry. "I did learn something interesting."

"Oh? What was that?"

"Simon had his eye on more than a historical district."

"More properties?"

Bibi's eyes opened wide. "Merry told me he wanted to open a museum."

"In Winsome?"

Bibi nodded. Her eyes still on the rambling Merry, she said, "Members of the Historical Society were split. Some thought it was a good idea; others felt like it would be a waste of tax dollars. Even Lenora couldn't understand his insistence. She thought Simon should have been content with the historical designations and questioned what they would display in a museum. It was clear Merry agreed." One white eyebrow shot up. "I think Merry did it."

"You don't like Merry."

Merry looked sharply at Megan and Bibi. "Well, that may be

true." Bibi glanced at Merry demurely, hands folded on the table, the picture of respect. They both focused their attention on the makeshift stage.

"And now for Roger, who will explain our plans to enact a preservation ordinance," Merry was saying. "Just the first step in putting Winsome on the map."

"You ass!" rang from the back of the tent. "How *could* you?"

All heads turned to the voice, and then back toward Roger. Merry motioned for silence. A woman was crying. The tent door opened and three people ran outside, one after the other—Amelia Dorfman, her husband Dave, and Neil Dorfman. It had been Amelia's voice that they'd heard. The blond woman who Megan had met outside the restroom was watching them, open-mouthed, her face twisted with grief.

"That's another thing I heard," Bibi said, making less effort to whisper in the din of voices that ensued after the trio ran out. "Dave wants to sell the business."

"To Neil?"

"I'm sure Neil would like it, but he doesn't have that kind of money. He's been working odd jobs all around Winsome, trying to make ends meet. How could he afford it?"

Megan thought about the rest of the barn renovations, the house plans she'd designed for the future. "Dave hasn't mentioned a word to me."

Bibi shrugged. "Guess he's yet to convince the missus."

Curious, Megan thought. But she didn't have time to ask any more questions. A young police officer in uniform stepped into the tent, closing the door against what was now a harsh wind and driving rain. All discussion stopped. He looked at the crowd, clearly uncomfortable. Finally, his eyes settled on King. He nodded at King and the police chief rose.

They conferred by the tent door for a few minutes, and then King went back to the table and grabbed his belongings. He glanced in the direction of Megan's table, his expression unreadable.

Up front, Roger was clapping his hands for attention.

But Megan, attuned to watching witnesses and reading their lips and body language, had caught enough of the conversation between the two officers to know what was going on.

They'd found Brian Porter.

More precisely, Denver had found him.

Megan and Bibi returned home after eleven, exhausted and edgy. Megan had wanted to leave after King did. She was going to call Denver and find out what was going on. But Bibi had talked her out of it, convincing her that it would look suspicious if she left—and with this much attention focused on the farm right now, she needed to be at the fundraiser.

Acknowledging her grandmother's wisdom, she'd stayed.

"That gentleman friend of yours," Bibi said on the way home, "Dr. Finn. Know how he got Gunther?"

"As a matter of fact, I do," Megan had said.

"He pushed Sauer into a wall, held him like that until the man agreed to give up the dog."

"Okay, *that* I didn't know."

"Then he called King and admitted to what he'd done."

"That part sounds like Denver."

Bibi stared at her, her face half-shadowed, half-illuminated by the streetlamps outside. It was still raining. Waves of water lapped over the road, and Megan was on the lookout for washed-out blacktop, especially in the low-lying areas. It wouldn't do to get stuck in overflow, not with her grandmother in the truck.

"Sauer probably deserved it, but a man's got to keep hold of his temper."

"Weren't you the one who said you'd wanted to kill my father on multiple occasions?"

"Wanting and doing are two very different things."

Megan turned onto Canal Street. The streetlights appeared to be soft, glowing orbs, their light seeping into the blackness of this rainy night. Megan passed the café, checking to be sure there'd been no more mischief, and then kept driving in the direction of the farm. She felt a headache creeping along the edges of her skull. Her suit, damp from the run to the car, felt binding and burdensome on her shoulders.

"What are you trying to say? Are you concerned about Denver?"

"No, I'm not. I just thought you should know. A man with a strong sense of justice is a good thing—when balanced with perspective."

Megan glanced at her grandmother. "Do you know Eloise Kent?"

"I do."

"Do you know her well?"

"She and her husband stay to themselves, mostly. I know she's Dr. Finn's aunt. I know her husband is a big-shot broker in New York City. Commutes back and forth. Makes a lot of money."

"Do you know why she doesn't seem to like my father?"

Bibi took a long time to answer. She busied herself digging through her handbag for a tissue. After wiping the tissue along her brow, mopping up the raindrops still trickling down her scalp, she said, "They may have dated at one point or another."

"May have or did?"

"Did."

"I thought Eloise came to Winsome with her husband."

"Your father has not always been known for his good judgment."

"Was that one of the times you wanted to kill him?"

Bibi smiled. "It may have been."

So Megan's father had an affair—nonsexual, according to Bibi—with Denver's aunt. Just dandy, Megan thought now as she was giving Sadie and Sadie's new best friend Gunther some water. And Denver is willing to play the hero using a little extra physical persuasion. She wasn't surprised. Underneath that kind exterior and those shockingly blue eyes lurked a certain lone wolf danger that Megan found attractive. It'd been the same with Mick.

With Bibi in her bedroom and the dogs attended to, Megan dialed Denver's number. It was late, she knew, but she was hoping he'd still be awake.

He didn't answer. After two tries, she clicked off her phone and went to bed.

Thirty-One

Megan spent the morning working side by side with Clay: mulching potatoes, weeding the crops, and picking an assortment of vegetables for the café. She and Alvaro had worked up a simple five-item menu, and she was picking, weighing, and bagging accordingly. They'd decided every day they would offer a soup, a salad, a sandwich with homemade potato chips, a hamburger or bean burger platter, and a blue plate special. The actual item would vary daily, depending on ingredients from the farm and Alvaro's whim that day. Alvaro had what he needed for today; she was picking for tomorrow.

Around eleven, she decided to head to the café. She and Clay loaded the cooler onto the truck while Sadie and Gunther played and wrestled around them. Gunther had some puppy left in him. Although a huge dog, he still had growing to do—physically and mentally. Megan thought about what Bibi told her the night before, and while part of her didn't like that Denver had resorted to physical confrontation, she'd seen the Gunther he'd saved. For someone like Denver, someone who viewed his role as protector and healer, that would be a lot to handle. And he'd helped Carl Sauer find the puppy in the first place...added guilt. Added rage.

"I heard you had some excitement at the Society's fundraiser last night," Clay said as they loaded the last of the goods into the truck. He wiped his long, slender hands on his jeans and smiled playfully. "Sorry I missed it."

"Where were you? I knew Clover wasn't going, but I thought maybe I'd see you there."

Clay waved his hand. "Nah, too expensive. Anyway, I got lost in a project." He raised his eyebrows. "Surprised you went."

"Keeping an eye on the enemy."

Clay laughed. He glanced at Sadie and Gunther, then beyond them at the barn. "Clover told me they nabbed Porter last night. The police are charging him with the break-in. More charges could be pending."

Megan wasn't surprised. She said, "Denver found him."

"Where?"

"He didn't tell me." Megan looked beyond the barn toward the old Marshall house. "But I have a hunch."

Denver still hadn't called her back. His receptionist said he hadn't gone into the vet clinic today and had cancelled all his non-urgent appointments. It was unlike him to ignore her phone calls. It was even more unlike him to ignore his patients.

Stomach tight, she pulled up on Canal and was surprised to find the road packed with parked cars, not a spot to be found. She drove the length of the street, past The Book Shelf, and into the alley behind the shops. Once parked, she pulled the first of the coolers out of the back and went in through the kitchen. She stopped when she heard the voices coming from the next room.

She left the cooler on a stainless steel work station and went into the shop, through the entrance by the lunch counter. The place was packed. Clover had a line of six or seven people in the store, but a majority of patrons were in the café. Some were seated at the lunch counter, eating and reading newspapers; the rest were crowded around the long farmhouse table, talking and laughing and—best of all—eating. And in the middle of it were Alvaro and her grandmother, bickering over something.

"That's too many meat selections," Bibi was saying. "And you need pie. I can make pie."

"Do you want pie?" Alvaro shouted at the men seated around the farmhouse table.

"Absolutely," one said. The rest nodded their agreement.

"Fine, old woman," Alvaro muttered. "Make pie."

"And all that meat?"

"Do you care if there's meat in the soup *and* the panini?" Alvaro shouted.

"No," was Oliver Craft's reply.

But Ernie Doyle shook his head. "The missus says I can only have meat twice a week."

"And you're a damn wuss for listening to her," Craft responded.

"Oliver Craft, be nice in my store," Bibi said, quieting the men. "Or I will tell Dolly you've been sneaking ice cream again. Though she'll figure it out when she sees your cholesterol levels."

Everyone laughed. Bibi turned to Megan. "You're here with Alvaro's vegetables for tomorrow?" When Megan nodded, she said, "Thank goodness. Maybe now this old man can stop his crabbing and get back to work."

The café customers lingered until nearly one o'clock. They seemed to like the combination of fresh food, unlimited coffee, and a place to stretch and talk. Most of them were local shopkeepers or workers from the town center. Megan didn't much care if they stayed to chat. They paid their bills and seemed happy with the service—despite the bickering of her cook and grandmother—and that, right now, mattered most. Given the shadow death had cast over Winsome, she'd take happy wherever she could find it.

Megan helped clean up the kitchen and restock the shelves. She couldn't afford another employee, but if today was any indication, she might need to hire a waitperson sooner rather than later.

"I can handle it." Clover pulled down her micro-mini so that it covered the top of her thigh. "It's not like I have anything else to do with Bobby this preoccupied."

"Anything new with Simon's murder?"

Clover nodded. She was counting cash and moving some of the bigger bills so Megan could move them to the safe in the kitchen.

"Porter?"

"Sounds that way. So horrible." Clover stopped counting, her long fuchsia nails still picking through twenties. "I don't know that I could have been as brave as you and Bonnie, remaining at the farm."

"Clover, do you know anything about reenactors?"

Clover shrugged, her slender shoulders, slightly hunched under normal circumstances, bent nearly double. "I know some people who are into it."

"Besides Simon?"

"Yes. Roger, Oliver, Merry, the Dorfmans, especially Neil—"

"They really love the historical elements?"

"Maybe. They've been doing it since I can remember. Roger's a cache hunter too. He and Neil have been looking for goods for years."

"A cache hunter?"

"You know, digging around for remnants of the Revolutionary War days. Artifacts." Clover shrugged. "Back then, I guess people hid their valuables by burying them. These guys go out with metal detectors and shovels. It's their thing."

"Have they ever found anything?"

Clover smiled, showing off her glacier-white teeth. "Damn if I know. It's all part of the thrill, I guess."

Megan nodded, curious. "Do you know Amelia Dorfman?" Megan asked, recalling their brief conversation and the scene at the fundraiser.

Clover had finished counting the money and was clipping together stacks of twenties. She handed the stash to Megan. "She attends the Pilates class I teach. Why?"

"A good student?"

Clover considered the question. "Kind of whiny."

"Whiny about what?"

"The Pilates position, her abs, the kids, Dave's job, the weather. You name it."

"She sounds like a peach."

The front door opened and three teens walked in. "More like a lemon," Clover said quietly. "Poor Dave."

"Then why would she care if Dave sells his business? If she hates Winsome that dramatically, that could be the ticket to freedom she's been looking for."

Clover smiled, flashing those teeth again. "When I was in the commune, it seemed like the people who complained the most stayed the longest. Only they couldn't see a way out of their predicament, even when it hit them in the face. That's Amelia."

Megan nodded. Sometimes Clover showed wisdom well beyond her years.

"Let's finish up here. I have more work to do at the farm." Megan glanced back at the lunch counter, where Bibi was doing a crossword puzzle with Alvaro, the two of them arguing over every clue. "Apparently Bibi will be here for a while. Give her a holler if you need something while I'm gone. She has her car and can see herself home."

Only Megan got sidetracked before she reached the farm. Her phone rang while she was driving, but it was Eloise, not Denver.

"Megan, could you come down to the stable?"

"Why?"

"Denver."

"Is he asking for me?"

"No, but...I think seeing you would be good. Can you stop by?"

Surprised by Eloise's show of vulnerability, Megan agreed to drive over. At the 7-Eleven, she made a U-turn and headed toward Eloise's farm.

Eloise met her at the truck wearing a yellow tunic, black leggings, and no makeup. She looked older than she had before—

older and worried.

"Thank you," she said. "I wouldn't have called you, but...You see, Denver and I don't really communicate. I've never known how to talk to children, not having my own."

"He's not a child anymore."

Eloise gave her a wan smile. "Maybe not in your eyes."

"Where is he?"

Eloise led her toward the stable. She stopped before going inside. "Riding. Just go through the barn to the paddock on the other side." She turned away. Megan stopped her.

"Is it Porter?"

Eloise shrugged. "He didn't say, and I didn't ask."

Megan found Denver outside with the Quarter horse. He was brushing the horse with long, gentle strokes, muttering comforting things to him under his breath. Both man and horse were sweat-covered.

"Eloise called you?"

He spoke with his back to her. Megan took in his long torso, long legs, strong arms, and the windswept auburn waves of his hair. His spine was rigid, his shoulders tense. "She needn't have," he continued. "I'm fine."

"I've been calling you since yesterday. First you didn't show at the fundraiser, then I heard about Porter." She stopped, seeing the way his shoulders tensed. "Are you okay?"

Denver turned around. His right eye was black, and scrapes marred one cheek. "Aye, I'm fine."

"You fought with Porter?"

He looked indignant. "Just a bit of an argument." Denver rubbed his jaw. "He clocked me a few times while under the influence of alcohol." He gave her a crooked smile. "A lot of alcohol."

She could imagine. "So why are you hiding out here?"

"I'm hardly hiding. I just need to think about a few things."

"I called the clinic. Your receptionist said you canceled your appointments."

Denver walked closer. Dark hollows encircled his eyes; his face was unshaved. He bit his bottom lip, contemplating his words. Finally, he said, "I was wrong about Porter. And it could have put you in danger."

"But it didn't."

"It could have."

Megan took his hand, which felt as tense as his shoulders looked. "I'm a big girl, Denver. Any choices I made were my own. What happened?"

The horse whinnied, his full lips back, and square, yellow teeth protruding. He stomped on the floor and brayed again. It was an overcast day. Brooding clouds marred a smoky blue sky. Denver looked up. "More rain soon," he said. "The horses are acting off, and back home the dogs were wound."

"Denver, tell me what happened."

With one foot on the split-rail fence and the other on the ground, he said, "Porter called me to check on Sarge. I convinced him to tell me where he was." Denver turned toward Megan. "I went there, tried to get him to give himself up and get help. He ran at me." Denver rubbed his face, gave Megan a crooked smile. "Clocked me good."

"I'm sure you were able to handle him."

"I let him take some of his anger out on me. Then he settled down. Not so different than a dog that's been cornered."

"Poor kid."

"Porter wasn't in control of himself. He felt threatened. I should have known better." He shook his head. "Worse, he was staying near you, in that abandoned house."

"I knew it! The Marshall house. When I heard he'd been found, it made sense. The footprints. He'd been there before."

"He could have hurt you."

"But he didn't." Megan stood on tiptoe and placed a hand on either side of Denver's face, forcing the veterinarian to look her in the eyes. "Stop blaming yourself, please. Anyway, I don't think he killed Simon."

Denver's eyes narrowed. "You said it yourself. He's a trained soldier."

"But he has no motive. I think Simon's death and Lenora's attack were done by the same person. And that person doesn't want Lenora's paper to come out. But even more critical—Porter was there the day of the murder. For a legitimate reason." She told him what she'd found: the photograph of the house, the confirmation that Porter had been subcontracted to take those photos. "Don't you see? Porter saw something he shouldn't have. That would have made someone very nervous, maybe nervous enough to threaten Porter in order to keep him quiet."

"Leaving the flask at your store?"

Megan nodded. "Porter's gate. Sarge."

Denver's eyes widened. "You think someone hit Sarge intentionally?"

"No, but I do think someone came by that night and left the gate open. Maybe to warn Porter. Maybe to threaten him. Maybe to get to Porter without the dog there to protect him. Porter knows something, but he's scared to say anything. And with one person dead and another in the hospital, I can't say I blame him."

They looked at one another, each lost in their own thoughts. Finally, Denver said, "But there is another angle, Meg. One that could damn Porter."

Megan had already thought of it. "That photo also puts him near the scene of the crime. Which means he may have had the opportunity to kill Simon."

"That's right."

Megan thought about the police investigation that first night after Simon's death. She remembered the crime scene investigator making a cast of a footprint—and the police having a suspect other than her or Bonnie relatively early on. Porter's shoe? It could have tied him to the scene.

She said, "Porter's not stupid. Why would he publish the photo with a time and date stamp if he'd recently killed someone? Even if he had acted impulsively and didn't know what to do? Plus, there's the little matter of the flask. What if Porter had been taking pictures at the house and he left it there? The killer saw him—or saw someone—and went up to the house to look around."

Denver's brow creased. "If they were from Winsome, they'd know whose flask it was."

"Exactly. What they think Porter saw would determine their next move. Threats or visits. Leaving the flask at my store could have been a warning to Porter—or a test. 'Open your mouth and you're a dead man.' Porter could have gone back to the store to see if anything else had been planted."

"Hence, the broken window." Denver patted the horse, leaving his hand on the animal's neck. "I'll give you one thing, Megs, you have an active imagination. Your logic makes sense, though."

"I don't want to see an innocent man go to jail. And if it wasn't Porter, as we suspect, then whoever killed Simon and attacked Lenora is still out there."

"You don't trust the police to find the culprit?" Denver asked the question without hinting at his own feelings on the subject.

"This isn't about trusting King and his crew. It's about protecting my own." She smiled up at Denver. "Everyone needs support now and then." She brightened. "Come with me to the reenactment on Saturday."

"Are ye going to dress up, then?" Denver grinned.

"No." She smiled, ignoring her baser instincts. "I'm going to find a killer."

Thirty-Two

The first Saturday in June started out with promise. Megan woke before five to the sound of her rooster crowing and the feeling of early sun warming her face. She turned over, hugging the pillow close to her chest, and thought about the day. She had a lot to do, but more than that, she was hoping to gain some insight into Lenora's paper and this society of Revolutionary War buffs in Winsome—and any tie they might have to Simon's death. First things first, she needed to get to the farmers market with a fresh crop of produce.

She climbed out of bed. Smells of cinnamon and yeast wafted from downstairs. Bibi couldn't bake for the café in their kitchen because of the dogs and health regulations, but she was making a fresh batch of goodies to share with her worst critic and new friend, Alvaro. Megan smiled. Her grandmother certainly seemed happier now that she was working at the café. She didn't go every day, and she didn't always stay for long, but she had extra kick in her step on the days she did go.

After a quick shower, Megan slipped into jeans and a plaid sleeveless button-down. She kept her hair down, pulling it behind her ears, and rubbed some sunscreen onto her skin. Sadie, who'd been downstairs with Bibi, was now hovering in the doorway, tail wagging. There was no sign of Gunther.

Downstairs, Megan found Clay already at the kitchen table, digging into a large plate of strawberry strudel. The flaky, buttery pastry looked amazing and Megan agreed to have a piece.

"Pizza farm," Bibi said. She was slicing the strudel with a sharp knife, a "Winsome Weighs In" apron around her waist. Gunther sat on one side of her, Sadie on the other. The begging crew. "That's what we should do next. Clay and I were just discussing it."

"Last I heard, pizza doesn't grow in the ground."

"Ha ha," Clay said with his mouth full. He swallowed, took a long sip of coffee, and added, "Friday or Saturday nights we could make pizza using ingredients from the farm. All you need is a pizza oven."

"All I need, huh?" Megan sat down at the table, coffee and strudel in front of her. "That and thousands of dollars."

"Clay priced it out. He can build it himself, cheaply. We can put some picnic tables in the old part of the barn, get the Dorfmans to do some work in there. I think it's a lovely idea."

"If the Dorfmans are still in business." Bibi and Clay looked as though someone had just poked a hole in their favorite balloon. "But I love the idea. Maybe that can be the next phase, after the farm and café are more stable."

Clay nodded. He stood, washed his dishes in the sink, and said, "I'll be outside loading the truck."

"Will you be going, Bibi?" Megan asked.

Her grandmother shook her head sheepishly. "Sarah invited me to play Bridge at her place. I'm going there for a few hours, and then I told Alvaro I would help him with the lunch rush."

Lunch rush. Megan liked the sound of those words.

"So I'll meet you back here after the reenactment?"

"You're definitely going?" Bibi asked.

Megan nodded. "Denver's meeting me there."

Bibi didn't respond, but she didn't need to. The look on her face said she thought it was a foolish idea.

The farmers market had a strange, timid joviality, as though visitors were afraid to be *too* happy to attend after last week's attack on Lenora. Winsome officers were stationed in the parking lot, and

Megan recognized one of King's baby-faced men in jeans and a t-shirt by the soap maker's stand. A plainclothes detective? Perhaps King was not convinced that Porter was the killer.

Despite the presence of the police, the morning's sales were brisk. By noon, they had sold out of most vegetables and what remained would be packaged up and sent to the café for use with the next day's menu. Megan had made small Washington Acres recipe cards showcasing the day's fresh picks, and they were out of the sugar snap pea and homemade hummus card as well as the one for spinach and white bean gnocchi.

"Not a bad day," Clay said. He was putting away boxes and packing the truck while Megan reconciled the cashbox.

Next to them, Merry was placing the last of her rosebushes in the nursery van. Neil Dorfman, red hair matted with sweat, was pulling down her tent. He wrestled it into the case, then stood by the van, huffing and puffing. "Anything else?"

"No, that should do it, Neil."

Neil turned to Clay. "Need help?"

"We're okay. Hey, I have a question to ask you." While Clay worked, he laid out his plans for the pizza oven. "But the barn will need a bathroom and some work in the old portion. Megan isn't sold on the possibility, but I'd like to know what it would cost." Clay glanced at Megan. "If that's okay with the boss."

"Sure," Megan said. "But I'm not making any promises."

"No promises. Understood." Clay turned back to Neil. "What do you think?"

"I'll take a look next time I'm at the farm. Dave and I still have a few things to finish up."

Across the parking lot, Megan could see a group gathering. Most of the men were dressed in the uniform of an enlisted man, although she could see a few brightly colored officers' uniforms sprinkled throughout.

"Participating today?" Megan asked Neil.

"I guess." He frowned. "If the weather holds out."

Megan looked up. Gray skies—again. So much for promise.

"Should be clear until tonight."

"Hope it's not a soaker. The river is already at capacity and most of the area streams are at saturated. Remember the floods of 1991?"

Megan nodded. It was the year the roads around the farm washed out. She had been young, but when you're cooped up on your property for days on end, the memory sticks.

Clay was on the ground, pulling up a particularly stubborn tent stake. "I checked the creek by the farm this morning and it had already overflowed its banks by several feet."

"You didn't mention anything to me," Megan said, alarmed. While an overflowing creek wouldn't impact the crops, it could flood the road leading to the farm again—which would make transporting goods difficult.

"Figured you have enough on your mind. Nothing we can do about it in any case." Reading her thoughts, he said, "There's the road down by the Marshall house if you really get stuck."

"Well, if you folks don't need me, I guess I'll go look for my brother." Neil tipped his Yankees cap toward Megan. "Later."

"Will this be it for the reenactment?" Megan asked, looking at the slender crowd.

Neil laughed. "Lord, no. Half the town will be here. Weather holds up, you'll see. What else is there to do in Winsome?"

Neil had been right. By two, the church's grounds and lot were full. The Historical Society had set up a small registration tent for participants near the church entrance. The church had set up a refreshment area in the basement and was selling lemonade, cookies, and small cakes they were calling Johnnycake, even though Megan was quite sure the original Johnnycake contained neither chocolate chips nor vast amounts of sugar.

Adults and children were lining up behind a red rope set up along the sidewalk, watching the participants in costume as they huddled together by the church, talking. The participants were divided between Tories and Patriots, although the Patriots well outnumbered the Tories. Megan noticed Merry by the registration desk. She was dressed in period costume, complete with a white cap and apron, and was giggling at something Oliver Craft was saying. Megan headed in that direction.

She was intercepted by Roger, who, Megan had to admit, looked surprisingly dashing in his officer's uniform.

"Megan! You decided to join us after all." He squinted at her jeans and plaid shirt. "Where's your costume?"

"You wouldn't let her dress as a soldier, and our Megan isn't suited to traditional women's work."

Megan smiled, turning to see Denver behind her. To Becker's obvious disappointment, Denver was wearing jeans and a Nike t-shirt, not a British uniform.

"Well, Merry will handle your entrance fee. But next time, come dressed and be part of the festivities. The more the merrier." He smiled.

"I'm glad you came," Megan said to Denver once Roger had left.

A quick grasp of her hand was Denver's only answer. He pulled a ten out of his wallet and plopped it in front of Merry. "I'm taking this fine lady on a date, ye see. Nothing but the best for our Megan."

Megan elbowed him and he laughed. She liked the way he laughed, his eyes crinkled and his smile wide. Merry, however, didn't laugh—whether because one of the few eligible bachelors in Winsome was on a date with the town's only female farmer or because she thought they were making fun of the event, Megan wasn't sure.

Megan said quickly, "Where do we go?"

"Behind the red line."

"Tell me again why we're here," Denver said as they climbed over a section of red rope. They moved along the waiting crowd until they found a spot directly behind the rope, by a massive oak tree.

"We love history?" When Denver shook his head, she said,

"We're looking for clues. What do we have to lose?"

Denver scanned the parking lot, focusing on the participants chatting by another oak, their rifles by their sides. "A few perfectly respectable hours of the day."

"You don't like this stuff?"

"I like being with you."

Megan laughed. "Good answer. Maybe there's hope for you after all."

A whistle blew and one of the Patriots came by dressed in an officer's uniform. He asked everyone to stay behind the rope. "Things can get rough," he shouted. "Stay clear of the action."

What action, Megan was thinking, when suddenly a group of Tories came charging toward her. They turned at the last minute, chased by a smaller group of Patriots waving rifles. Shouts and cheers erupted from the crowd. One little boy, dressed in his own Patriot costume, hung from the red rope, his tiny legs swinging back and forth, until his father pulled him back.

The sky had darkened to the color of ripe plums, and surly clouds were moving in from the west. The wind had picked up too, lending an authentic air to the happenings before them.

"Won't be long before it's pouring again. They'd better move it along," Denver said.

Another group of Patriots came running through. Dave was "bleeding" from the arm, a soaked bandage wrapped loosely around his bicep.

"Merry must be playing nurse," Denver whispered. Megan laughed at the thought of Merry playing hospital with Dave. She could only imagine the frown on Amelia Dorfman's face if she saw that.

"You know, they asked to borrow Eloise's horses for this. I had to say no, of course. They would be terrified by all the noise and clamor."

And it was noisy. In addition to the excitement of the onlookers, fake gunshots rang out, accompanied by smoke and soldiers falling dramatically in all directions. In the rear of the parking lot, under the trees, someone had set up a cannon, and the roar of fake cannonballs being fired at intervals added another layer of clatter to the chaos. Every tree, every crevice near the church, was a potential hiding spot, with blue, brown, and red-clad soldiers whipping between them. It truly looked like a battle scene, and for a moment, Megan forgot where she was.

A flash of yellow on the far side of the church caught Megan's eye. She turned to say something to Denver, when a loud pop ensued, followed by a low, ominous roar. The yellow flickered red and orange. Someone shouted, "Fire!" and the crowds dispersed in every direction. Roger stood on the church steps. He screamed into a megaphone, demanding that everyone stay calm. It was no use. Panicked onlookers were running every which way.

Denver said, "Go to your car, Megan. I'll join you in a minute."

"Oh, no," she shouted. "We stay together."

She and Denver jogged past the church and toward the flames. Megan recognized the young officer who showed up at her house days earlier. He was standing within ten feet of the fire. "Stay back," he shouted. "There could be more explosives in there."

Denver said, "The flames are contained. Whoever set these explosives meant to scare, not kill." He looked around, his gaze falling on a shed in the back of the church. "Wait here."

The flames climbed and flickered their way out of an old carriage, placed at the church as a prop. Now that the threat of a massive explosion seemed past, a few onlookers drifted over. The young officer glanced at them. "Everyone, get back. Go to your cars and stay there. There could be bombs planted in other locations."

He had a point, Megan thought. Although there could also be explosives planted in cars. The church really looked like a war zone.

Denver was back a few seconds later with a long, coiled hose. "We need the hook-up."

"Over there." Megan pointed to the side of the church, near the entrance to the cellar.

"Megan, please go to your car," Denver said.

But Megan had already taken one end of the hose and was

busily unraveling it, pulling it straight. Denver shook his head and headed to the spigot. Megan could hear sirens in the distance. While the officer managed the crowd, which was newly emboldened by the containment of the fire to the wagon, Denver attached the hose to the spigot and turned the metal handle. Megan aimed the water at the fire, barely making a dent in the blaze.

Denver took the hose from her. He ventured closer to the flames, glancing overhead at low-hanging branches. The recent rain meant the trees were saturated and less of a threat, but she was sure Denver was thinking about the danger of open flames near old trees and an old church—a potentially disastrous combination.

Megan, unsure what to do with herself, spotted a little boy crying by the tree line. She ran over and knelt beside him.

"I can't find my daddy," he said. His tricorne was crooked, his t-shirt smudged with dirt. Megan recognized him as the little guy who'd been hanging from the rope, excited by the soldiers who were charging by. He must have gotten separated from his father when the crowds panicked.

"Wait with me," she said. "And don't worry. We'll find him."

In short order, the boy's father joined her, his face rash-red with worry. King and Denver walked over too. King's mouth pressed into a stern line.

The firefighters arrived to finish what Denver had started. Megan could see the young officer combing the tree line behind the blast, presumably looking for any other explosives. Rain began to fall. Cold, fat drops that did nothing to dispel the tension in the air.

The boy and his father reunited. The father thanked Megan before heading toward his car.

"Stay in the parking lot," King called. "I'd like to ask you and your son a few questions."

Megan, Denver, and King watched the pair walk away, hand in hand.

"Any idea who did this?" King asked.

"Not Porter," Denver said evenly. "You have the boy locked up."

King nodded, looking troubled—a good sign, in Megan's estimation. If the police weren't convinced they had their man, they'd keep looking, and clearly whoever was causing trouble in Winsome was still at it. Megan had to believe the explosion and the attacks were related.

King looked toward the carriage, now a twisted shell. "This explosion seems more of a statement than a targeted attack."

"Or a distraction," Denver said.

Distraction. Megan's mind flitted to the broken window at the store the night someone had been in her barn. What if she had been wrong? What if Porter had thrown that rock into her store to distract her from what was really happening?

King said, "A distraction from what?"

Denver shrugged. "While the police are tied up here, someone could be up to no good somewhere else."

King looked worried. Megan turned her attention from the police chief to the two officers bagging samples near the burned-out carriage. She was thankful no one was hurt.

This time.

Thirty-Three

The police had kept the remaining onlookers for questioning, allowing them to leave one at a time. Megan and Denver gave what little information they could and then departed, both thankful to be vacating the site. There had been too much violence as of late, and that burned-out carriage was a reminder that their little town wasn't *really* safe.

Denver wanted to stay with Megan, but she insisted he return to his own responsibilities. She'd be fine. Back at the farm, she fed the chickens, checked on the fields, and made sure the goats were warm and dry, longing for a sense of routine. The drizzle had continued on and off, but now lightning flashed in the distance. Gunther accompanied Megan on her rounds, an attentive and playful guardian. He was a smidgen too interested in the goats, and so Megan had to keep him outside of their pen. His white fur, difficult to keep clean on the driest, sunniest days, was painted with streaks of mud. He didn't seem to mind, but the furniture—and Bibi—certainly would.

Satisfied that the animals were faring well, Megan was heading back toward the house when she decided to take another look at the old house next door. If Jeremy was determined to make something out of it, maybe she'd beat him to the punch. The house was barely livable; surely she and Bibi could scape up the funds to buy it. It was too close to her property. She didn't like the idea of someone else's business right nearby, especially Jeremy's business.

The yard between the two properties had not been mowed, and the wet grass looked daunting, even with her muckers on. The drizzle was picking up. Megan thought about Porter holed up in the old building; she remembered the eerie feeling she'd gotten last time she visited. This was as far as she'd go today.

On her way back toward her house, something about the barn caught her eye. Since Simon's death and the subsequent intruder, she'd been careful with the barn. Everything had to be closed and locked, and Clay and the students knew that. Today, however, the rear door was unlatched on the outside: closed, but unlatched.

Her stomach clenched. *Not again.* She'd made sure these doors were closed and latched when she and Clay had left earlier, and the students hadn't been in today. She doubted Bibi would come down to the barn, and if she had, she would have used the front door. Megan pulled her phone out of her pocket and had it ready. She and Gunther made their way toward the rear door slowly, carefully. Megan's heart pounded into her throat. At the barn, she listened for movement or voices. Nothing. Gunther was sniffing the door, but his hackles weren't up. Taking that as a good sign, Megan opened the door slowly. Inside, nothing seemed out of place. She let out her breath. Gunther ran in ahead of her.

The back door led into a small utility porch. Beyond that was an old portion of the barn. Dark and musty, with a dirt floor and crumbling stone, it didn't get much use—and wouldn't, unless Clay had his way about the pizza ovens. Megan was walking through this section into the larger, newer portion when she noticed Gunther sniffing excitedly in the corner of the room.

"What is it, boy?"

At first, she didn't see anything. But as she got closer, she noticed that the dirt in one section near the wall was lighter, as though it had recently been disturbed. As though someone had been digging there. Her mind flashed to Simon's skull, bashed and bloody—and the shovel that had been used for something other than its intended purpose.

She thought about Denver's words at the reenactment: "*Or a distraction.*"

Had someone staged today's explosion? Certainly not Porter.

Everything appeared to revolve around Washington Acres. But why?

Megan dialed 911. Her fingers shook. Whatever was at Washington Acres, it was apparently worth killing for.

Not surprisingly, the police couldn't do much. Once on her property, they asked whether she was certain the digging had been done today and she wasn't. She *was* certain someone had opened the door, and calls to the high school students and Clay reassured her it hadn't been them, but other than that, she was clueless about the timing of the excavation. The old portion of the barn was generally ignored. She suggested the police contact the Dorfmans—perhaps they'd had reason to be in there.

The police agreed, searched the property, and took a few soil samples. Other than that, the uniformed officer in charge suggested she leave Gunther outside and call if she saw anything suspicious.

"Anything else, you mean?" she asked.

The officer shrugged. What could they do?

Back at the house, Megan called the café. Bibi had left a few minutes before and would be home soon, pulling up the driveway in her Subaru wagon. The rain was falling harder now, leaving more muddy pools of water in the courtyard between the house and barn and streaming from the new gutters. Megan remembered Dave's concern about flooding. She hoped the creek didn't overflow. She hoped her grandmother wouldn't have trouble getting home.

She was about to go look for Bibi when she heard her grandmother coming in through the porch.

"I heard the news," Bibi said as soon as she saw Megan. "Truly, I don't know what's come over this town."

"Did you have trouble getting here?"

"It's raining hard, but the roads were mostly clear." She scrutinized Megan's face, looking at her the way she would when Megan was younger, in the days after Charlotte left. "What's the matter, Meg?"

Megan told her about the barn.

Bibi's frowned. "So that explains it."

"Explains what?"

"They're digging for treasure."

"Treasure?"

"The cache hunters. They must think something is buried in the barn."

With dawning horror, Megan realized that made sense. She recalled that Roger Becker was a cache hunter. She was sure there were others—local men for whom cache hunting was simply a harmless hobby. Or had been—before it became a deadly pursuit. Her mind flitted to the glove in her goat's mouth that first fateful day, and the one left near Simon's dead body. She thought about the open gate on the goat enclosure, the cat in her kitchen, the light in the barn. If someone was looking for something in the barn, they'd be ghost-like residents, hiding in the shadows, biding their time. They may have even snuck up to the house, accidentally letting in Mutton Chops. The thought made her shudder. It all made sense.

Appalled, Megan said, "Would someone really kill over war trinkets?"

"Stranger things have happened," Bibi replied. "Believe me."

The rain didn't let up. By ten that night, the water pouring from the gutters had become torrents, and the yard and fields were a soggy mess. Megan brought both dogs inside, shutting the door against a howling, angry wind.

"Tornado watch," Bibi called from the parlor. "Until midnight."

Thunder boomed. Megan was regretting her decision to put off a generator for the farm because she'd used the funds to hardwire one for the café instead. If this kept up, she and Bibi would be in the dark.

Feeling edgy and wide awake, and with little else to occupy her time, Megan turned on her laptop and started searching. She began with the little she knew about the farm—the names of the prior owners, the location, even the coordinates of the farm's location, anything that might hint at a motive. She found nothing new. Frustrated, she sat back and stared into space, her eyes taking in everything in the kitchen and nothing at all.

She knew this kitchen like she'd known the ridges and plateaus of Mick's body, the curve of his smile, the laugh lines around his eyes. Since her mother left, and until Mick, Bibi had been her world. Bibi and the farm and everything in it.

Since her mother left...What had Jeremy said? The original owner's husband had abandoned his wife. Paul Caldbeck had abandoned Elizabeth Caldbeck? That certainly hadn't been part of the family legend. Megan did a search for Paul Caldbeck, but nothing definitive turned up. She tapped into the local library's online resources, broadening her search and adding various terms like "merchant" and "farmer." Nothing other than a reference to Paul's English roots, and a few references to his wife Elizabeth, the daughter of a wealthy lumber mill owner and a Patriot zealot. Her father had financed armies from Pennsylvania up through New York.

If Lenora was right and Washington had stayed at the farm, it would've meant Caldbeck was important to the Patriots. Megan found no references that said Caldbeck was a soldier—so his support may have been financial. But if Jeremy was right, Caldbeck had left his family to fend for themselves *after* the war was over. The period after the war was a dangerous one for many people. What would have led a man during the 1700s to leave his family, especially during a time of such turmoil?

Megan considered the look on Lenora's face when Megan had mentioned Caldbeck in passing during the farmers market. Perhaps Caldbeck *was* the Washington connection—but how?

He could have been sharing information with the Patriots. But then why would he desert his family? He'd be a hero.

Unless he was also sharing information with the Tories.

Caldbeck may have been a spy.

Megan included the word "desertion" in her search, and it didn't take her long to find what she was looking for. After the war, former loyalists often fled their properties out of fear of reprisal. She wondered: what if Washington had stayed here because he thought he was getting information from a sympathizer—someone who was, in fact, a loyalist? What if Paul Caldbeck had really been loyal to the Crown, and after the war, when the Patriots won, he'd fled? The Winsome area, heavy with farmers and others anxious to be rid of the British and British taxation, would have been a very inhospitable place for a Tory, especially a Tory spy.

And a rich Tory merchant? He may have buried his treasure somewhere the locals wouldn't find it. Somewhere like the barn.

But would it still be here all this time later? Megan remembered the painting at Aunt Sarah's house. Sarah had said Eddie found it at the farm. Was it original? If so, what else was here?

Megan laid her head on her arms. It felt like a stretch, but somehow Washington's visit to this farm and the attacks on the Duvalls were connected. Megan kept coming back to Caldbeck's desertion of his family. If Caldbeck left, it must have been because he was no longer welcome. Which likely meant he had been on the side of the British.

The house was silent except for the gentle snores of the two dogs at her feet and the occasional rumble of thunder outside. Megan's eyes were getting heavy, but she couldn't go to bed—not yet. There was something else, something she wasn't quite putting together. A dead zoning commissioner, a critically injured historian, and an explosion at the reenactment. If Bibi was right and this was related to cache hunting, it would have to be a hell of a cache. But a rich Tory merchant fleeing for his life might have left something quite valuable...silver, or even gold. Maybe enough to risk your freedom for.

Especially if you were desperate.

Megan thought about all of the people in Winsome who had

something to gain from finding a treasure like that. While everyone liked money, certainly, only one person had been working extra jobs to make ends meet. On a hunch, Megan started delving into Neil Dorfman's financial history. Years of legal research had given her access to databases the general public didn't know about. She rarely used them; she did tonight.

To her frustration, Neil came up clean. No criminal history that she could find, and almost no social media presence. At least based on her search, he was living the life he appeared to live: a hard-working bachelor with a limited social life and few assets.

There had to be *something,* maybe even something unsavory. A tree branch hit a kitchen window and Megan jumped. Her nerves were on edge. She started searching public court records, beginning with local files, working more to calm the jitters than because she actually hoped to find anything.

Nothing on Neil.

Her head hurt. A glance at the clock told her it was well after midnight. She was tired of chasing smoke.

Megan was about to close up for the night when she decided to try one more search. Knowing the idiosyncrasies of court clerks, she put in "N. Dorfman" and then simply "Dorfman," in case Neil had another official name.

To her surprise, she got a hit with "Dorfman"—only it wasn't for Neil Dorfman. It was for David John Dorfman. She skimmed the proceedings quickly. Dave Dorfman had been sued for failing to complete a construction job. The customers had paid up front; he never delivered. She kept searching and found two more suits against Dorfman, one for $8,000 (failure to deliver windows) and one for $13,657 (failure to complete a bathroom remodel). All were relatively recent.

Megan thought back to what she knew, shifting the puzzle pieces in her mind. What if Dave was the one in financial trouble, not Neil? He might have killed Simon over the cache. But if yesterday's explosion was a diversion, then he had an accomplice. Neil. Neil, in typical brotherly fashion, could have been trying to help his brother by making extra money and giving it to him, and by helping him cover up a murder—or two.

And then there was the scene with Amelia Dorfman—the public arguments, a well-heeled wife, and a bank account that couldn't afford a well-heeled wife. Dave Dorfman's life was unraveling. Gold and silver could be worth a lot, even sold on the black market. He could sell the business, have a new life. It all made more sense.

Megan wished she could pull Dave's credit score, but without his permission that was illegal. She could access property records, though, and a quick search told her what she needed to know: his house was listed as a short sale.

Gambling? Poor money management? Drugs? Did it matter? She still felt like she was missing something.

Lightning flashed outside, first in the distance and then closer, thunder following seconds later. Sadie was asleep, but the thunder startled Gunther, and he picked his head up, alert. Megan looked outside, but she saw only blackness and the unrelenting rain. She thought about making herself a cup of tea but decided against it. At some point, she'd need to sleep. Tomorrow would bring new challenges, including eroded fields and wind damage.

She settled back in her chair, thinking. Did she have enough to call King?

Yes. Better to look like an idiot and err on the side of safety. She dialed Clover's number, figuring King would be there. A sleepy-sounding Clover answered.

"Let me talk to Bobby."

"It's almost one," Clover said. "Is everything okay?"

"Yes, but I need to talk to Bobby."

"He's not here, Megan. The storms have everyone in a panic. The Sauers lost a roof, and Marshall Pond Road is completely flooded. Norm Kennedy got himself stuck in flood waters coming home from the brewery."

"Damn."

"Call Bobby's cell." Clover gave her the number.

Reluctant to call his personal cell when he was out dealing with true emergencies, Megan tried the station. She left a detailed message with the dispatcher and waited. King would call her back eventually.

When King rang, he sounded tired and irritable, but Megan forced herself to calmly lay out her theory about the Dorfmans.

King mumbled, "Dave had an alibi for Simon's murder and for the time of Lenora's attack."

"Was his alibi Neil, by any chance?"

King was silent.

"Look, I can't access Dave's credit scores or bank records, but you can. I saw enough online to know that Dave has financial issues, which can be a powerful motive for murder."

"Megan, you're basing all of this on an unproven assumption that there is treasure buried on your property."

"I know it sounds far-fetched at first, but if you really stop to consider it, it makes sense." Megan recounted what she'd pieced together about Elizabeth Caldbeck and her husband, Paul. "If Simon had shared his suspicion with Dave Dorfman, the temptation may have been too much."

"But murder—"

"Simon was killed with a shovel. I saw the crime scene, remember? It looked like an impulsive act, an act of passion. They argued first, and then Dave killed Simon."

King sighed. Megan was expecting more protests, but instead he said, "Dave avoids eye contact. It's always bothered me." He paused, sighed again. "We have Porter in custody. He has just as much motive if the motive is, indeed, financial in nature."

"But Porter didn't have free access to my property. The Dorfmans did."

"He had access to the Marshall house. The photographs, the footprints."

"Not the same."

Another pause. King said, "Do me a favor? Write down what you have and I'll be by when I can to pick it up. I'll do some searching of my own."

"In the meantime?"

"Don't drive anywhere. Local roads are flooded."

Thirty-Four

At two fifteen, the power finally went out. Megan wasn't surprised. A greenish glow lit up the sky. The lightning had hit a transformer, likely taking with it the electricity for most of Winsome.

My cue to go to bed, Megan thought. She stood, stretched, and after finding the small flashlight Bibi kept in the kitchen, turned off the laptop. She thought about checking on the goats and chickens, but the idea of being alone out there in this storm gave her a chill that went beyond the damp weather. On her way upstairs, she checked on her grandmother. Sound asleep. Gunther had relocated to the floor beside her. Ignoring a nagging sense of foreboding, Megan continued up the stairs.

She washed her face, brushed her teeth, and traded her jeans for sweatpants and a t-shirt. No pajamas for her tonight. One never knew what misfortune a storm could bring.

She lay in bed for what felt like hours, unable to sleep. Outside, the storm had dulled to a steady downpour, but the wind still battered the old lead windows. Megan turned on her side toward the window. She thought about Mick. She thought about Denver. She thought about what she'd read, and about how desperation may have led to murder. The more she thought about it, the more convinced she became that the Dorfman brothers were the perpetrators. And the thought of them out there, working on the barn, sickened her.

A boom startled her from her thoughts. Megan sat up, listening. She heard it again. Heart racing, she walked to the window, keeping the flashlight off. She couldn't see anything at first, but a flash of lightning lit up the sky, giving her a momentary glimpse of the farm. The noise was coming from the goats' enclosure. It looked like the gate was loose and swinging in the storm. The goats must have gotten scared and kicked it open with help from the wind. Little hellions.

Megan pulled a raincoat and a baseball cap from her closet. She should have checked on them. They were still babies, not used to weather like this. Or she should have brought them into the front porch—with all the tempting things for them to chew, swallow and get sick on, she reminded herself. Not a workable solution.

But then, neither was leaving them alone in this storm.

Sadie followed her downstairs, but she left her with Bibi and called Gunther to join her outside. For one, his white fur would make him more visible in the pitch black night. And he was meant to guard. Tonight, Megan would trust him to do his job. He could guard the goats.

Outside, the wind howled. Rain pelted her face and whipped at her clothes. The light from the battery-powered lantern she carried barely impacted the night, illuminating only a few feet in front of her. Megan walked in the direction of the barn, praying that Heidi and Dimples had stayed inside their enclosure.

No such luck. Gunther found Heidi outside, huddled against a tree, cold and scared. Megan picked her up and carried her back toward her pen. She followed Gunther into the pen, relieved to see Dimples still inside, laying on a bed of hay. Megan placed Heidi beside her, reclosed the now-battered gate, leaving Gunther with the goats, and went toward the barn in search of some rope to secure the gate.

Despite the hat and jacket, her hair was dripping wet and her clothes were soaked through. She shivered, pulling her jacket closer, and opened the barn door.

She stopped cold. She heard noises—scraping noises—coming from the back of the barn, in the old section. In the murky light emitted from her lantern, she saw what looked like a sheet of white canvas strung between the old and newer sections of the barn.

Someone was behind that canvas.

She firmed her grip on the lantern. Her mind danced with possibilities for her next move. Leave quietly and call the police. Barge through and announce herself. Find a weapon. She had decided the first was the most prudent when the wind pushed the barn door shut. It banged once, twice, and then settled back against the façade of the barn. Megan's breath caught, her vision narrowed. She was about to run when she heard footsteps.

She looked around for anything that could be used as a weapon. Her eyes settled on a small ax Clay used for splitting boards. She stuffed the wooden handle into the back of her sweatpants, under the rain jacket, and hoped like hell she wouldn't need it.

Someone pulled the edge of the canvas aside. A shadow fell across the threshold. One footfall, then another. Dave Dorfman emerged holding a flashlight. Their beams crossed. Megan could see the look of confusion pass on Dave's face. It wasn't Megan he was expecting.

"Don't you ever sleep?" he asked Megan.

"Don't you ever knock?"

They stared at each other for a few heartbeats before Megan's fight or flight response opted for flight. She sidled toward the door. Dave sprang toward her. She was halfway outside when she felt his hand on her wrist, hard flashlight metal grinding into her back.

"I'm sorry, Megan," Dave said. He sounded like he meant it.

Thirty-Five

"I'm not a monster."

Megan stared at Dave, wide-eyed. He was sitting on an overturned paint-mixing bucket in the oldest section of the barn, his dark, curly hair matching the black circles under his deep-set eyes, a gun pointed toward her. Two lanterns had been strung up by wire attached to nails in the old support beams. The canvas was meant to keep the light from reaching the house. It had worked.

"No?" she asked. "Then what do you call this?" Megan motioned toward the deep holes in the barn floor. A flash of silver could be seen through the dirt.

"A solution-oriented approach."

Megan searched for irony in his voice but heard none.

"You actually killed a man over buried treasure?"

Dave rubbed his face with his left hand, keeping the right hand on the gun. "Simon's death was an accident. He was being impossible and he pushed my buttons one too many times." He glanced at the holes in the ground. "Do you have any idea what you have here? What your family has had here all along? All those years your dad struggled, all those years your grandfather and uncle struggled before him? Needless suffering."

Megan glanced at the holes, at the hint of silver buried deep beneath the dirt. A box? Something else? The wind whipped through the trees outside, howling like a wounded animal. Inside, there were only shadows.

"What do you care? You were going to steal whatever it is."

Dave stayed silent for a moment, studying Megan's face. Finally, he said, "Neil and I had known for a long time that there may be a cache of stuff buried around here somewhere. We thought it was at the old place," he shrugged a shoulder in the direction of the abandoned Marshall house, "but Lenora's work convinced us otherwise."

"George Washington's visit."

Dave nodded. "Caldbeck's wife's family had connections. Washington visited here, and Caldbeck fed him false information. Only Washington knew he was a traitor and used it to his advantage. That's the focus of Lenora's paper."

"I heard enough bits and pieces to string this all together. I wasn't sure about the last piece, the false information, but it makes sense. Washington knew Caldbeck was loyal to the English. Otherwise, why would Caldbeck have run?"

"Leaving his Patriot wife behind."

"And his silver and gold."

Dave's eyes narrowed. "He didn't leave the silver and gold. She did."

Surprised, Megan said, "Elizabeth?"

"She buried her most treasured belongings and took off shortly after Caldbeck did. She and her parents had been Patriots, so she would have been safe here, despite her husband's actions. But maybe she felt ostracized, married to a Tory and all." Dave shrugged. "Who cares? In the end, she left the loot behind."

"Says Lenora."

"And others."

"Simon?"

"I'm getting tired of chatter, Megan." Indeed, he looked ready to fall over with exhaustion. But she needed to keep him talking.

"Lenora and Simon were in on this together?"

"Not Lenora. She only figured it out later, or was starting to see the big picture. She and Simon didn't see eye-to-eye, but she needed him for her research. The man was a genius when it came to historical records. He could find anything." Dave shook his head, clearly admiring the man, even now.

"So why kill him?"

"He wanted the treasure for Winsome. First, he tried to buy the house. When Bonnie refused, he decided to go for preservation status. His plan was to locate the treasure and convince Bonnie to donate it."

"How did he find out Bonnie was even selling the house?" Before the words were out of her mouth, Megan knew. The work at Sarah's home. Neil had been the one to tell her about Bonnie's discussions with Simon. Neil must have overheard something at Sarah's and told Simon, giving him the ammunition he needed to go to Bibi.

Dave smiled. "Neil."

Megan thought about the expression on Dave's face when he saw her. He was expecting Neil to show up tonight. Which meant that Neil could be here, listening. Or he could be down at the house. Bibi was there, alone. Megan needed to do something. Fast.

But what? Dave was holding a gun.

She stood, hands on her hips, looking at the holes along the back side of the room. "Can I see what you found?"

Dave stood up, nervous. He waved the gun. "Sit back down."

"Really, you're going to *shoot* me?" Megan shook her head, making a *tsk, tsk* sound and forcing herself to sound way braver than she felt. "That's way too obvious. I thought you were smarter than that."

You could drown me, she thought—hard to prove it wasn't an accident in this weather, with the rising stream waters. Drown me and a goat and everyone will think I died trying to save her. But Megan kept those thoughts to herself. No use giving Dave ideas.

"Don't make this harder than it is."

"Oh, right," she said sarcastically. "Stealing from us should be easy. Killing me should be easy too."

"No one needs to kill anybody."

"You're simply going to leave here, go back to Amelia, pretend you're an upstanding Winsome citizen with me still around to say otherwise?"

A shadow passed over his face at the mention of Amelia. "In return for your life—"

"I don't want to live that way, Dave. Always looking over my shoulder in case I become too much of a liability? Nah." Megan stared at him, hard, forcing him to make eye contact and see her as a person. "So is this all because of Amelia? Tastes getting too expensive for you? Maybe there's another man lurking in the shadows?" The specter of doubt deepened. Megan took advantage of his distraction and inched her hand toward her back. "Maybe she's tired of Winsome? Of the same old, same old. And that same old is you?"

Mean words, but Megan needed to get out of here, back to the house.

"Stop."

"I hit a nerve." Her hand was almost there...

"My wife has nothing to do with this."

"And what does? You're not paying your mortgage, Dave. Your business isn't able to meet its obligations. Where is the money going?"

"I made some bad investments. Lent money to my sister, who couldn't pay it back. Amelia hates Susan. I couldn't let her know."

"And you've been juggling funds around ever since, stealing from the home to pay the business, and vice versa."

He nodded. She almost felt sorry for him. *Almost.*

His eyes narrowed to slits, his lips compressed into a slash. "Enough."

Her hand reached the ax in her pocket and tightened around the handle.

He pointed the gun at her head. "Outside."

Outside anything could happen. She could slip in the muddy yard. He could catch her, gun her down, hide her body in the sodden woods, throw her body downstream. No, she'd take her chances here.

Dave yelled, "Outside, Megan. Now!"

She pulled the ax out of her back pocket and flung it at him, aiming for his chest, the biggest target. It hit his head instead, leaving a gash. Surprised, he stumbled, then fell, dropping the gun. Megan dove for it.

Forcing her hand to stop shaking, she held the gun on him. She pulled her phone from her pocket and called 911, keeping her voice as steady as possible and her eyes on Dave. There was rope in the front room, the rope she'd been fetching when this started.

"Come on," she said to Dave, keeping the gun pointed at him.

"You don't know how to shoot."

"Oh, Dave," she said. "I was married to a soldier."

She *didn't* know how to shoot, but her words were enough to convince him otherwise. He walked in front of her, arms up. In the newer portion of the barn, Megan tied him to the workbench, careful to secure arms, feet, and midsection. She thought he'd fight, but he didn't. Maybe he's relieved this is over, she thought. Or maybe he knows help is on its way in the form of Neil.

Either way, she needed to hurry. Outside, she held the lantern up, half jogging toward the house. The police would take forever in the weather, if they could even get to her on the flooded roads. She was climbing the small hill by the house when she slipped, falling into muddy grass and back down the hill. Her ankle twisted painfully under her.

"Damn," she muttered.

She tried to stand, wobbled, and then put another foot on the grassy, muddy slope, digging in with her heel. One foot after another. She ignored the pain.

She was focused on getting up the embankment and didn't hear someone come up behind her. A knife point jabbed her back, digging in between her shoulder blades. She screamed. A hand clamped over her mouth.

"I'm afraid I won't be quite as easy to fool," Jeremy said behind her. "Drop the gun."

Megan froze at the sound of his voice—so cold, so calm. Of

course—Jeremy was the missing link. His knowledge of this farm, his interest in the Marshall property. Megan's pulse raced. She dropped the gun. He meant business.

"Shall we go for a swim?"

Megan bit his hand, then tried to elbow him in the ribs the way Mick had taught her to handle an attacker what felt like ages long ago. He moved his hand and she screamed again. And again. She could hear Sadie barking frantically in the house. She hoped Bibi would call the police.

He recovered, clamping his hand down on her mouth, harder this time. "I don't know who you're trying to call. Your eighty-year-old grandmother?" He laughed. "Let her sleep, and she gets out of this alive."

He started up the slope, toward the tree line, dragging Megan with him. "You're a pain in the ass, you know that? Now my shoes are a muddy mess."

Megan couldn't talk. Her ankle hurt, and her head was pounding with adrenaline. She listened for the sound she hoped to hear. But the wind and rain, although calmer, made hearing next to impossible.

They were at the tree line when Jeremy moved the knife from her back to her throat. "Let's make this easier, shall we? Don't struggle and it's quick. Give me a hard time and—"

Megan stomped on his foot. Jeremy let out an annoyed yelp and dropped the knife. He didn't have a chance to go after her again before Gunther was on top of him, mouth wide and teeth bared. The dog went right for his throat, knocking him over into the mud. Gunther stood on his chest, growling deeply. Megan felt tears of gratitude well up in her eyes. Good dog.

She felt along the rain-soaked grass for the knife. Finally finding it, she tucked it into her pants. With Jeremy well-pinned by Gunther, she pulled Dave's gun from his pocket. He must have been Lenora's attacker. Clearly, he preferred the knife.

"It's empty," Jeremy said. "Dave doesn't like guns. No bullets."

Gunther growled.

Jeremy moved and the dog went for him.

"I'd stay still if I were you," Megan said.

"Get this damn beast off me."

"The beast has a name."

The dog let out a low snarl. He clearly didn't care for Jeremy.

Megan looked back at the house. She could see her grandmother coming toward her, near the embankment, King with her. Bibi was carrying a rifle. Megan didn't even know they owned a rifle.

"What's here is mine," Jeremy said. "All of it."

"Yeah, well, explain that to the cops."

"You don't understand."

"I don't need to," Megan said, pulling Gunther off Jeremy so King could handcuff him. "And where you're going, it doesn't matter anyway."

Thirty-Six

The storm system had left behind a trail of destruction in Winsome, claiming barns, roof tops, and windows, and downing trees. All things considered, the farm had fared well. A morning-after inventory uncovered a ruined flower bed, a ripped hoop house, and a sapling that had fallen on the greenhouse, breaking a window. Other than that and some minor flooding in the lower fields, the farm withstood the elements, as it had, Megan thought, for several hundred years.

The animals were fine too. The chickens, snug in their tractor, had been largely undisturbed. The goats survived, although Bibi spent her first morning after the storm with Heidi. She'd escaped again after Gunther knocked open the gate, and she wandered into the barn—cold, wet, and with a sudden interest in eating rope. Apparently, she'd kept Dave company until the police took him away.

The café was the only restaurant along the canal with a full generator, and the lunch counter and store remained open—and busy. So busy that Megan moved Clay there for a few days, ringing up groceries and maintaining a steady stock of vegetables and eggs for the wilted townspeople.

The first day after the storm, Denver visited. Megan was behind the counter, wiping down the serving area after the lunch crowd had left. Bibi was in the kitchen, chopping onions and garlic for Alvaro's black bean chili, and Alvaro was with her, preparing the beans. Megan could hear them arguing over the correct way to hold the knife. Denver, hearing them too, laughed.

"Have a few minutes?" he asked.

Megan threw her towel to Clover, who was chatting with Lydia about hair products. She took off her "We Do It Better in Winsome" apron, placed it behind the counter, and said, "Make yourself useful," to her store manager.

"Outside?" Denver asked.

"Sure." Megan led the way outside, past the men drinking coffee at the farmhouse table, past Clay, who was ringing up Merry's two dozen eggs and bag of green beans, and out into the sunshine. Despite the lack of electricity, Canal Street was alive with people—walkers, bikers, runners, mothers and fathers out with babies in strollers. It was as though the storm had reminded them all to be thankful for days like this.

Denver crossed the street and Megan followed. They strolled along the canal walkway, in silence at first. A car passed, and Megan saw Roger at the wheel. Megan waved and then looked away, down toward the water, which rushed through the old canal at a thoroughbred's pace, its waters still muddied from run-off and rain.

"Feeling okay, Megs?" Denver asked.

"Yes."

His eyes searched hers for the truth. Seemingly satisfied, he took her hand and continued walking.

"I'm glad you weren't seriously hurt."

He was talking about her ankle, and the small stab wound in her upper back, where Jeremy had poked the knife through her clothing. Three stitches and she was all sewn up.

"Me too."

"You're quite brave for a gentleman farmer, ye know."

Megan smiled. "Brave, or reckless?"

"Maybe a bit 'o both."

They laughed. "So it was your chef all along?" Denver asked, his tone once again serious.

"Talk about a lapse in judgement." Megan sighed. "Their vision was impressive. Find the gold and silver, take it without anyone knowing, and move it to the abandoned Marshall house. Jeremy would buy the Marshall house and no one would ever know the treasure had been at our farm in the first place. Both homes had been part of the same parcel when the Caldbecks owned it. I didn't realize that until I saw the painting in my aunt's home." She smiled. "Quite a devious plan."

"And Simon?"

"Simon, believe it or not, was the hold out. He wanted to make a Winsome historical museum." Megan squinted, looking past the canal to the park on the other side. She watched a mother swing her daughter on a new cedar swing set purchased by the Beautification Board. The mother was smiling; the child had a look of unabashed glee on her pretty round face.

Megan continued, tearing her eyes away from the mother-daughter pair. "Simon and Jeremy had hired Dave to find the cache. Simon was stalling on my permits because Dave had been unsuccessful when he pulled the old flooring up in the newer portion of the barn. He wanted Dave to dig in the old section. Dave refused unless Simon agreed they would sell what they found. Dave needed the money. Simon said no, things got heated and...well, the rest is history."

"Pun intended?"

Megan smiled. "Perhaps."

"I don't understand Jeremy's role, Megan. Why would he involve himself in this nonsense?"

"Because Elizabeth Caldbeck was his great-great-great-great-grandmother. After three failed restaurants, he wanted to come back to Winsome and create something that was his own. He needed the right place, but even more than that, he needed funds."

"How did he know about the treasure?"

They came to a bench and Megan sat down. She was wearing a long skirt and fitted wrap top, and she pulled the skirt tight around her knees, enjoying the security of cotton against skin.

"He had some old journals, kept from generation to generation. When Simon told them about his mother's findings—that Washington had been to the farm—he looked back through them. He and Simon compared notes. Elizabeth wrote that she was leaving and would hide 'her most precious belongings.' They decided to act in concert. Only Jeremy wasn't willing to see the money go to a museum either. He wanted it for his own."

"He stabbed Lenora."

"Yes. She was on the verge of figuring out what had happened, according to King. He wanted her silenced." Megan stared at her feet, thinking. "It looks like she'll make it."

"That could have been you." He squeezed her hand. "I hate the thought."

"Gunther may very well have saved me."

"Aye. He's a fine dog."

"You bought him back from Sauer, didn't you?"

"How did you figure that out?"

"Bibi told me you pushed Sauer. I believe you did. But I also figured you wouldn't want any chance that Sauer could have a claim against you and regain custody of the dog. You paid him for Gunther and gave him to me."

"There's nae pockets in a shroud."

"And that means?"

"It's an old Scottish saying." Denver grinned. "You can't take it with you, sweetheart."

Megan looked at him, eyes watering. She or Bibi could have been hurt. The thought had occurred to her many times. Things could have been much worse. By entrusting her with Gunther, Denver had, in fact saved her life.

"I came by for a favor, Megan."

She waited for him to say more. When he didn't, she said, "Whatever you want."

"Brian Porter."

"He didn't kill anyone, Denver. He was a witness. They tried to threaten him, just as we thought. Made him break into the store to create a distraction. He ran so he wouldn't have to do any more of their bidding."

"Aye, ye were right about that, then."

"But you're still concerned."

"The man needs a job. Something to keep him busy. So much idleness is not good for anyone, much less an alcoholic. I will try to find something around the clinic, but I thought maybe there might be something at that gentleman's farm of yours for him to do. Physical labor."

"We can always use help, but does he want to work?"

"He says he does."

Megan thought about that. Porter was strong and could make a good worker. Plus, Mick would have wanted him to have a chance. Mick with his soft heart and soldier's strength. "I'll make Porter a deal. If he gets help—and we both know he needs some professional help—I'll hire him. But he'll have to prove himself."

"Ta. Sounds like a fair deal to me."

They sat quietly next to each other, Denver's hand still on her own. She liked the heft of it, and the warmth. His fingers, incredibly long and strong, were a mite rough.

A child rode by on his bike, speeding along the canal path. Denver watched him. "Did they ever discover what was under your barn?"

"Not yet." Megan glanced at her watch. "They're pulling it out in an hour. It seems that Dave had struck something—a box of some kind. I need to be present when they remove it from the ground. Even though it's evidence, it belongs to us." She turned, moving her head and torso so that her face was close to his. "Want to join me?"

"In an hour? Sure." He tilted his head. "Would you like dinner tonight?"

Megan smiled. "Maybe. I still owe you a dinner."

"And dessert?" He grinned, that boyish smile giving way to dimples.

She kissed him lightly on the cheek. "We'll see."

Thirty-Seven

A crowd had gathered at the farm. There were police, media, and a few members of the Historical Society whom Megan had invited. Plus, she and Denver and Clay and her Aunt Sarah, who stood alone at the far side of the barn, her earthy features a blank canvas. Was this hard for her, Megan wondered. The farm should have been hers. Does it matter to me? Yes, she decided. It did matter. They had no relationship now—Megan was still digesting her aunt's presence in her life and her role in her mother's leaving—but maybe someday. Maybe.

The barn was once again a crime scene, and the old portion of the barn had been taped off until the police could dig up the box. For her part, Megan didn't much care what was in it. Gold and silver would be nice, of course—she could use the money to fix up the farm, maybe even buy the old Marshall estate. Or she could give it to Aunt Sarah, her portion of a rightful legacy denied.

Beside her, Denver moved from foot to foot, impatient. His broad shoulders and lanky form looked even bigger in the small space. He caught her looking at him and smiled.

"Ready?" he asked.

"Sure," Megan said.

King, donning gloves, was the one designated to do the honors. A pair of uniformed officers, also gloved, pulled the metal box from the earthen floor. It was large, maybe three feet by two feet, and decorated with tiny scroll engravings. There was a lock, but it had long since rusted. King took a deep breath, looked around the room, and then clipped the lock with wire cutters. He opened the box. Only he could see the contents, and he stared for a long moment into the abyss of the container.

"Well?" Roger said.

King turned the box so the crowd could get a look at the contents. It took Megan a moment to register what she was seeing. It wasn't a box of coins, nor was it full of anything of obvious value. There was what appeared to be a wedding portrait, presumably of Elizabeth. She wore an extravagant magenta dress set with purple panels and a plunging, gold-trimmed neckline. Her plain oval face gazed out with an innocence that was at once heartbreaking and endearing.

There was also a set of candlesticks, a trinket box, and an elaborate tapestry of the Washington Acres farmstead as it must have looked in the mid-eighteenth century—much like the painting in Sarah's living room. Carefully, King opened the trinket box. A silver chain and locket, severely tarnished, lay inside.

"Open it," Merry whispered.

King looked at her and nodded. Everyone remained silent as King worked the lock, springing the ornate oval to make the picture inside visible. King motioned for Megan to come forward. She gazed at the miniature portrait inside. It was a man. In the fashion of the day, he wore a brown suit and frilly white shirt, and his thick dark hair was swept back from his broad, open face. The face of a husband. The face of a traitor.

"Is that Paul Caldbeck?" Megan asked.

Roger peered at the picture over her shoulder. "I believe so."

"There's no treasure," Merry Chance muttered. She and Roger looked devastated.

"Hold on, folks. There's a letter attached to the back of the picture frame," King said. Carefully, he untucked yellowing parchment, surprisingly intact for such an old item. The letter was secured with wax, the imprint of a crest pressed firmly in the center of the red circle.

"Open it," Merry whispered.

A hush had descended over the room. King looked around from face to face, seemingly unsure whether he should break the seal here, in the barn—or at all.

"Would you like me to do it?" Megan asked.

King nodded. He handed the letter to Megan, who ran a finger across the crisp parchment and the hard wax. First, she took a photo of the seal with her smart phone—for future's sake. Then Denver handed her a Swiss Army knife from his pocket, the knife blade open. Megan used it to work the seal free. She read, first to herself, then aloud.

My dearest Paul,

If you are reading this, my love, we are together once again or you have returned home alone. I pray that the former will be our fate, but I am afraid the latter is a more likely course. I waited as long as I dared, but time was not on our side, and without my father's protection, I feared for my life and the lives of our children. In either case, you must know that should we return, Mr. James has agreed to terminate our contract and return our home to us for the original sum plus 10% as one last favor to my father. Be well, my Paul.

Always, in love and marriage,
Elizabeth

The hush continued. Megan stared at the paper, turning it over in her hand. A memory box, filled with one woman's sentimental treasures. It hardly seemed worth killing for.

King said, "You'll need to think about what to do with this once we're done. This stuff belongs to the house, Megan."

Megan glanced at Denver, then at Sarah. She'd talk to Bibi, of course, but she knew already what was right. "Simon's museum," she said with a glance at Merry. "Once the Historical Society sets it up."

Merry nodded. "We can do that."

"I'd like to keep the letter, Bobby. If that's all right with you."

"We'll need to make a copy for the records."

"Of course." Megan took a deep breath. Everyone was looking at her expectantly, but she was at a loss for words. She walked out of the barn, back toward the greenhouses. She wanted to get back to work. To normalcy.

Denver followed her to the greenhouse. Her heart felt leaden, her mind numb. He took her hand at the entrance, spinning her around toward him. He ran a finger along Megan's jawline and smiled. "It's not quite the treasure Jeremy was after, was it?"

"Love letters and sentimental keepsakes? No, I don't suppose it was."

"Are you disappointed?"

"Not in the way you might think."

Megan pulled the letter from the pack she was wearing on her back. "Read it," she said.

His eyes widened when he reached the end. The portion she'd omitted when reading it aloud had no doubt caught his attention: *You will find the money necessary to repurchase the house in the place we discussed the night you left.*

"So there *is* money hidden on these grounds. This was a ruse."

"Here, or on the old Marshall property, most likely." Megan gave him a wan smile. "You understand why I kept that quiet, don't you?"

"Aye, and ye were smart to do so, Megan. You don't want another bloody brigade of people sneaking on your property to try and find the treasure. As we've seen, greed can bring about one's baser nature." His face softened. "But what about you and Bonnie? You could no doubt use those funds. And what about the preservation district?"

"We'll deal with that when the time comes. Otherwise, we're doing fine. Besides, I don't even want to think about treasure for a long, long time. If we happen to come across it—" Megan smiled "—well, then I guess we'll decide what to do."

Inside the greenhouse, the air was hot and humid. Trellised tomatoes wound their way up toward the ceiling, their hanging fruits in various stages of ripeness. Megan glanced around, her gaze falling on the table in the back, up against the windows. A bin of fresh potting soil mixed with compost sat on one side of the table, potting blocks on the other. Clay had placed packets of seeds next to the potting soil.

"Know your way around a garden, Denver?" Megan asked.

He smiled. "Aye, a bit."

"Want to help me plant some annuals?"

Denver nodded. "Sounds like a perfect afternoon."

"What time is your next appointment?"

"Besides dinner?" Gently, Denver pushed Megan up against the wall so that her back braced against warm glass. He kissed her while his hands trailed gently down her sides. "Not until tomorrow."

Megan smiled. She kissed him back. "All the time in the world."

Bibi's Farmers Market Pasta Primavera

The version of pasta primavera is versatile. You can add whatever vegetables you've just picked from the garden or selected from the farmers market. Just remember not to overcook the vegetables so they remain crisp-tender. And Bibi's not afraid of a little butter or cream. Go ahead, indulge. Life is short. You'll work it off in the garden tomorrow.

Serves 8

Ingredients
1 pound dry pasta, any variety, cooked al dente
5 Tbsp. extra virgin olive oil, divided
1 pint cherry tomatoes, halved
2 cups yellow squash, roughly chopped
1 large onion (about 2 cups), roughly chopped
6 cloves of garlic, peeled and minced
1 carrot, washed, peeled and sliced in thin rings
1 red pepper, thinly sliced
6 cups bite-size broccoli florets (1 small head)
1 cup kale, chopped, tough inner ribs removed
½ cup vegetable broth or white wine
5 Tbsp. salted butter
1 pint heavy whipping cream
1 cup half and half
1 cup (or more!) good quality parmesan cheese, grated
Handful of fresh basil, chopped
Pepper to taste

Heat your oven to 375 degrees

Bring a large pot of salted water to boil and cook your pasta according to the directions. It will be warmed in the sauce later, so be sure not to overcook it.

While the pasta water is boiling, wash and prepare your vegetables so they are ready to be cooked.

Toss the cherry tomatoes and squash with 2 Tbsp. olive oil. Add pepper to taste. Place in the oven on a cookie sheet and bake for 13-15 minutes. Turn the heat to broil and cook for an additional 5 minutes, until the tomatoes and squash are slightly caramelized. Remove from oven and set aside. The tomatoes and squash can be cooked a few hours ahead of time and refrigerated.

Heat 2 Tbsp. of olive oil in a Dutch oven over medium heat. Add the onion and sauté until tender and slightly brown. Add the garlic and stir for 1 minute. Add red pepper and carrots and cook until just tender (3-5 minutes). Remove the vegetables from the pan using a slotted spoon and transfer to a plate.

Add the final Tbsp. of olive oil to the pan. When hot, add the broccoli. At this point, you can add a little pasta water to the broccoli and place a lid on the pan to steam the broccoli. Don't overcook. Add the kale and cook for an additional 2-3 minutes, until kale is tender. Remove the broccoli and kale from the pan and add them to the plate.

Add the broth or wine to the Dutch oven and scrape up any bits in the pan. When most of the liquid has evaporated, add the butter. Melt the butter, then add the heavy cream and the half and half. Bring to a simmer, stirring constantly with a whisk. Add the parmesan cheese and cook until the mixture thickens to the desired consistency. If it's too thick, add more broth/wine or half and half. If it's too thin, cook it down further (slowly—don't scald the cream) and/or add more parmesan cheese.

When the sauce reaches the desired consistency, add the vegetables (including the tomatoes and squash), the pasta and the basil. Stir to combine. Add pepper and additional parmesan cheese to taste.

Gardening Tips

Want to extend your growing season? Consider low tunnels. Low tunnels, which you can make yourself using PVC hoops and heavy plastic, can be used to shelter young, cold-hardy crops (such as spinach) through the winter for an early spring harvest.

Organic straw can make a terrific, inexpensive mulch for your garden. Oftentimes, though, hay—straw with the seeds still intact—is grown using pesticides and herbicides that can infiltrate your soil and impede the growth of your plants. Make sure you only purchase straw from farmers who don't treat their hay with pesticides and herbicides. Organic straw may be harder to find, but it's worth the additional effort.

Garlic is a wonderful plant to add to your home garden. Healthy, delicious and prolific, garlic can be stored up to a year, depending on the variety and the storage conditions. But how about the flower buds that appear before the garlic is mature? Those buds are called garlic scapes and they are edible and delicious. Clip the scapes in June and use them in recipes just as you would garlic. We love them chopped and added to salads. You can also add scapes to flower bouquets. Their curlicue designs make for an interesting addition to traditional floral arrangements.

WENDY TYSON

Wendy Tyson's background in law and psychology has provided inspiration for her mysteries and thrillers. Originally from the Philadelphia area, Wendy has returned to her roots and lives there again on a micro-farm with her husband, three sons and three dogs. Wendy's short fiction has appeared in literary journals, and she's a contributing editor and columnist for *The Big Thrill* and *The Thrill Begins*, International Thriller Writers' online magazines. Wendy is the author of the Allison Campbell Mystery Series and the Greenhouse Mystery Series.

Henery Press Mystery Books

And finally, before you go...
Here are a few other mysteries
you might enjoy:

FATAL BRUSHSTROKE

Sybil Johnson

An Aurora Anderson Mystery (#1)

A dead body in her garden and a homicide detective on her doorstep...

Computer programmer and tole-painting enthusiast Aurora (Rory) Anderson doesn't envision finding either when she steps outside to investigate the frenzied yipping coming from her own back yard. After all, she lives in Vista Beach, a quiet California beach community where violent crime is rare and murder even rarer.

Suspicion falls on Rory when the body buried in her flowerbed turns out to be someone she knows—her tole-painting teacher, Hester Bouquet. Just two weeks before, Rory attended one of Hester's weekend seminars, an unpleasant experience she vowed never to repeat. As evidence piles up against Rory, she embarks on a quest to identify the killer and clear her name. Can Rory unearth the truth before she encounters her own brush with death?

Available at booksellers nationwide and online

Visit www.henerypress.com for details

NUN TOO SOON

Alice Loweecey

A Giulia Driscoll Mystery (#1)

Giulia Driscoll has just taken on her first impossible client: The Silk Tie Killer. He's hired Driscoll Investigations to prove his innocence and they have only thirteen days to accomplish it. Talk about being tried in the media. Everyone in town is sure Roger Fitch strangled his girlfriend with one of his silk neckties. And then there's the local TMZ wannabes stalking Giulia and her client for sleazy sound bites.

On top of all that, her assistant's first baby is due any second, her scary smart admin still doesn't relate well to humans, and her police detective husband insists her client is guilty. About this marriage thing—it's unknown territory, but it sure beats ten years of living with 150 nuns.

Giulia's ownership of Driscoll Investigations hasn't changed her passion for justice from her convent years. But the more dirt she digs up, the more she's worried her efforts will help a murderer escape. As the client accuses DI of dragging its heels on purpose, Giulia thinks The Silk Tie Killer might be choosing one of his ties for her own neck.

Available at booksellers nationwide and online

Visit www.henerypress.com for details

MACDEATH

Cindy Brown

An Ivy Meadows Mystery (#1)

Like every actor, Ivy Meadows knows that *Macbeth* is cursed. But she's finally scored her big break, cast as an acrobatic witch in a circus-themed production of *Macbeth* in Phoenix, Arizona. And though it may not be Broadway, nothing can dampen her enthusiasm—not her flying cauldron, too-tight leotard, or carrot-wielding dictator of a director.

But when one of the cast dies on opening night, Ivy is sure the seeming accident is "murder most foul" and that she's the perfect person to solve the crime (after all, she does work part-time in her uncle's detective agency). Undeterred by a poisoned Big Gulp, the threat of being blackballed, and the suddenly too-real curse, Ivy pursues the truth at the risk of her hard-won career—and her life.

Available at booksellers nationwide and online

Visit www.henerypress.com for details

THE SEMESTER OF OUR DISCONTENT

Cynthia Kuhn

A Lila Maclean Mystery (#1)

English professor Lila Maclean is thrilled about her new job at prestigious Stonedale University, until she finds one of her colleagues dead. She soon learns that everyone, from the chancellor to the detective working the case, believes Lila—or someone she is protecting—may be responsible for the horrific event, so she assigns herself the task of identifying the killer.

More attacks on professors follow, the only connection a curious symbol at each of the crime scenes. Putting her scholarly skills to the test, Lila gathers evidence, but her search is complicated by an unexpected nemesis, a suspicious investigator, and an ominous secret society. Rather than earning an "A" for effort, she receives a threat featuring the mysterious emblem and must act quickly to avoid failing her assignment...and becoming the next victim.

Available at booksellers nationwide and online

Visit www.henerypress.com for details

CPSIA information can be obtained at www.ICGtesting.com
Printed in the USA
LVOW10*1448020316

477477LV00013B/114/P